I0549286

I AM AUTOMATON

A NOVEL

Edward P. Cardillo

Acknowledgements

I would like to thank my wife, Sandra, who is my partner, my manager, and my coach. She helped me progress in my development as a writer and never let me succumb to the self-doubt that writers periodically feel. I would like to thank my son, Alexander, who inspires my imagination to roam free; Thank you to Alan Basso, Arno Kolz, Robert Rubicco, Charlene Nunez, James Nunez, and Jim Taylor for their feedback and support as I shaped this work into what it is. I would also like to thank Gary Lucas for giving me my shot and making the process so easy.

In memory of my mother, Terry, who passed away suddenly, leaving behind a rich legacy of love and kindness.

Part I
Danger and Opportunity

Chapter I

Tijuana, Mexico

Command Sergeant Major Peter Birdsall and his squad of ten were baking in a beat-up, unmarked van parked on the street. The men were hot, sweaty, and growing antsy.

They were all recovering from the night on pass cut short. They were a tight squad. Their motto was the squad that fights together, raises hell together, and last night they didn't disappoint.

They were not supposed to deploy today, but apparently, the brass had received some new intelligence that made it imperative that they mobilize.

It was almost time. The sun was beginning to rise and bathe the cesspool of a town in golden light, purging the sins of the night prior.

The only remaining illumination was that of the holo-panels on parked cars flashing ads for Mexican beer and strip clubs. The cars were obsolescent models, the first generation of electric. The United States was already in its third generation.

Soon the streets would be bustling with people. If they were going to maintain a low profile, they had to move now. Peter cleared his throat.

He was consulting his Mini-com Multi-tasker. Only the size of a pack of gum, it projected a screen that was flashing information.

"Alright, listen up. Intel says that some major players in the Navajas gang are staying in the second floor apartment across the street. There are reported to be only three of them, high ranking members, maybe even a capo, so this is going to be a simple smash-and-grab."

There was backslapping, high-fiving, and a flurry of macho remarks. Peter put his hand up. They listened.

"But keep in mind that our Special Forces were down here not long ago training the Navajas to help the Mexican government in the war on drug cartels. Unfortunately, these Navajas realized that they could make more money using their new training as security for the cartels, and then eventually they became the cartels.

"These are not debutants. They know our tricks, they know our tactics, and they're sure as shit going to use them against us."

Corporal Apone was wearing a sly grin.

"Yeah, well, we've learned a few things since then. They haven't tasted army tough yet."

The other men hooted and hollered in support. They sounded like a football team in the locker room before the championship game.

Peter raised his hand again, half in recognition of Apone's sentiment, and half to impress upon his men his point.

"While that is true, these Navajas are not to be underestimated. So listen up. We need to cross the street fast while keeping an eye all round us. Squad Vee formation. Once we breach the building through the front, we switch to two fire teams in squad column formation and take the second floor."

Corporal Apone nodded, and the men grunted in affirmation.

"Remember your training, because it is that very training that will keep you alive. This ain't amateur hour, and it's no time for mistakes. Am I clear?"

The men grunted.

A bead of sweat ran down the side of Peter's cheek. He checked his watch. He then extended his hand vertically and pointed in each direction. The men dispersed out of their van, covering each other, and proceeded across the street in Vee formation, Peter leading and Apone bringing up the rear.

There was a light breeze, and a stray paper was blowing down the vacant street. In the distance, a three-legged dog was watching them with lazy interest. But its attention quickly shifted to a dog biscuit ad flashing on the side of the nearest car.

They splashed through the filthy gutter as they approached the front door of the storefront. Peter produced his Mini-com Multi-tasker and activated the lock pick application. He began working on the digital lock quickly, but quietly. It was an outdated algorithm, no challenge. The flanks were scanning the quiet street.

All was still. The prostitutes, criminals, and morally licentious were all sleeping off a wild night of drunken debauchery. The city almost seemed decent in the tranquility of morning.

Peter disarmed the lock with what seemed like a pop, but he realized quickly that digital locks don't pop.

Two men on the right flank were dropped—Spottiswoode and Bertucci.

"SNIPER," Apone yelled.

Before Peter could bark a command to switch formation, Allen on the left flank was dropped.

"COLUMN FORMATION."

The men quickly rearranged into two fire teams, and Peter pushed into the building. He felt something graze his shoulder as he dove into the store.

It was some kind of a general store with aisles and shelves. The store was lit, digital sales and prices were flashing on the walls and above the aisles, creating the effect of a consumerist discotheque.

Men filed past him, and each fire team went down an aisle past rows of antibiotics and various controlled substances that were illegal in the States. His squad was yelling all around him, and there was yelling in Spanish from inside the store.

This was going all wrong. The Navajas knew they were coming. Somehow, the bastards knew, and they were ready for them.

Before he could process the scene before him, his men were being cut down in the store by controlled gunfire. By being corralled into the aisles, the Navajas were able to take them out two at a time.

Peter ran down the aisle behind Apone, and in minutes, Navajas surrounded them on either side of the aisle with carbines. Apparently, they were putting the American weaponry they received to good use.

Peter had to make a snap decision. Fight or surrender?

"Throw your weapons down," he ordered his men.

Apone looked back at his friend, multi-colored lights reflecting on his face. There was doubt in his expression. But Peter was in command. He placed his M-16 down to the floor slowly and put his hands on his head. The remaining three men followed suit.

One of the Navajas advanced and gestured with the barrel of his carbine for them to kneel. Peter nodded and they complied.

There was yelling in Spanish all around them. Before the situation got too out of hand, Peter figured he'd try to communicate.

"We are United States Army. I am Sergeant…"

The man with the carbine in his face told him to shut up. Peter's Spanish was not the best, but he understood that much.

Apone looked at him nervously. Privates Wilson, Rodriguez, and Wilcox shifted nervously behind, but they remained silent, awaiting the lead of their sergeant.

The man with the carbine in Peter's face was speaking rapidly in Spanish to another man, who then gestured for him to stand and come down the aisle.

"Rodriguez, you make anything of that?"

"They want you to go in the back while they watch us. They know we're US Army."

The man yelled for Rodriguez to be quiet, and then he gestured aggressively to Peter.

Peter stood slowly, his hands still on his head, sweat trickling down the side of his face, and began to follow the man. When he reached the end of the aisle, the man pointed for him to go into a back room.

Peter didn't want to go. He was unarmed, and totally at the mercy of these Navajas. He knew what would happen if he went into the back room. Moreover, he knew what was going to happen to his men kneeling in the aisle.

Once again, he was at a decision point. He could try to fight back, but then he would probably lose and his men would surely be executed. Nevertheless, if he complied, they were surely dead…most likely, anyway.

It was a judgment call, and Peter had no time to make it.

Peter turned and began to walk towards the door to the back room. He heard the swish of the man's clothing and Apone yell his name when he felt a blunt object hit the back of his neck.

He went down hard, his face smashing into the tile floor spilling blood and shards of teeth onto an advertisement for aspirin.

He tasted copper as blood ran over his broken teeth before he blacked out.

***

Peter felt like he was floating in darkness as his head swam. When water splashed into his mouth, he realized that he was literally floating.

He screwed his eyes to clear his vision, and he was apparently in some kind of cave. As he looked forward, he saw the ceiling drop towards the water until the two met in the distance.

Suddenly Peter heard several loud splashes behind him, as if cinder blocks were being dropped into the water. He did not know why, but something inside him very urgently told him to move deeper into the cave, away from the splashes.

He began to wade deeper into the cave, the splashes echoing off the ceiling, and as he did so, his feet left the ground and the ceiling was beginning to drop towards the water.

There was splashing behind him, but not the splashing of things dropping. Concentric ripples made their way towards him and splashed gently against his neck. Someone was in the water with him, and they were now wading towards him.

He swam farther and farther in. He could now see the guano on the ceiling and stalactites. The water was very cold from lack of direct sun exposure.

The splashing grew louder…closer.

He pushed further into the cave until the rock ceiling was practically scraping the top of his head. In his haste, he was now swallowing water.

He closed his eyes and commanded himself to remain calm. His training told him that he had to assess the situation and evaluate his options. Panic was not one of them.

He opened his eyes and saw that there was no room to progress unless he went underwater. He would have to turn and face his pursuers if he was to get out of this cave.

Therefore, he turned in the other direction and found himself gazing into blackness. He couldn't even see a few feet in front of him.

The splashing stopped. Were his pursuers just treading water in darkness, waiting for his next move?

Hand-to-hand combat in deep water without oxygen was clumsy, but he was ready. Perhaps he would make it through the gauntlet by being evasive and just focusing on getting through rather than engaging.

He felt something bump against his foot.

He looked down into the black water, but he could not see beyond the surface.

He felt it again.

He began to kick his feet and swim forward when a hand wrapped itself tightly around his right ankle and began to pull him down.

Peter struggled against the grip to stay afloat, kicking wildly. A second hand wrapped itself tightly around his other ankle, and he was able to yell as he was being pulled under the water.

He grabbed frantically at his ankles and at the hands holding him, trying to pry them off, but the grip was unnatural.

Other hands began to reach out of the darkness and pull at his clothes and tear at his skin as he sank further into the dark void.

He knew he was going to die.

He looked up towards the receding surface and let out a loud yell as water rushed into his lungs and there was an awful burning in his chest—

***

Peter woke with a start to darkness. He heard voices around him in Spanish. His hands were bound tightly in front of him with rope, and his own breath was hot against his face. He was sitting on hard wood, a chair of some kind.

Suddenly something was pulled from over his face, and light flooded his vision. As his eyes adjusted, he saw men kneeling in a row in front of him facing in the other direction...*his* men.

There was a cartel member standing between him and his men. He was holding the burlap sack that was just removed from Peter's head. There were two men with AK-47's guarding the door, and another to Peter's right polishing a machete with a dank rag.

Peter looked around and guessed that they were in some kind of a shack. It was close quarters, the walls were made of dilapidated corrugated tin and through the chinks in the walls and joints, he could see daylight and hear nothing but the breeze.

They were out of the city.

His head was spinning, but he recalled storming the store. He remembered shots being fired from within the store as soon as they breached the front door. He remembered his men being cut down.

The Navajas had gotten the drop on them. There would be no reinforcements. Not in time for what was left of them.

The man with the burlap sack spoke first.

"Well, good morning, senor."

"My name is Sergeant Major Peter Birdsall of the United States Army…"

"I know who you are, pig."

The other men chortled.

There were four of Peter' men left kneeling in front of him. They had their hands on their heads and their legs crossed. They were in a perfect row. This was to be an execution.

"There are others on the way. If any harm comes to my men, you will be hunted to the ends of the earth."

Peter tried to sound confident and forceful while trying not to choke on the dust flying around the shack.

The man tossed the burlap sack into Peter's lap. "Senor, you are out in the middle of nowhere, no one knows where you are, and you are all alone."

"Well, I suggest you run now while you have the chance. Reinforcements are closing in."

"Oh, we have enough time, you gringo pig."

He produced a pistol and brandished it behind the captive soldier's backs. Coward.

"When your reinforcements do show, they will see that it was not wise to interfere."

He turned, placed his pistol to the back of one soldier's head and—before Peter could voice any protest—pulled the trigger. Blood and grey matter sprayed the wall of the shack in front of them.

It was Corporal Apone, husband and father of two young girls. Hell of a pool player. Peter's friend.

"You BASTARD…"

The man smirked and proceeded to stand behind the next man.

"STOP. I won't tell you anything you want to know. Shooting my men will be useless," Peter said hurriedly.

All of the Navajas laughed out loud. The man with the pistol spoke.

"Know? I don't want to *know* anything from you, Sergeant."

And he pulled the trigger. Private Wilson. Only child. Practical jokester and squad clown. Just last night he was trying to hit on a pair of rather buxom blonde twins and making a spectacle of failing at it.

Peter felt helpless. He could do nothing to slow this down. The man was going to shoot his squad in the head one-by-one to save time for working on him. Peter knew the machete was reserved for him to send their message.

The man walked up behind the next soldier who was now sobbing so hard that he was shaking violently. It was Private Rodriguez. Husband and father of three. Two boys and one little girl.

Peter didn't know what to say.

"My name is Command Sergeant Major Peter Birdsall of the United States Army. Be advised that reinforcements are en route…"

"Is that so?" the man mocked, and he blew Rodriguez's brains out.

The last man, Private Wilcox, must've decided that he would rather chance an escape than be shot execution style in the back of the head.

He did not even make it to a standing position. The man with the machete buried it in his neck. Wilcox dropped to the ground and began writhing around and squirting blood all over the walls and dirt.

These savages were using nineteenth century melee weapons, farmers' tools. It was their reputation, and it was supposed to serve as a deterrent to government, police, and outsiders.

The screams. Peter would never forget those screams that seemed to go on for minutes, his own personal eternity. The machete landed one final blow, silencing them forever.

The man with the machete was wiping the blood off the blade with his rag and grinning wickedly at Peter. Peter now lost his cool. All of his men were gone, and he knew what was coming next.

"I'm going to kill you bastards!" His mouth foamed as he spat his very well meaning but futile threats, "Goddamned sons-of-bitches!"

His captors and would-be executioners laughed. One of the men by the door to the shack cracked it open and peeked out.

"Nada."

"Well," gloated the man with the pistol, "it looks like your friends are not coming for you. You're alone."

That word was like a dagger in Peter's heart. It sealed his fate, and any will he had left to survive evaporated in the hot summer air.

No. He had to keep strong. He had to remember his training. It was all he had right now. He attempted to focus on his surroundings.

He noticed some farming tools hanging on the walls, rusted blades hanging all around him. His chair was rickety and in all likelihood could easily be broken. The ground consisted of dry dirt that could create dust when disturbed.

The two men watching the door now came around to either side of Peter. They grabbed him by his shoulders and restrained him, pressing him hard into the seat of his chair. The chair creaked in protest and wobbled under the weight.

The man with the machete was now brandishing it, toying with Peter like a cat toys with a mouse before the kill. He pulled out his own Mini-com unit, toggled the rotator button with a filthy thumb, and pressed play.

The shack was filled with the sounds of loud music. Trumpets blared as a man wailed over them in Spanish. The song was meant to camouflage Peter's own wailing. In his terror, Peter almost found it comical.

The man put the Mini-com on the dusty floor and walked up to Peter. But Peter remained silent, and he struggled against the grip of his restrainers, testing their strength. He was seated, and they were putting all of their weight on him. There was no way he was shaking loose.

"Well, mi amigo," jeered the man with the pistol, "you have the honor of being our message to the United States to stay out of our business. Now how about you give me head."

The other men chuckled at the pun. At least Peter hoped it was just a pun.

Peter did not look at the machete. He kept it in his periphery. He glared at his tormentor, who nodded to the man with the machete.

The two men holding Peter bent him forward in his chair, sticking his neck out. Peter's pulse was pounding in his ears. His muscles wanted to tense, but he used his will to keep them loose. It was important that he stayed loose.

The man with the machete stepped forward, lining the blade up with Peter's neck. Peter began to slacken as the man brought the machete over his head.

All of a sudden, Peter lurched upward. The two men restraining him reacted by pushing him down with all of their weight...

And he let them.

The chair broke apart under the force, sending Peter crashing to the ground and his two restrainers falling over him as the third man brought the machete down on them.

The one on Peter's right had the back of his neck cleaved. The shack was filled with more blood and shrieks.

Peter rolled from underneath the other man, snatching up dry dirt in his hands as he stood, and he threw it in the eyes of the man holding the pistol.

"Matalo!"

Peter, hands still bound, sidestepped a machete strike and double hammer-fisted the attacker, breaking his right clavicle. The Navajas dropped the machete as his right arm became useless.

Peter snatched the machete from the gang member's limp arm. He turned and slashed at the man with the pistol and then the other man who had restrained him in the chair in a frenzy of self-preservation…

Peter, covered in other men's blood, caught his breath, as he stood in the red-spattered room full of slain men to the sound of a bad trumpet solo.

Grateful that he was alive and the singer was taking a break, he kneeled in the dirt. He placed the machete in between his knees, blade facing up. He rubbed his bindings back and forth until they were severed.

He stood up, machete in hand, and stumbled to the door of the shack. He peeked outside and saw that he was in one of several tin shacks on the side of a steep dirt hill. At the top was a house.

He had to move, as there would be other Navajas. The music likely served its purpose, and they probably heard nothing. However, once they found their dead compatriots in the shack, they would be looking for him.

He summoned what was left of his strength, and he crept out of the shack. The bright sun stung his eyes, and flies buzzed around his ears.

He made his way down the hill, stumbling to keep his balance, kicking up dust as he went. He tried to run from shack to shack, minimizing his exposure to those that might be watching in the house above.

He was weak, his muscles ached, and he likely had a concussion, but he staggered down the hill. Behind him, he heard men yelling in Spanish.

He made it to street level and began frantically waving his arms for cars to stop, but they only swerved around him. He was nearly run down by a car flashing an advertisement for coffins on its hood holo-panel.

He crossed the road, passing cars be damned, and descended another hill and began to wander towards town.

***

Peter wandered into town, and having put some distance between himself and the Navajas house, he began to slow his pace so as not to draw attention to himself.

En route, he had stripped down to his undershirt. Walking in camouflage pants and a sweat-stained undershirt, he looked like a local...or so he hoped.

He thought he heard a commotion down the block behind him, so he ducked down an alleyway where a prostitute was with a man behind a dumpster.

He shambled past them, his exhaustion catching up with him, and they did not pay him any regard. His head began to pound, his muscles ached terribly, and the alley before him began to spin.

As he collapsed to the ground and leaned against the wall, he fingered his broken teeth. The dumpster now blocked his view to the street and the street's view of him. He leaned his head back against the wall as he listened to the sounds of the couple struggling next to him.

A young woman, another prostitute, poked her head out through a shabby storm door into the alley and saw Peter lying against the wall. He figured that he must've looked awful.

She said something to the other prostitute in Spanish, who gave him a quick look, shrugged, and continued her work. Her customer was now looking uncomfortable at the sight of Peter.

They all heard yelling from the street—Navajas—and the customer pulled himself away from his date and fled the other way down the alley. The abandoned girl, having already accepted payment, only shrugged casually at the premature evacuation.

The one in the doorway yelled something to her. Peter thought he heard the word "Navajas," but in his condition, he couldn't be sure.

The other one was arguing with her, huffing in protest, but in the end, both girls hoisted Peter up and threw each of his arms around each of their shoulders. They half-carried, half-dragged his sorry carcass into the cathouse.

Peter slipped in and out of consciousness. He remembered being lowered onto a bed. As they undressed him, he saw a pile of used towels huddled in a corner.

When he woke again, he was naked, and the girl who poked her head into the alley was washing him with a wet rag.

He tried to speak, but she put her fingers to her lips and said "Shhh." He did not argue. He closed his eyes.

He was jolted awake by some kind of commotion in the front of the house. He picked his head up and looked around at the cracked plaster walls painted in a faded yellow. There was a condom advertisement flashing up on the wall next to where he lay. He was alone.

He wanted to call out, but given the commotion, thought better of it.

The girl who was nursing him burst into the room and started telling him something frantic in Spanish. She was holding his Mini-com Multi-tasker in her hands trying to operate it, but she didn't know how. She wouldn't—it was army issue.

"Ma'am, what are you doing with my…"

She was muttering to herself in frustration until she finally pressed a button and the payment kiosk by the bed registered with a tone indicating that payment had been made.

She began to take off her clothes. When he tried to say something, she shushed him again. She was young and firm and in her early twenties. He was so confused. Why was she…?

She got onto the bed and mounted him, but she did not move. She only looked anxiously at the doorway, waiting.

They heard two men yelling commands in Spanish, and she began to lower herself over him. He was limp, but he understood what she was doing.

Two men with carbines surged into the room—Navajas. They yelled at her in Spanish, and she sat up and raised her hands compliantly.

The men looked them up and down and looked at Peter. He obviously was not Mexican. With sudden panic, Peter wondered where his clothes were. If they saw the camouflaged pants…

Shit. The Mini-com Multi-tasker. If they saw it, they would know he was no local. He wasn't paying attention. Where the hell did she put it?

Everything was happening faster than his concussed mind could understand. And they were staring at him suspiciously, sizing him up.

Peter did not know what to do, so he smiled.

The Navajas saw this pathetic gringo under this whore with his broken smile and an ad for a popular erectile dysfunction pill flashing next to them.

He must've looked like a real travesty because they snickered. One man called him names and used the words "carajo" and "mariposa" liberally. Satisfied with their derision, they left.

The girl sighed heavily in apparent relief, and looked down at Peter. She smiled and whispered something in Spanish.

Peter picked his head up slowly. "I don't know who you are, but thank you."

She smiled, looking upon him with pity, and whispered, "Mi nombre Lucita."

That was her name. It was like music to his weary ears. The name of his savior was Lucita.

Then he suddenly felt very tired. The immediate danger had passed, the adrenaline was waning, and Lucita would look after him.

He was too exhausted to think about what had just happened and that his men were all dead. For the moment, he did not care what was going to happen next, or how he would get back. He succumbed to sweet oblivion, if only for a moment.

Chapter 2

Peter was sitting in Molly Apone's kitchen sipping lemonade. Her two girls were running around in the back yard playing, undeterred by the unrelenting heat of the summer sun.

Molly was looking towards the back screen door, lost in some private reverie. "I can't believe Mya's going to be starting the fourth grade this year."

"And Courtney's starting second?"

Molly nodded.

Peter sipped his lemonade. Molly made the best. It wasn't overly saccharine like store bought and man did it kill a good thirst.

He had been to their house on base on many an occasion, where they had worn out Delroy's eight-foot, regulation pool table.

"What're you making?"

There was a savory aroma filling the kitchen. "Oh, I was just making some pecan pie," Molly said absent-mindedly, "for after dinner."

Molly's dinners were the stuff of legend. They were all in for a treat. Delroy…where was…

All of a sudden, the girls' laughter turned to screams from the backyard. Peter stood up in alarm, but Molly remained seated. She was crying, mascara running down her face. She began to tear at her clothes violently.

"Molly, the girls…"

However, she would not stop. She tore at her dress and then her hair, screaming bloody murder. Peter did not understand.

He crossed the kitchen and flung the screen door open. A strange man cornered the girls. Peter crossed the yard quickly. "Hey, you! What do you think you're doing?"

The man did not turn around. He only continued to advance on the girls slowly. They were holding each other and screaming.

Peter descended the old wooden steps and crossed the backyard yelling at the man. "Hey! Get away from those girls!"

But the man never turned around.

Peter put a hand on the man's shoulder and whirled him around. "Hey…" He was stunned by what he saw. It was Delroy.

However, it didn't look like Delroy. The man was practically grey in color, his skin ashen. His eyes were dead, but wild with some kind of feral hunger.

Peter didn't notice it before, but Delroy's clothes were disheveled and ragged. He smelled of bile and looked like a hobo.

Recognizing his friend, Peter's demeanor quickly softened. "Delroy, what are you doing? You're scaring the girls."

Only Delroy did not answer. He grabbed Peter by the shoulders and began to pull him close, as if to intimate some kind of secret, something that would explain all of this. His grip was like a vice.

The stench was overwhelming. It was a sweet, sickly, rancid stench, and it was coming off his friend. Peter's viscera contracted as the aroma of pecan pie was chased out of his nostrils. He wanted to retch.

However, as Delroy pulled Peter close, his mouth began to open, revealing stained teeth. Peter twisted and pulled away from Delroy and out of his grasp. "Delroy, what happened to you?"

Delroy lurched forward, arms extended, reaching for Peter. His mouth still hung open. Molly was screaming hysterically from the steps outside the kitchen, pulling at her hair. "You let him die, Peter! I trusted you. You promised to take care of him. I trusted you!"

Peter was caught between his friend and his wife. What the hell was going on? The daughters were now taunting Peter. "You let our daddy die. You let daddy our die. Hi-ho the dairy-o, you let our daddy die."

Peter had been Delroy's commanding officer for the past five years. In that time, they had become friends. They had seen some action in Iraq, but they had always looked out for one another.

"I did my best. There was nothing I could do."

"I trusted you, Peter."

"Molly, we were taken prisoner. There was nothing I could do."

"…hi-ho the dairy-o, you let our daddy die!"

"Girls, I didn't want your daddy to die."

"Ashes, ashes, NOW YOU FALL DOWN!"

Delroy lunged forward and grabbed Peter, falling on top of him. "Delroy, I'm so sorry." Delroy opened his mouth.

"As I lay me down to sleep, I pray the Lord my soul to keep…"

"I'm so sorry, buddy."

"And if I die before I wake, I pray my dad your brains to take."

Peter closed his eyes as he felt jagged teeth clamp down on his nose, sending blood rushing back down into his throat. He gasped for air…

***

Peter woke sitting straight up, his eyes overwhelmed with the whitewash of his surroundings. He heard the blips of monitors nearby. He was in a hospital.

It was just a dream. Where was Lucita? How did he get here? Was he still in Mexico? He knew he was back in the States when he saw a nurse enter the room with Major Lewis.

"How are you, son?"

It was such a big question. His body ached, and he was a bit disoriented. It took a moment to review in his mind all that had happened.

"The whole squad was wiped out."

His own voice sounded strange to him.

"I know, son."

"Those bastards knew we were coming. How did they know we were coming?" His question was more of a demand, and to a Major no less.

Major Lewis was a forgiving man, given the circumstances, but his tolerance had its limits.

"I don't know how they knew."

"Well, now all my men are dead because you don't know."

"You're lucky to be alive."

Peter was filled with rage, not at anything Major Lewis was saying, but at the notion of being the lone survivor. Why did *he* deserve to live? To carry around the guilt of the loss of his squad? He would've given his life for his men.

Mostly Peter was angry at himself for feeling relieved about being alive. The relief made him feel worse than anything.

"Funny, sir. I don't feel lucky."

Did Molly Apone feel relieved? What about the families of the other men? Did they get to feel relieved? He did not feel lucky at all.

Major Lewis paused, choosing his next words carefully. "You should be out in a week. There'll be some physical therapy afterwards, but nothing you can't handle."

And…That was it? Peter was waiting, as it was a pregnant remark. But Major Lewis only stared at him. Was he really going to make him ask?

Peter was so worked up that he took the bait. "And?"

Major Lewis revealed nothing, all poker face. "And what?"

"And what then? After I finish my physical therapy?"

Major Lewis smiled. "We have something for you, a new assignment."

"Oh, no. You're not putting me on some rubber gun squad. I want at those Navajas."

"I figured as much. This new assignment will be in that vein, but I cannot discuss it at the moment. It's, frankly, above your pay grade."

Was this man kidding? Above his pay grade?

"Sir," Peter was doing his best to restrain his outrage, "with all due respect, you should…no, you *owe* it to me to keep me in this fight. They need to pay for what they've done."

Major Lewis looked Peter right in the eye. "Work hard on getting better, son. We need a man as tough as you in this program. If you complete your therapy and are up to the challenge, I'll have to see about promoting you…"

"Sir, I…"

"…to First Lieutenant."

Peter was speechless. That was certainly another pay grade. He had been hoping to make First Lieutenant, just not this quickly.

Stunned, he did not know what to say. "Thank you, sir. I won't disappoint you."

"I'm sure you won't. Rest up, Sergeant. You're going to need it."

Then the Major turned and began to leave the room, but he paused halfway to the doorway. "I'm sure you'll want to tell some loved ones that you are okay. Remember that our activities in Mexico are classified."

"Yes, sir. Of course, sir."

Then Major Lewis left the room.

He would tell his parents that he was all right. He would tell them that he was injured in a training exercise at Fort Bliss, so they wouldn't worry too much.

The world was a crazy place. The United States was spread thin. There was a war on terror in Afghanistan, Iraq, Iran, Egypt, Pakistan, Greece, and South America. Iran had successfully developed nukes. North Korea was rattling its saber, as it periodically did, near the border.

Then there was the war on drugs. Every American knew there was a war on drugs, but most didn't know what that meant. Most Americans probably thought it meant patrolling the border, which was a joke, and enforcement within our own borders.

Your average American had no knowledge of the efforts in Mexico itself, with the cooperation of the Mexican government, of course. Drugs needed to be stopped before they crossed our borders.

There were sectors of the Mexican government that were in league with the cartels and gangs. The handful of politicians that wanted them routed out wanted...no, needed the help of the United States. As far as the press knew, Special Forces had gone south of the border to help train the Mexican government's military to fight the war on drugs on their end.

Of course, when those that were trained defected to the other side, the press went nuts over the story. They spared no ink in tearing the administration a new one for botching the training objective.

They preferred nation building to outright war and occupation, but they never hesitated to criticize when it failed. The only example of truly successful American nation building was in Japan after World War II.

However, despite the public's dissatisfaction with how the government was handling the war on drugs, they would certainly be critical of military operations in Mexico involving hunting down the cartels.

The liberal press would accuse the administration of being warmongers. The Tea Party and Libertarians would tout a noninterventionist standpoint. The Republicans would only be interested in occupation to profit off Mexico's natural resources and reconstruction.

So the operations in Mexico were hush-hush. What the citizenry didn't know wouldn't hurt it, and that was for its own good.

College kids and yuppies saw the drug problem as a harmless joint on Friday nights or an occasional line of coke in the executive bathroom at work. No one saw all of the death that surrounded the drug trade.

It also involved one of our borders, and therefore was a matter of national security—especially since what had evolved into the Order for International Liberation (a global terrorist organization) had taken to providing security for the cartels in running the drugs across the border.

Peter wondered about the new program that Major Lewis was referring to. He thought he knew about all of the operations going on in Mexico. This program must've been something brand spanking new, cutting edge even. He was looking forward to getting back in on the action.

First thing's first. He picked up the phone in his room and dialed his parents.

"Hi, Mom…yeah, I'm okay…there was an accident…no I'm fine. It was a training exercise on the airfield…"

***

Major Lewis was looking in his right desk drawer when there was a tone at his door.

"Enter."

Captain Fiona London entered the room, closed the door behind her, and strode up to the Major's desk. She removed her headgear and saluted smartly. "Captain London reporting."

"Have a seat, Captain."

She took a seat in one of the two chairs in front of his desk. He continued to rummage through files on his Cybernetic Digital Organizer Clipboard, while she sat there feeling somewhat awkward.

Fiona was a young captain and was in the army to help pay off graduate school. Psychologists entered the army at the rank of captain and usually worked their way up from there. As noncombatants, after passing muster at Basic Training, they served as medical staff.

"Oh, here it is." Major Lewis turned his Cybernetic Digital Organizer Clipboard to face Captain London. It was Peter's personnel file.

"Sergeant Peter Birdsall. A tough young man. Shows a lot of promise. But his squad took a nasty turn in Mexico with one of the major drug cartels, the Navajas."

Captain London reached forward and took the clipboard.

"Captain, I want you to assess Sergeant Birdsall."

She looked up from the file. "PTSD? Acute Stress Syndrome? The usual?"

"No. I know he won't have any of that."

Now she was curious. "Oh? So what should I be looking for?"

"I'm sure you've heard of the ID Program?"

Her eyes grew wide. "Yes, I have, sir. It's…operational?"

"Almost. We need a leader. Someone to learn the ropes and train a platoon in the methods."

"I see."

"This Sergeant Birdsall is one tough bastard. His whole squad in Tijuana was wiped out in front of him, and he almost bought it himself, but somehow he made it out. He's smart, quick, and resourceful. He can take a hell of a lot of pain, too."

"It sounds like you've already made your own assessment, Major."

"Well, this program is not for the weak or psychologically ill-equipped. It takes a strong constitution and an extraordinary ability to deal with loss."

"So you're asking me to assess if a man, who had his whole squad murdered in front of him and somehow survived to tell the tale, has an extraordinary ability to deal with loss?"

Major Lewis smiled. This man will be filled with piss and vinegar, and driven by thoughts of revenge, but I'm not sure if he's ready for the ID's...methods. I need to know that he'll keep a level head. If he can't then it would be..."

"Dangerous."

"Yes, Captain. That would be putting it mildly."

"Does he know he's going to be meeting with me yet?"

"No, and he won't be pleased, but that's a small matter. I'll just dangle the carrot of the new program in front of him. He'll do it. The rest is up to your ability to get inside his head."

"So he's aware of the ID Program?"

"No. Not yet. Not until he's ready. You'll tell me if he is."

"Yes, sir."

"And, of course, all of this is confidential, and you'll report only to me. Is that clear, Captain London?"

"Yes, sir."

Major Lewis flashed a warm smile at her. "I knew you were the right person for the job."

"I'll do my best, sir."

"If we can get this program off the ground and run successful pilot tests in Mexico, the implications for unconventional warfare will be quite profound."

"I understand, sir."

"Dismissed, Captain."

***

Peter was sore from his physical therapy session and was irritable. He was in no mood to see a shrink.

He detested army shrinks. They could not possibly understand what a real soldier went through. They were noncombatants and never saw any action.

He winced as he walked down the corridor to her office. Captain Fiona London. She sounded to him like an actress or model, or a WASP who enlisted in the army to piss off daddy.

He pressed the blue button for the retinal scan. A beam scanned his eye, and a tone signaled the confirmation of his identity.

"Enter," he heard from inside.

He stepped into the room, closed the door behind him, and saluted the captain at her desk.

"That won't be necessary, Sergeant."

She gestured for him to sit down in the chair in front of her desk.

As he sat, he took in her office. It was different from the other officers' offices. It wasn't minimally decorated with that Spartan sensibility so characteristic of the army.

No, Captain London apparently was going for homey, but only as much as the military would permit. There were curtains on the window, even a valence. Impressionistic paintings hung on the walls, probably by famous painters, not that he would know the difference.

Then it dawned on him. It was his parents' living room from his childhood. Nice touch. Just enough to make him feel at home.

He sized up his new therapist. Captain London obviously had some sophistication to go with her fancy degrees, and she was not terrible to look at either.

"So, Sergeant Birdsall…may I call you Peter?"

"Yes, ma'am."

"I think that we can dispense with the formalities. I think that it is important that you feel comfortable in here."

"Well, I've never been to a…shrink before."

"That's okay. I think you'll find I'm the least painful army doctor."

There was something very easy-going about her demeanor. Peter felt that it was almost as if she was flirting with him, but there was no flirtatious body language. She was being folksy.

"Let's see." She was poking the touch screen of her Cybernetic Digital Organizer. "Sergeant Peter Birdsall. Age 24, 6'4", 220 pounds. Texas native. Played high school football. Hobbies include hunting, fishing, and camping. Good all-American boy."

"Yes, ma'am."

She put down the Cybernetic Digital Organizer and looked him right in the eye. "So, Peter, I see from your file that you had experienced the loss of your squad in Tijuana."

Boy, she didn't mince words.

"Yes."

"And Corporal Delroy Apone was a friend."

Peter swallowed hard. "Yes, that's correct."

"I'm very sorry to hear about that."

"Thank you."

Captain London paused briefly, deciding which route to go with the session. She wanted him to open up, but she didn't want to be too direct and shut him down. "If you don't mind me asking, how on earth did you manage to get out?"

"I believe it's all in the file."

"Yes, in the file it states that you fought off your captors with hands bound and fled to the city where someone had apparently taken you in."

Lucita. He never saw her again, was never able to thank her. "Yes, that's correct."

"Well, Peter, you are very lucky to still be with us."

He hated that everyone said that to him. "I don't feel lucky."

"What do you mean?"

"I mean that I walked my men into an obvious ambush. I saw my men gunned down...no, *executed* in front of me. And now I get to live with that the rest of my life."

"Peter, I'm not going to bullshit you. You were squad commander. You were responsible for those men. Now, I can say that it wasn't your fault that the Navajas knew you were coming. But that wouldn't change what happened or how you feel about it."

Peter began to tense his hands and clench his jaw. "No, it wouldn't."

"In fact, it would probably just piss you off."

"Yes, it would."

"And it would be equally ridiculous to remind you that as a soldier in the United States Army, there is the distinct statistical probability that any of your squad will or will not make it back from any given mission."

He was now gripping the arms of his chair. "Yes, it would."

"And why would that be ridiculous, Peter?"

"Because it wouldn't help me fix anything."

"It wouldn't bring back your friend, Delroy."

His eyes were welling up. She could see the sadness of loss and heat of vengeance in his glare.

"So what do I do, Doc? What *can* I do?"

She now leaned forward, meeting the intensity of his eyes with determination in hers. "What would you like to do?"

Peter was now visibly attempting to control his feelings. "Permission to speak freely."

"Peter, you can say anything you want in here."

"I know you report to Major Lewis, so I want him to hear this."

She nodded in encouragement.

"I want to kill the bastards. I want to hunt every single one of them down. I want to burn their entire drug running operation to the ground. Is that what you wanted to hear?"

She paused thoughtfully, letting his words hang out in the air. It was important to let his own words register with him.

"You're not ready yet."

The digital curtains and paintings glitched.

"I know; I have to complete my physical therapy."

"I wasn't referring to your physical recuperation."

"Oh, here it comes. So I'm not *psychologically* ready."

She leaned back in her chair, her voice now softer but firm. "Peter, you're very angry and looking for revenge, and you haven't dealt with the loss yet."

Peter was growing tired of the psychobabble. "And…"

"And that would make you dangerous. Dangerous to any soldiers we would put in your charge, particularly for the program that Major Lewis has in mind for you."

"Yeah, no one's exactly told me what this program is actually about. How do I know that I even want to be a part of it?"

"For the exact reasons that you have just elaborated. You want revenge, but in time, I'd like to modify that motive a bit. Eventually, you can come to the conclusion that it is important that your men…your friend, Delroy Apone…didn't die for nothing."

Peter nodded in agreement.

"Right now your vengeance makes you reckless, impulsive. You would run into any fight to exact your revenge. But it has to be about more than that."

"What do you mean?"

"I mean that it has to become more than about you and your guilt and making yourself feel better."

He stood up out of his chair, shaking. The paintings distorted momentarily. "How dare you imply that I'm being selfish."

She stood and met his gaze. "So far, all I've heard about is how *you* feel. How sad *you* are. How angry *you* are. How *you* miss *your* friend."

"What the hell else am I supposed to say?"

"It's not all what you say, Peter. What are you going to do? Are you going to deal with your loss and move on so that you can do the right thing for your men and your country?"

Peter slowly lowered himself into his seat. He had never thought of it that way before. She was right. He couldn't just return to Mexico, guns blazing, shooting up the place.

His men in Tijuana deserved more, and if he were to return, the new soldiers in his charge would deserve more too. They deserved a CO who would have a clear head and show good judgment.

"And...how do I go about doing this?"

Captain London sat down and smiled. "You've already begun. That's what you're here for, Peter. You can't do this alone."

Peter nodded silently.

"Peter, the Chinese have a saying: 'In every crisis there is danger and opportunity.' The danger is that you're too traumatized by what happened in Tijuana and you'll wash out, but there's an opportunity. Deal with you grief, your guilt, and your loss and return to Mexico wiser from experience."

She hesitated, choosing her next words cautiously. "And this new program is like nothing anyone's ever seen before. It needs competent leadership. It needs you, Peter."

"I understand."

She sized him up for a moment, registering his sincerity, but she wondered if he had the will. They would both find out soon enough.

"I think that's enough for today, Peter. We'll meet again next week. We have a lot of work to do."

"Yes, I suppose we do."

"By the way—standard question—I don't have to worry about you hurting yourself or anyone else, do I?"

"Just the Navajas."

"Good. See you next week."

He stood and saluted, and she dismissed him. He left and the digital curtains and paintings from his youth switched off. After he left her office, she sighed heavily and opened his file. Before she registered her session note, she dialed Major Lewis.

"Hello, Major."

"Did you see Sergeant Birdsall?"

"Yes, we just concluded our first session."

"So, what do you think? Is he ready?"

She paused. "No, he's not ready yet, sir."

"How long?"

"I'm not sure how long, if ever."

"You'll keep me abreast of his progress?" It was an order more than a question.

"Of course, Major."

"It is important that he get back on the horse. If not, he'll wash out."

"I understand, sir."

"Good day, Captain."

She hung up the phone and stared into thin air, lost in her thoughts for a moment. Rehabilitation of Sergeant Birdsall was certainly possible. Soldiers in combat situations had to deal with trauma and loss all of the time.

Part of her worried about what she was preparing him for. Sending this man into the ID Program was like sending a snowball careening into hell. If he wanted back in, he would get it. However, at what cost to him?

She had to follow orders. Besides, he wouldn't be compelled to join the program. He could always be reassigned, but she saw that look in his eyes. He would not give up. He would not quit. She was a good enough judge of character to know that he would pursue this to the end.

She picked up her pen, began to compose her analysis, and she registered her first session note with Sergeant Peter Birdsall.

***

The next few months, Peter faithfully attended his physical therapy sessions, and his perseverance paid off. His injuries were minimal given the situation, and he progressed rapidly.

His psychotherapy with Captain London was also going well. She had a practice of cutting through the garbage and addressing things head on, and he respected that.

They had discussed his relationships with each of his men, his guilt, and his anger. He was beginning to find some closure about what had happened in Tijuana.

She had taught him how to compartmentalize his feelings and memories about what had transpired. She taught him the Buddhist philosophy towards loss—that in death people gave back that which never belonged to them in the first place.

She talked about entanglements, and how worrying about loss would cause a self-fulfilling prophecy in combat. He learned to let go of worry about dying and focus on staying alive.

Captain London had his file open in front of her on her desk. He was shifting uncomfortably in his seat. "Well, Doc…what do you think?"

"Well, Peter, you've made significant strides in our sessions together. You managed your grief; you confronted your guilt…"

"And…"

"And, I'll be recommending you for the ID Program."

Peter jumped up so quickly that he startled her. He shook her hand enthusiastically. "Thanks, Doc. I really appreciate it. I won't let you down."

"You worked hard, Peter. Of course, my recommendations are only recommendations. Major Lewis will read them and make a final decision."

Peter suddenly felt awkward. "Well, Doc, I guess this is it."

He was confused by the consequent expression on her face. If he wasn't mistaken, it was…amusement.

She chortled, "Oh, no, Peter. This isn't goodbye."

Peter stood there, some of the wind obviously taken out of his sails.

"I-I don't understand."

"Peter, if Major Lewis approves you for the ID Program, you'll definitely need to be continuing sessions on an on-going basis. I'll need to evaluate your on-going mental status and fitness for duty."

"I still don't understand."

"Major Lewis will explain everything to you. In the meantime, you're due for some R&R. I recommended some leave time, and if Major Lewis approves it, I suggest you take it."

He was not sure what to make of any of this. "Yes, ma'am. And thank you."

Peter left her office a new man, although he was unsure of what was in store for him, but he was grateful to Captain London and what she did for him.

In the days that followed, he anxiously awaited Major Lewis' response. He was lying in his bunk when his com unit beeped…he had a message.

He touched the screen. It was from Major Lewis. Excited, he opened the message. It was the approval of the leave time. That was it. No mention of the ID Program or Captain London's recommendation.

He was disappointed, but no news was no news, not bad news. He decided that he would go out, raise some hell, and worry about the ID Program, whatever it was, when he returned.

He had the ominous feeling that he was going to get what he asked for, but he was not exactly sure if he wanted it.

Chapter 3

Peter pulled up in a cab to his childhood house. It was late and the block was quiet. Living room windows flickered with television light, like fires in hearths.

He swiped his Mini-com over the payment kiosk in the back of the cab and thanked the driver. Shouldering his duffle bag, he closed the door quietly and strode up the front path as the taxicab pulled away.

The living room was dimly lit from some secondary light source—his parents must have been in the kitchen.

He paused before he reached the front door. He took in his neighborhood. Once the stomping grounds of his youth, the block felt familiar, but no longer like home.

He stepped up to the front door, placed his palm on the security lock panel, and it registered his print. A soft tone sounded, and the door lock disengaged.

He quietly slipped into the house. He heard conversations coming from the kitchen table. He silently crossed the living room and stood in the archway to the kitchen, placing his duffle bag quietly on the floor.

His mother, sitting at the kitchen table facing him, was the first to notice. She stood up and put her right hand to her mouth as if to silence an outcry.

"Oh, Peter, you're home."

His father was sitting at the table with his younger brother, Carl. She ran over to him and threw her arms around him. "Oh thank God you're alright."

"I told you it wasn't that bad, Mom. A little physical therapy and I'm good as new."

His father came over and put his arm around him. "How's my man doing?"

"Fine, Dad."

His father backed away, making room for Carl, who stepped up and hugged his brother. "How's the army treating you?"

"Shitty as usual, Carl. How've you been?"

"Well, we were just discussing that," Peter's mother interjected rather tersely.

"Now, Marla, we don't need to burden Peter with Carl's…situation," his father admonished.

Peter wondered what kind of conversation he had just interrupted. "Why? What's going on with Carl?"

Carl put his hands up in exasperation. "They just don't understand, Pete. Maybe you can help me explain it to them."

Peter leaned against the kitchen counter. "Explain what, Carl?"

"He thinks he's dropping out of school and joining the military, Peter." His mother's eyes were welling up with tears.

"No, not dropping out," Carl corrected, "just postponing."

Peter didn't understand. "Why, Carl? I thought you liked school."

"I do, Pete. It's just that I'm halfway through, and I can't afford it anymore. And Mom and Dad can't afford to help me out either."

This was happening all over again. The first two decades of the new millennium saw a freezing in credit, an exponential increase in college tuition, and predatory lending from banks with double-digit interest. On top of that, unemployment had been hovering between nine and fifteen percent over the years in what economists were calling the Rollercoaster Recession.

This was the same discussion Peter had with his parents several years ago, only he never entertained the notion of attending college. This was a wound for his parents that had not yet completely healed, particularly for his mother, and now his brother Carl was opening it up again and pouring on the salt.

"Carl…"

"Don't 'Carl' me, Peter. You of all people should understand. My half scholarship is no longer cutting it. In order to take out a bank loan, Mom and Dad would have to cosign…at 22 percent. *Twenty-two percent*, Pete. I can't let them do that."

"I told you I'd find a way to pay it, Carl," his father said. "The military is not an option."

"It was for Pete," Carl retorted.

"Carl, do you know what joining the military means?" Peter implored.

"So what, now *you* can do it, but *I* can't hack it?" Carl was sounding hurt and defensive. So much for a nice, quiet visit home.

"Carl, in case you forgot, we are at war. A war on many fronts." Peter had to be careful—no mention of Mexico. "It's not like you'll be at a base in training exercises all day. They'll ship you off to Iran, Iraq, Afghanistan, or some other God forsaken part of the world where you'll be shot at by the very same people you're trying to help."

His mother was pleading with Carl, "Honey, listen to Peter. You'll be shot at, bombed. There are decapitations."

"Well what am I supposed to do, live in your basement unemployed? For how long? There are no jobs. College is a waste."

Peter sized up his younger brother. He was about as tall, but thin and soft from an easy life. He wouldn't even survive boot camp. Then there were the horrors of war.

"Carl, if you enlist, you'd be putting yourself in harm's way every day for people halfway around the world who don't understand freedom or democracy."

"So, is that how you feel about what you do, Pete?"

"Yes, Carl. Yes it is. It is exactly how I feel."

"So, then why do you do it?"

Peter knew there were two answers to this question. He was doing it for freedom and democracy. He was doing it to fight villains all around the world who threatened the American way of life. Then there was the other reason, a much less romantic one.

"Carl, I wasn't a good student like you. I didn't have any other option."

His mother glared at him. She apparently believed otherwise, but she had lost that argument years ago.

"Well, Pete, I don't have any other option either. I only have two years of school under my belt, and there are no jobs."

This was true, and in the past decade, many other young people found themselves in the very same shoes that Carl was standing in at that moment in the middle of his parents' kitchen.

"There's another way, Carl," his father pleaded. "I'll make some phone calls. I know people who owe me favors."

"Carl, please. Listen to your father."

"Mom, we've been through this already. There's no other option for me. The military could train me in engineering. They need people, and it would be good on-the-job training."

"For what?" his father asked. "The private sector? The private sector doesn't give a damn about anything you learn in the military."

"That's not true, Dad."

Peter was leaning up against the kitchen counter taking this all in. He had been here before, and this all resurrected memories of intense arguments over the dinner table and the horrible guilt of what he did to his mother.

He wanted very badly to shake his brother and discourage him from enlisting, but his brother was grown and this was not Peter's fight. At the moment, he was content to be a noncombatant in this battle.

"Pete, I know you understand."

"Carl, my situation was different."

"Different? How?"

"It...it just was, Carl."

Carl threw up his hands in surrender.

"Well, I see I can't reason with any of you." He stormed out of the kitchen, slamming the storm door behind him.

Peter's mother grabbed his hands and squeezed them in hers. "Please, Peter. You have to *explain* to him…"

"What, Mom? What am I supposed to explain to him? What could I possibly say that wouldn't make me look like a hypocrite?" Tears streamed down his mother's face. "Mom, I don't want him to enlist any more than you do, but what could I say?"

Her eye makeup was running down her face. Peter felt awful. He felt awful for what Carl was doing to her, and more so, he felt awful again for what he had put her through. He knew she suffered every day, worrying about where he was and if he was okay. She never admitted this to him, but his father had related it to him during quiet moments alone.

They heard the sound of Carl bouncing a basketball in the backyard. His father put a sympathetic arm around his wife. "Well, I don't think Peter wanted to come home to this. Let's give him a chance to settle in. He must be hungry."

"Yeah, Mom. I've been dreaming about your meatloaf since the last time I came home. You wouldn't have any of it handy, would you?"

His mother wiped her eyes, sniffled, and nodded, smiling uncontrollably at her son's flattery. "Yes, Peter. As a matter of fact, I do. I'll warm some up for you."

Peter smiled at his mother. "Sounds good, Mom."

He shouldered his duffle bag and walked out of the kitchen, ascending the steps to his room. As he unpacked his bag on his old bed, he heard his parents continuing the discussion in hushed whispers as Carl dribbled the ball furiously on the patio out back.

Peter looked out his old bedroom window as Carl took a shot that hit the rim and ricocheted away from him. Had things gotten so bad that even his egghead brother was now considering the army? He was the one who was to become some kind of a doctor or engineer and make his parents proud.

However, part of Peter was relieved that he was no longer the black sheep who disappointed his parents. Now he was in good company, but that did not stop him from worrying about his little brother.

When he finished packing, he went down stairs and wolfed down his mother's leftover meatloaf. She stood there clutching a cup of coffee and watching him eat with maternal satisfaction.

It was a small satisfaction, but some of the only satisfaction she got these days. She tried her best to be content at home, but she missed the days of working in the office. A casualty of the recession, she became a shell of her former self, smiling through her domestication and feeling helplessly inadequate.

Peter's father was sitting with him at the kitchen table. "Peter, this accident you had…"

"Nothing that would happen again, Dad. A freak accident. The Major called it a 'low probability event.'" He hated lying to his father. "I'm okay, really. So how've you guys been?" Change of topic.

"Good, I guess. The hardware store's doing okay. Business has been a bit slow, but it's a living. It's good to see you again."

His mother jumped in. "It's always good to see you, Peter."

"Thanks, Mom."

All things being equal, Peter felt good. He was home, he was stuffed to the gills, and he was ready to hit the town. "I'm going to grab Carl. I've been itching for a night out on the town."

He remembered his last night on the town with Apone and his squad.

His father put his hand on his shoulder. "Can I offer you gents a lift? Frisky's I presume?"

"Yeah, Dad. Thanks. We'll walk back." Peter got up and hugged his mom.

"Be careful, Peter. Look after your brother."

"Will do, Mom."

He and his father went into the backyard to fetch Carl.

***

Peter and Carl got out of their father's car and waved as their father drove off. Ah, Frisky's. It was a local dive—small, smoky, a total dump—but it was theirs. Every single local knew Frisky's, only some would ever admit to frequenting it, but the beer specials were unmatched.

Carl gestured for Peter to lead the way. Peter opened the front door and held it for his little brother, and they walked in.

Inside, it was packed, a typical Friday night. There were men and women, mostly in their twenties, and a few middle-aged husbands who snuck out of the house for the night to have some suds with the guys or just find temporary respite.

The MP3 shuffler was belting out a Wave Punk tune, what people in the 1980's would have considered a blend of new wave and punk music. It was old wine in new wine skins, but it was the popular genre of the moment.

Peter led his brother to the bar where he ordered two domestic beers. Forty dollars. Couldn't beat it. Townie bars had their merits. The boys sat there and canvassed the bar enthusiastically with their eyes. There were pretty girls everywhere, townies mostly, but that's all there ever was around there.

Peter appreciated that one thing about the army. It got him the hell out of Texas. He mused that nine point five out of every ten patrons in the bar probably never left the state.

Carl was watching his big brother. He knew something was weighing heavily on him. "Pete, everything alright with you? You look like you're carrying the weight of the world on your shoulders…"

No, just the weight of ten men and their families.

"…I'm sorry you walked in on that conversation."

"It wasn't that, Carl."

However, Peter saw the look of relief on Carl's face and didn't want it to look like he was condoning Carl's decision. "But I agree with Mom and Dad. You can do better than the army."

"Pete, you've been in the army so long, you haven't been keeping up with what's going on in the private sector."

"What private sector?"

"Exactly."

"But, Carl, men die in the army. Good men like you."

"So what do I do, hide away in safety in our parents' basement? Pete, I've never been anywhere. You've been places, seen things."

"You have no idea, Carl. I've seen many things. I've seen dead bodies. Not just of the enemy, but children…*children*, Carl. Comrades, friends, fellow Americans…good people."

Carl was now starting to feel genuinely concerned. He knew his brother, and he knew there was definitely something wrong. "Pete, what happened to you?"

"The same thing that will happen to you if you enlist, Carl. You'll lose people. You'll make friends, get close to men in your unit, and then you'll lose them. If you're lucky, you're the one who will eat it, and then others can worry about feeling bad for your death."

Carl looked confused. "I thought you were spending the past year in training exercises."

Crap. Peter underestimated how sharp his brother was. He needed a topic change. "How about you, little bro? How are things in the ladies department?"

Carl looked away defensively, pulling his drink closer to him. He pretended that he was scanning the room. Peter knew this was a sore topic for Carl, but it did the trick. It took the focus off him.

"Well, not many women want to date unemployed, broke students living with their parents."

"Carl, it doesn't mean that you can't have any fun."

"So what am I supposed to do, lie to them?"

Peter smiled. "No, just don't tell them the truth."

He saw Carl eyeing a beautiful brunette by the MP3 shuffler. Some local hick was making a royal mess out of hitting on her.

He leaned over and talked in Carl's ear. "She's way out of your league, bro."

Carl laughed and brushed his shoulder off. "You were the one who played in leagues, Pete. I'm going to dazzle her with my intellect."

Peter slapped him on the back. "Go for it, tiger. I'll be there to catch her on the rebound."

Carl took one last slug, draining his pint, and slammed it heartily on the bar. "You assume I'm going to fail. You assume too much."

"Go get her, Romeo."

Carl started to walk away when Peter grabbed him by the sleeve and reeled him in.

"What now, Pete?"

"Wait a minute, hot shot. What's your approach?"

"I'm just going to go over there and introduce myself."

"That's it? You're just going to…say hi?"

"Yeah, introduce myself. You know, like civilized humans do."

Peter looked over at the target. Long legs, ample rack, curves in all the right places. "I don't think she's so civilized, Carl. She's some kind of predator."

"Classy, bro. Real classy."

"Hey, I just call it as I see it."

"Let me do my thing."

Peter let his brother go and watched in amusement as he sauntered over to the brunette by the MP3 shuffler. They had only just arrived, and already Carl was trying to show up his big brother. It had always been that way, even though Peter thought his parents favored Carl.

Peter was always bigger, more athletic, and better looking. Carl wasn't bad looking, but he was more ordinary. However, when it came to intelligence, Peter admitted that Carl out-classed him.

Peter was not quite sure what Carl said to the girl, but her body language already indicated that she was not interested. She was trying desperately to look around the bar for a friend to bail her out, but she wasn't so lucky. Carl was floundering.

Peter finished his beer and placed his glass on the bar. Big brother to the rescue. He crossed the bar over to where Carl and the brunette were standing. Peter addressed the girl, ignoring Carl entirely. "Hi. Is this guy bugging you?"

The brunette looked at him to gauge if he was serious. So did Carl. She nodded tentatively.

He grabbed Carl by his shirt. "Get lost, dude." And he shoved him several feet away. Okay, so it wasn't exactly Carl he was rescuing. "Hi, my name's Peter."

The brunette smiled, obviously impressed by his brawn and assertiveness. It was pure animal magnetism. "Hi, I'm Amanda."

Carl, his pride wounded from being upstaged by his big brother yet again, went back to the bar and ordered a shot of whiskey and a beer chaser. He looked on helplessly as his brother charmed the pants off the knockout brunette. He figured that girls like that just responded to sophomoric bravado, something he decided was not in his constitution.

He turned to face the bar and wallow in his self-pity when he saw her. She was an attractive blonde. Pretty, athletic, and she had an air of self-confidence. She was looking across the bar. Perhaps she was waiting for someone. Nevertheless, at the moment, she was alone.

Carl pulled himself together, took one last swig of his beer, and he summoned the courage to dismount his bar stool. He crossed the bar, apparently acting before his mind could catch up. He was frantically searching for the perfect introduction, but he was in front of her before he could come up with anything.

He stood there awkwardly in front of her, and it wasn't long before her gaze shifted from across the bar to him. He didn't know what to say. He held out his hand. "Hi...I'm Carl."

Not facile at reading the opposite sex, Carl was not sure how to interpret her reaction. It was somewhere between confusion and displeasure, but the look quickly faded, and she smiled politely. "Hi, Carl."

"Do you mind if I join you?"

She began to fidget. "Well, actually I am supposed to meet someone…"

"Yeah, I'm supposed to meet my brother," he pointed to Pete making time with the brunette, "but he's obviously busy at the moment."

"Oh, I see…" she looked over at Peter and then at Carl. She appeared to have an inexplicable sudden change of heart. "What're you drinking, Carl?"

"At this point, whiskey."

"Rough day?"

"You have no idea."

The girl summoned the bartender. "Two whisky shots, black label."

Carl was impressed. This girl knew how to order drinks.

"So, Carl, what was so rough about your day?"

"Well…I decided that I was going to enlist…in the army." Dammit, he forgot…he wasn't supposed to tell the truth.

"Oh, the army. Impressive."

Wow. He wasn't expecting that. She looked actually impressed.

"Yeah, well, my parents weren't too happy about it."

"No, I suppose they wouldn't be."

"Even my brother, who's actually a sergeant in the army."

"Really? Well, that seems hypocritical of him, doesn't it?"

"Yes. Yes it does."

He couldn't believe it. He was actually having a real conversation with a beautiful woman, and she was so easy to talk to. The night was looking up.

"So why the army, Carl? You don't seem like the army type."

Now he was embarrassed. Apparently sensing his insult, the girl clarified her remark. "I mean, you seem like someone who'd do well in the private sector."

"Yeah, that's what my brother seems to think. But the economy is so bad, I can't afford any more tuition, and there are no jobs."

"So the army seems like your best option at the moment."

"Well, I want to do something with myself. I don't just want to sit around and do nothing. I am my own man. I want to see the world."

"Well, Carl, you know the army isn't a vacation."

"I know that, but maybe I want to do some good, and perhaps I'll learn some skills on the job."

"What were you studying in school, Carl?"

"Engineering. I figured that there's plenty of on-the-job training, and the army can pay the rest of my tuition."

"Well, there are other skills you can learn too, besides engineering."

"Oh?"

"Like leadership, independence, discipline."

Carl thought he was falling in love. Here he was talking to a beautiful woman who understood him and what he wanted to do. Was this actually going somewhere? She seemed older, but he wasn't sure how much.

Then he realized that he knew nothing about her. Here he was droning on about himself and his existential quandary. He suddenly felt self-conscious and rather clumsily tried to change the topic to her.

"So, I've been going on and on about myself, I don't even know your name."

She was looking over his shoulder. "Oh, I think I see the person I was supposed to meet."

Oh great. She was blowing him off. He screwed up, blathering on about enlisting, unemployment, and his parents.

"Let's go say hi." Unexpectedly, she grabbed him by the arm and nearly yanked him off his bar stool. She pulled him through the crowd, through the smoke, and across the tiny dance floor until she was standing in front of Peter.

Peter looked away from his brunette as he saw some blonde pulling his brother across the bar. He almost did a double take when he saw who it was.

"Hi, Peter."

Carl was confused. "What? You know my brother? Pete, you know her?"

Peter, embarrassed by his company and completely unprepared for this encounter, straightened up. "Captain London."

Peter didn't know why, but he was disconcerted. He didn't want Captain London seeing him with this bar fly. Part of him found her attractive since their first meeting, even though romance wasn't an option. She was his therapist after all.

Carl couldn't believe it. He was finally able to maintain a conversation, with a total knockout no less, and she was here to meet his brother. What was it with this guy? What did Pete have that he didn't?

"I was just talking with your brother, Carl, over at the bar."

Peter didn't quite know what to say. The brunette, no longer the center of Peter's attention, looked flustered.

"What are you doing here, Captain?"

She sized up the brunette contemptuously. "Major Lewis sent me to personally tell you that your leave has been cut short."

Great. Again?

"He has approved you for…that program we were talking about."

It took a moment for the meaning of her message to register with Peter. At the moment, it was really the last thing on his mind.

Carl was lost. "Program? What's she talking about, Pete?"

She was staring him dead in the eye, no doubt gauging his reaction.

"Nothing, Carl. Yes, thank you, Captain. I'll report tomorrow morning."

"At 08:00, Lieutenant."

What? Did he hear her correctly?

"Lieutenant," he repeated tentatively.

"Yes, it appears you have been promoted."

Carl stood there stunned. The brunette, her ego bruised, was losing interest fast. Carl was happy for his brother. "Pete, this is great! Lieutenant. Congratulations!"

"08:00 hours, Captain."

Captain London turned to Carl and shook his hand. Her skin was soft to the touch, but her grip was firm. "It was nice meeting you, Carl. Peter, you never told me your brother was cute."

Then she turned and left the bar.

Now Carl stood there just as flabbergasted as his brother was. The brunette had already left the scene and was now talking to some other jock. Both brothers basked in the glow of accomplishment, and each would have argued that his was more significant.

They left the bar shortly thereafter and began their half-drunken walk home. Carl was dissertating about how smooth he was in his introduction and conversation with the illustrious Captain London. Peter was unable to discuss his promotion and what it meant, so all he could do was listen to Carl. Unfortunately, the effects of the alcohol were waning, rendering Carl's soliloquy nearly unbearable.

Carl noticed his brother squirming. "Hey, listen, I understand if this makes you uncomfortable, she being a senior officer and all."

Peter didn't respond. Carl studied his big brother's face, and then his face lit up as if struck by a great epiphany. "It's not that, is it?"

Peter just kept looking forward as he walked.

"It's not that at all," Carl continued in delight. "You *like* her."

"Carl, she's my goddamned therapist."

"She's a shrink? Why are you seeing a shrink?"

Peter looked annoyed. "Carl, haven't you heard of confidentiality?"

Carl was practically squealing with delight. "You *like* her. And she said *I* was cute, and that just burns your ass."

"Yes, Carl," Peter responded sarcastically, "it really burns my ass, even though she's my shrink and there's no prospect whatsoever."

For Carl this was Christmas come a little early. "Oh, it burns your ass alright. A girl actually chose *me* over you."

"She didn't choose anything, Carl. She just said you were cute."

Then it was as if Carl was told that there was no Santa Clause. "Crap...crap, you're right."

Peter felt bad at Carl's disappointment, but he was happy it shut him up.

"Hey, Pete, do you think I'll see her again?"

Peter just looked at his brother with exasperation. Weary from a night of drinking, he put his arm around his brother and they walked the rest of the way home in silence.

Chapter 4

Peter tossed and turned that night in his old bed. He was dreaming furiously. Visions of Apone, Marx, Spottiswoode, and the others danced in his head. They stared at him, through him, boring into his soul and exposing his guilt to the light of day. He could not hide from their collective gaze and consequently his own shame.

He awoke in a cold sweat with bitterness on his tongue. He sat up and swung his legs over the side of the bed, putting his feet on the floor. His shirt was drenched. He rubbed his eyes thoroughly, as if it might rub out the bad memories.

He looked at the clock—three twenty-two in the morning, only a couple of hours before his alarm. He wiped the tears streaming down his face with his forearm, sniffled, and reached for his duffle bag under his bed. He reached in and pulled out his pistol. He felt it in his hand. It was like an extension of his body. But that was his training.

He placed the cool barrel on his forehead as he fought back sobs. He struggled to keep quiet; he didn't want to wake his parents or Carl. He rocked back and forth, contemplating the unspeakable as his body convulsed with suppressed sadness. He wanted to scream, but he fought the urge.

He slowly slid the barrel of the gun down his forehead until it reached his mouth. He then slowly opened his mouth wider and slid the barrel in. He was now shaking violently as he sat there in his childhood bedroom with a gun in his mouth poised to pull the trigger.

This was the bedroom where he played with his action figures, read his comic books by flashlight, and fantasized about several girls in his class. Life was so much simpler then. It was filled with such possibility.

However, as potential cannot sustain itself indefinitely with the passage of time, all individuals are forced to make choices. And with each choice made, potential erodes, possibilities are left behind, and one's life path narrows. Then one must face the life he has chosen for himself and all that goes with it. Nevertheless, at three twenty-two in the morning sitting in his childhood bed, Peter could not stomach the absurdity of his situation and the horrors he had unknowingly chosen for himself.

He yearned to sleep forever, to join his fallen comrades, but they had died an honorable death. What he was about to do was…cowardice.

He slid the pistol out of his mouth and put it gingerly on his end table. He realized that suicide would bring further shame and dishonor on himself.

No, he would report back to Fort Bliss and jump head first into this "ID" Program, whatever the hell it was. He would hunt down every last Navajas until he took his very last breath.

Amused by what he almost did in his parents' house, he chuckled hysterically to himself as he sobbed in the dark. He placed his pistol back into his duffle bag, lowered his head back onto his pillow, and took advantage of what time he had left before the alarm would sound off.

His parents slept soundly in the next room, completely unaware of how close they were to tragedy. Then again, ignorance is bliss.

***

El Paso Intelligence Center
Biggs Army Airfield, Fort Bliss

Peter was in uniform outside Major Lewis' door at exactly 08:00 when the door gave its tone and he heard the Major shout, "Enter."

Peter walked into the room, strolled up to the Major's desk and saluted. "Lieutenant Peter Birdsall reporting."

"Be seated, Lieutenant."

Peter sat.

"Well, as you have likely guessed from your promotion, you have been approved for the ID Program."

"Yes, sir. Captain London had informed me in person."

"Yes…" Major Lewis hesitated for a moment, as if he wanted to lend gravity to what he was about to say. "What I am about to tell you is highly classified, so classified that most of the army itself does not have clearance to this information. The existence of this program is not common knowledge, and with good reason."

"I understand, sir."

"But the significance of this program is profound. If successfully developed, it will change the landscape of the war in the Middle East."

Now Peter was confused. The Middle East? He thought they were going to be operating in Mexico.

Major Lewis sensed Peter's confusion. "One of the greatest obstacles to hunting down terrorists has not been their decentralized nature, or the support of a network of disenfranchised countries around the globe, or anything of that sort."

Peter waited for the correct answer.

"It is the terrain. No matter how many drones we send in, once they retreat to the caves, it's game over. That's why we're still in Afghanistan. It's a haven for terrorists, but the cave system makes the terrain virtually inaccessible."

"I understand, sir. The army does not wish to waste lives sending soldiers into the caves."

"And bombing only affects the surface. But Research and Development has acquired a technology that would allow us to infiltrate the cave system in Afghanistan without needlessly expending lives."

Peter was fascinated, and he wondered what the technology was, but foremost, he wondered what the Navajas had to do with Afghanistan. "Sir, if you don't mind me asking, what does this have to do with the Navajas?"

Major Lewis produced his Cybernetic Digital Organizer and called up a file. He then slid it across his desk to Peter. "We have intelligence that the Navajas have moved their operations to Xcaret, Mexico. They apparently find the cenote cave systems to be optimal for hiding their operations from the authorities. We need to achieve maximum penetration of this system of underground caves.

You will pilot this new program in Xcaret. If it passes the field test, then we will likely get the green light for Afghanistan."

"I see. So what is this new technology?"

Major Lewis sat back in his chair and sized Peter up, as if he was gauging Peter's preparedness for the answer. "The technology is best shown, and then explained."

Why was the Major being so cryptic?

"Okay, sir."

The Major paused for another moment and then stood up. "Follow me."

Peter followed him out of the office and out of the building. They crossed the airfield to a large hangar. They entered through a small door.

Peter recognized the hangar from his training exercises on the base. Inside was a large replica of a building. It was used to train squads to infiltrate buildings and clear rooms. There were a few of these on the base, but this one was particularly vicious because it was set up like a maze, hence its nickname, the Labyrinth.

Major Lewis strode up to a man standing in front of the faux building. The man saluted.

"Lieutenant Birdsall, this is Sergeant Lockwood. He's in charge of many of the training exercises on base."

"Yes, I am familiar with Sergeant Lockwood." As a matter of fact, Peter had participated in some of Sergeant Lockwood's training exercises.

Major Lewis nodded to Sergeant Lockwood, who then addressed Peter. "Lieutenant, I ask that you step into the building."

Peter was taken off guard. "I'm sorry. You want me to step inside?"

"Yes, sir."

Peter was not sure what game they were playing, but he did as instructed. He stepped into the first room of the structure and turned to face Sergeant Lockwood. "So what am I supposed to do now, Sergeant?"

"Make it to the other side." Then the sergeant closed the door. Peter heard him engage the digi-lock from the other side.

What was the point of this? Was he just supposed to meander through the maze? He was pretty sure he remembered the way. If not, it wouldn't take much to figure it out in short order.

"Begin," he heard Sergeant Lockwood yell from the other side of the door.

Peter began to walk through the rooms. It was dark, so he used his Mini-com Multi-tasker as a light source. He strolled from room to room, feeling foolish. Was something supposed to happen? Was this new technology somewhere in the maze?

That's when he heard it.

Footsteps. But the gait was strange. It was a shuffling, if he was not mistaken. It was coming from one of the adjoining rooms. He crept quietly into the next room, put his back to the wall, and listened. Someone else was definitely in the maze with him, and the mystery guest was zeroing in on his position.

The footsteps sounded like they were somewhere in front of him, so Peter ducked into a side room. He then attempted to circumvent the room that was in front of him, all the while taking great care to be silent. He didn't want to give away his position.

The strange thing was that as he would cross a room and then stop, then cross another room and stop, the footsteps seemed constant as if his pursuer never stopped.

The effect was unnerving enough that in his attempt at circumvention, he cornered himself into a dead end. However, as he turned to exit the room, he heard the shuffling closing in on him. He cursed his sloppiness.

Peter was able to see a dark silhouette moving towards his room, but the silhouette appeared odd. It looked as if the person was hunched over, and it shambled around like a prisoner shackled at the ankles.

Peter readied himself for who was coming through the door. Would he be shot at? He prepared to make a dash around the figure and through the doorway once it entered.

Peter was not prepared for what wandered into the illumination of his Multi-tasker. In fact, he wondered if the dark was playing tricks on him.

There, by the dim light of his Mutli-tasker, was a man in a black, form-fitting suit. Was this some new kind of uniform? There was something off about his face. Perhaps it was a trick of the shadows.

"Okay, so you got me. Did I lose?"

The man did not answer, he only stared at him with the most vacant of expressions. Then he began to shuffle forward.

The gait didn't sit right with Peter. Why would a soldier shuffle, particularly in a combat situation?

"So what're you supposed to be?"

The man reached out a hand. Peter took it as a greeting and shook the man's hand, but the man's grip was unusually tight, and he began to pull Peter closer.

"Hi, I'm Lieutenant..." But Peter saw the glazed eyes, which now widened in some kind of frenzy. The man gripped Peter by the shoulder with his free hand and pulled him close.

He opened his mouth, and Peter smelt the sickly sweet aroma of putrescence on his breath. Something was wrong. Peter knew this feeling, and he became alarmed.

He struggled to pull himself away from the man, but the man possessed an unnatural strength. He remembered his Aikido and spun out of the man's grip, causing him to trip over his own limbs and fall to the floor.

Peter backed into a corner. "What the hell's your problem? This exercise is over."

But the man was hoisting himself up. When he was kneeling on his left knee, he looked up at Peter and let out a ghastly moan that sent chills up Peter's spine.

Peter knew at that moment that he had to get away from this soldier. He dashed around the man, barely dodging a swipe of the man's arm, and he ran out of the room.

He began to navigate the dreaded Labyrinth room-by-room with shuffling and moaning only a couple of rooms behind. As he struggled to remember his training and his past experiences with the Labyrinth, his mind ran wild with terror as to what was pursuing him.

The panic was inexplicable, but found its origin in the most primitive recesses of his mind. There was something definitely wrong with that soldier, and the knowledge that he was pursuing him triggered a potent revulsion and the most basic instinct to survive.

However, the terror was unsettling to the point of distraction, causing Peter to flounder about clumsily in the dark maze. As Peter ran and bumped against walls and found himself going in circles, the constant shuffling gait always right behind him never ceased.

Peter must have reached a room with an exterior wall, as there was a boarded up window. He threw himself at the window, hoping to go through, but the boards were fastened tightly and he ricocheted off and fell to the floor.

The man appeared in the doorway and saw Peter on the floor.

"Soldier, state your name and rank."

As if in response, the soldier reached out his hand and moaned. It sounded like when a strong breeze is caught by the mouth of a large empty jug. It was not a sound a natural man made with his lungs.

Peter stood up. "This exercise is over, soldier."

The soldier, ignoring Peter's declaration, reached out and grappled with Peter again, causing him to drop his Multi-tasker. He heard a crunch as he struggled with the man in the dark. The man must have stepped on it.

"What are you?"

The man only moaned as it opened its mouth. Peter wedged his forearm under its chin as it snapped its jaws at him only inches from his face and clawed at his clothes with his nails.

"Stand down, soldier! That's a direct order." He managed to wiggle out of his grip and ran towards what he estimated to be the back of the maze in relative darkness.

The shuffling continued, the moans bearing down on him sending his mind reeling to the brink of madness.

"Let me out! Sergeant Lockwood, this exercise is over!"

He ran frantically through rooms, slamming into walls and clipping his shoulders on sides of doorways, but his adrenaline was pumping and he was feeling no pain.

In his alarm, he must have gotten turned around and ran right into the soldier, who in reaction wrapped his arms around Peter, nearly squeezing the breath out of him.

He was face to face with the soldier, whose white eyes widened. He opened his mouth and hissed loudly at Peter.

"Sergeant..." He struggled, as the man's grip would not allow him to draw breath, like a boa slowly but surely constricting around its prey. "Get...me...out."

The man opened its jaws and leaned its head into Peter. Peter closed his eyes and no longer fought blacking out.

Suddenly he was dropped to the floor hard. It was dark, and his vision was blurry. He made out the silhouette of the soldier standing over him, but he did not move.

There was buzzing in Peter's ears, but as he regained his bearings he began to realize that the buzzing was not coming from within his ears. He stood up rather unsteadily and backed away from the buzzing soldier until his back hit the wall behind him.

Bright lights flashed on, and Peter was able to get a better look at his antagonist. The soldier looked like hell. His face was ragged, the skin pulled tight over his skull like tanned animal skin, and the eyes were severely clouded with cataracts. There was no expression on his face.

Peter heard the tone of digi-locks disengaging, and in a moment, Sergeant Lockwood and Major Lewis stepped into the room.

"What...what is this?" Peter asked to either man, still catching his breath.

Sergeant Lockwood was holding some kind of transmitter. "No worries, Lieutenant Birdsall. He's quite harmless at the moment."

"Quite harmless," Peter parroted acerbically.

Major Lewis put his hand up to Sergeant Lockwood in warning, "Sergeant..."

But he was too late. Peter lunged at Lockwood, punching him square in the jaw with such momentum that they both fell to the ground.

"What the hell is wrong with you?" Peter yelled hoarsely into Lockwood's face, sprinkling it rather generously with spittle.

Major Lewis was pulling Peter off Lockwood. The buzzing soldier just stood there stoically, frozen in time and rather unmoved by the drama.

"Lieutenant Birdsall, stand down."

Peter backed away from Lockwood, who picked up the transmitter that he had dropped and glared at Peter.

"I can explain everything," said Major Lewis. "Let's go to the debriefing room. Sergeant, put the ID away."

Lockwood nodded and saluted. Major Lewis left the room, and Peter followed giving the now still soldier a last glance on the way out.

He followed Major Lewis into the debriefing room and closed the door behind him rather abruptly. Major Lewis leaned up against the table in the front. "Have a seat, Lieutenant."

Peter sat. "With all due respect…enough riddles, Major. I want answers."

"I understand your confusion, son, but it was important that you saw it for yourself. The 'ID Program' stands for Insidious Drone Program."

"Drone? That man looked dead."

"Undead, actually," Major Lewis corrected.

"Undead? You mean…zombies, sir?"

"Yes, Lieutenant. I suppose you could call them that. In the twentieth century, in the early 1990's there was a civil war in what was then Rwanda, between the Tutsi and the Hutu."

"Yes, I remember something about it from Twentieth Century History class."

"Well, then you may have remembered the genocide perpetuated by the Presidential Guard, the Rwanda armed forces, and extremist militia targeting those who supported the Arusha Accord. Nearly one million Rwandans were killed. That was nearly ten percent of the population."

"Yes, but the Rwandan Patriotic Front got their revenge, didn't they?"

"Well, yes, but that's on oversimplification. In 1992, the production of coffee, their main export, went down, and since most of the land was dedicated to growing coffee, there wasn't enough food. What resulted was famine and disease."

Peter was wondering what this had to do with zombies.

Major Lewis continued his explanation. "Even after the Rwandan Patriotic Front (RPF) retook the capital of Kigali, disease was still rampant. In fact, there were reports of civilians becoming sick and turning to cannibalism. Soon RPF soldiers had fallen victim to this mysterious sickness. The Hutu fled to the Congo.

"Later, when the US-backed Alliance of Democratic Forces for the Liberation of Congo-Zaire entered the Congo with the RPF, they encountered what first appeared to be refugees wandering through villages.

"But these refugees were afflicted with the mysterious disease and were devouring everyone in sight. They were unsure if these were agents of the French, who were backing the Hutu. Curious about the phenomenon, the Alliance forces followed them, observing from a distance.

"They observed the afflicted hunting down and cannibalizing Hutu refugees. Thinking that the enemy of my enemy is my friend, they attempted to approach these afflicted individuals with disastrous results.

"So they captured many of the afflicted, killing some in the process out of self-preservation, and they were extracted secretly by US Special Forces. The press blamed the RPF for the slaughter of the Hutu refugees in the Congo, but it was written off as a justified response to the genocide."

Peter couldn't believe what he was hearing. Zombies in the Congo? It sounded like the plot of a bad black-and-white movie. "So…that soldier in the Labyrinth, he's a…"

"Yes."

That explained the blank expression, putrescent smell, and the man's constant attempts to try to eat him.

"Lieutenant, I know this must be a great deal for you to digest. But, we've found that they make the perfect soldiers, combining unconventional and psychological warfare. They never need to be fed, they don't dehydrate, they never show fatigue, and in numbers, they can swarm and overwhelm just about any position."

Peter recalled the footsteps in the maze. "The soldier in the maze was relentless."

"Yes, and it drove you to panic. That's the psychological component that we didn't even anticipate until the field tests."

"Field tests?"

"Just image your panic if we threw forty, fifty, or even one hundred of these Insidious Drones at you."

Peter didn't want to, but he got the point.

"And furthermore, they can be sent into terrain normally inaccessible to live soldiers. Just imagine, finally we can breach the cave systems of Afghanistan. All we'd have to do is pour a few hundred of these bad boys into the caves, and they would just keep wandering through, sniffing out terrorists…"

"And eating them?"

"But no lives of American soldiers would be risked. They are the ultimate drones. And we could apply this not only to caves, but any terrain not easily accessible by traditional means. It even has applications for urban warfare."

A few hundred? How many of these things did the army have?

"Well, Major, this all sounds good, but where do I come in?"

"Lieutenant Birdsall, we need a platoon of soldiers to funnel them into the buildings, caves, and the like. Like shepherd dogs directing sheep. They won't think on their own. In fact, they don't think at all."

"Like cowboys herding cattle."

"Yes, exactly."

"Well, isn't that…dangerous? I mean, how are these things controlled?"

Major Lewis pushed himself off the table he was leaning on. "C'mon, I'll show you."

Peter followed Major Lewis back out of the debriefing room. He submitted to a palm print and retinal scan at a heavy door with two armed guards and took Peter into a room that resembled a large freezer. "It's going to be cold in here, Lieutenant."

Peter nodded and followed. There was a clear, thick Plexiglas wall with a door built into it. Behind it, there were rows of shackled soldiers like the one in the maze in the same black suits. Major Lewis entered a code, and the door opened.

"This is our containment facility. The temperature is maintained at near freezing temperatures to arrest decomposition to the point where it's negligible."

"But what about when they're in the field, sir?"

Major Lewis pointed to one of the soldiers. "See the black suit?"

"Yes, sir."

"The suit is designed to reduce body temperature to retard decomposition, which is easy since these guys are dead and aren't generating any body heat. The suit is more of a protection from the surrounding environment."

Major Lewis paused so that Peter could take it all in. Then he beckoned Peter to follow him out of the room. They exited, and the door sealed behind them.

"I noticed that none of them were moving, sir."

"Yes. That's because they each have an Amygdala Inhibitor—or AI—installed in their skulls."

"Pardon my ignorance, sir, but what is that?"

"Follow me. I'll introduce you to someone who can explain it."

They crossed the hall and entered a laboratory. There were long, black-surfaced tables, beakers, microscopes, centrifuges, etc. Major Lewis waved at what was apparently a scientist (hence the white lab coat) and the man walked over.

"Lieutenant Birdsall, this is Dr. Gilbart. He's an organic chemist working on the project."

Dr. Gilbart shook Peter's hand.

"Dr. Gilbart, if you could be so kind, could you explain the ID's condition and why they need Amygdala Inhibitors?"

He bowed his head graciously. "Of course, Major Lewis." Then to Peter, "Lieutenant Birdsall, we don't know the origin of what has been dubbed the Tutsi-Hutu Virus, or THV, but we do know that those afflicted die rapidly from organ failure and re-animate with brain damage."

"Re…animate."

"Yes. More precisely, they re-animate with suppressed frontal lobe functioning due to oxygen deprivation and a nasty case of Kluver-Bucy Syndrome."

Peter's eyes were apparently starting to glaze over, and the good doctor took this as his cue to explain in simple, layman's terms.

"Lieutenant, Kluver-Bucy Syndrome was originally only seen in primates with lesions in very specific areas of their amygdala—the center of the brain in responsible for aggression—that would cause them to behave in a hyper-aggressive, hyper-sexual, and hyper-oral manner."

"I get the hyper-aggressive and hyper-oral—they basically want to eat you…"

"Yes, that's correct."

"But hyper-sexual?"

Major Lewis jumped in. "Yes, in early field tests they would sometimes resort to humping each other."

Peter stifled a laugh.

"Yes," said Major Lewis matter-of-factly, "we, too, initially found it amusing, but it became problematic during training exercises."

"Hence the Amygdala Inhibitors," added Dr. Gilbart. "They are set at a low enough level of inhibition to suppress the acting out of sexual urges, and we can turn them up to effectively stop any behavior as a safety mechanism."

"So that's what happened to the soldier in the Labyrinth?" Peter asked Major Lewis.

"Yes, we never had any intention of letting the exercise get out of hand. We were monitoring your progress and had our finger on the button at all times."

"We?"

"Sergeant Lockwood, actually. He's the one who turned the ID off and effectively saved your life."

"Remind me to thank him properly," Peter remarked with obvious sarcasm. He turned to Dr. Gilbart. "So where do all of these zombies come from anyway?"

"Ah-hem, Insidious Drones," corrected Dr. Gilbart, who looked at Major Lewis nervously.

Major Lewis quickly changed the subject.

"Come with me, Lieutenant Birdsall, I have to show you the equipment you'll be utilizing."

Peter was still pondering the brief moment between Dr. Gilbart and Major Lewis when the Major had left the room. Apparently, they did not intend to answer his question.

Dr. Gilbart bowed his head. "Good to meet you, Lieutenant. Welcome to the team." And he turned around and walked back across the lab to continue whatever he had been working on.

Peter left the lab and caught up with Major Lewis, who had been waiting in the hallway. He continued giving the tour. "Let's go to

Engineering. They've developed portable MRI's to help you when you are alone with the ID in the dark to tell the living from the undead."

They entered another security-locked room where there was a laboratory of another kind.

"Lieutenant Farrow…"

Farrow was at a stainless steel workstation, calibrating some kind of apparatus. When he heard his name, he put down what he was doing, walked over, and saluted the Major.

"Lieutenant Birdsall, this is Lieutenant Farrow. He's the engineer that supervised the development of MR.UD. Lieutenant Farrow, Lieutenant Birdsall will be leading the platoon of ID wranglers. Could you explain MR.UD to him?"

Farrow smiled enthusiastically. "Yes, sir. Lieutenant Birdsall, MR.UD is the Magnetic Resonance Undead Detector. Picture every atom in your body spinning like a top, but each in a different direction. The MR.UD uses a powerful magnet to align all of the atoms in your body so that they all spin in the same direction. Got me so far?"

Science was not Peter's strong suit, but he got the gist and nodded.

"Good," Farrow continued. "Well, when I turn the magnet off, all of the atoms return back to their original orientations in space. As this happens, they emit information revealing the location of each atom, in essence painting a picture of you."

"Got it."

"Well, one of the measures taken is the time it takes the atoms to snap back to their original orientations—we call it T1. In necrotic tissue, T1 times are longer, meaning it takes necrotic atoms significantly longer to snap back to their original orientation."

"So, does that mean the picture of a…ID…is going to be different?"

"We've calibrated the device to feed information into a monitor. If the T1 readings fall above a preset threshold, indicating an undead individual, the image of that person will appear red."

Farrow then walked over to a table with what was apparently the MR.UD and pressed a button on a control panel. A heavy metal door retracted into the ceiling, and behind it was yet another room separated by thick Plexiglas.

An ID lurched forward and threw himself against the Plexiglas, smearing blood and saliva on it.

Farrow handed Peter the MR.UD. "Here, point it at the ID and watch the monitor closely."

Peter did as he was instructed. There was a red image on the small screen.

"The black suit enhances and transmits the T1 reading," said Farrow.

The ID continued to attack the glass.

"It helps you in the field to tell who is who."

Peter gingerly handed the MR.UD back to Lieutenant Farrow. "Thank you, Lieutenant Farrow."

Farrow nodded.

Peter turned to Major Lewis. "I have a question." He felt as if he was in school again, and the sentiment was not a comfortable one. "How exactly do we *wrangle* these things?"

"Lieutenant Birdsall, follow me."

Peter accompanied Major Lewis, this time, to the firing range. Sergeant Lockwood was waiting for them.

Peter felt awkward. He was still pissed off about the exercise in the Labyrinth, but Sergeant Lockwood was the one who got him out in one piece.

Peter addressed Lockwood. "So, I understand that you are the one who was responsible for keeping me alive in the Labyrinth." That was the closest he could come to an actual apology for punching the man who saved his life.

Lockwood nodded tersely.

"Sergeant Lockwood, "Major Lewis interrupted, "I think it's time to show the Lieutenant what kind of firepower he'll be using."

"Yes, sir." He walked over to a table and picked up an unusual looking weapon. "This is the future of military weaponry. This is the FLASH electric ignition 12-gauge shotgun."

He handed it to Peter, who took it and immediately gauged its weight and feel. "This weapon was developed by a private corporation in the United States. Now let me ask you, Lieutenant, what's the biggest problem with conventional army weaponry?"

Peter looked up from the shotgun. "You mean carbines and AK's?"

"Yes."

"Jamming."

"Exactly. There are an unacceptable percentage of fatalities in combat situations due to jamming, because as you know, the rifles typically used involve moving parts."

"So how does this one work?"

"Well, let me put it this way. You felt how scary it was to have one of these ID attacking you."

"Yes," Peter tried not to look bitter about it.

"Well, imagine if you had fifty or one hundred ID swarming you. In such a scenario, jamming is not an option. This weapon has no moving parts. It utilizes an electrical ignition system. So, when you pull the trigger, a pulse is sent up to ignite the ammunition. Look…"

He took the weapon from Peter and disengaged a tube. "Because there is no need to stack ammunition, it is loaded in tubes where they are spring-loaded back-to-back. As one is ignited and leaves the chamber, the one behind it immediately slides up. No moving parts. No jamming. And you can get off more rounds quickly. It's semi-automatic, so wasting ammo in a panic is less likely."

"Wow," Peter was genuinely impressed, "that's amazing."

"Generally, in a swarm scenario you don't want to panic. You'll want to make every shot count. You'll also be equipped with FLASH handguns. Some of your team will have automatic rifles to address flanking by unfriendlies, insurgents, and such.

"The only kill shot with an ID is to the brain, which is why you'll be using blunt impact munitions rather than scattershot in the shotguns. Scattershot would normally have effective stopping power at close range, but for a live target. Scattershot won't even slow an ID down. You need to damage the brain."

Peter was doing his best to process all of the information being presented to him. "So when we're out in the field guiding these ID towards targets, what's to stop *us* from being the targets? You said so yourself, Major, that they do not have any thoughts. How do they know who the bad guys are?"

"Show him the suit," Major Lewis instructed Lockwood.

Lockwood unfolded and held up a black suit.

"That looks like the suit the ID was wearing in the maze," Peter reflected.

"It is," replied Lockwood. "But this one is modified to be worn by a live soldier." He held out an arm of the suit. "The live soldier's suit is designed to glow. There are fluorescent lines running up and down the arms and legs to help you see in the dark and identify each other."

Lockwood then pointed to the shoulder. "As you can see, this is a Corporal's suit because it has two fluorescent stripes indicating rank."

Peter reached out to feel the material of the suit. "What's it made of?"

"A synthetic material designed to keep the soldier cool while masking any heat signature given off."

"Heat signature? So this is a stealth suit."

"Exactly. It masks you from detection by the ID, so they'll ignore you and pursue the designated targets. Terrorists and cartel members will not be wearing these suits."

"So the ID will only pursue their heat signatures instead of us."

"Exactly. You'll be more like furniture to them. Oh, and you'll appear blue to the MR.UD, yet another way to tell who's who."

"So the weapons…"

"Plan B."

"Yes," Major Lewis interjected. "The army would appreciate it if the percentage of ID lost to 'friendly fire' could be kept to a minimum, given that they are quite expensive and don't grow on trees."

"Well, what about the targets? I'm sure they'll be shooting at your precious ID."

Major Lewis snickered. "Yes, but they will know next to nothing about the ID. In all probability, they'll mostly be firing at the body, as it's the largest target. A few will get lucky with some headshots, but neither terrorists nor Mexican cartel members are known for being marksmen."

This made sense to Peter so far. "But what about recovery? How do we get them back after the targets have been neutralized?"

"We trigger the Amygdala Inhibitors," Lockwood said, "to immobilize them temporarily. Then you would mobilize the bait."

"Bait?"

"Yes, pigs. There being nothing for the ID to pursue or eat, they'd return to pursue the pigs. Plus, one of your engineers will transmit a frequency that tends to attract the ID, to draw them back out."

"We want to minimize losses of ID, as we don't want this technology falling into enemy hands," Major Lewis added. "Not that they would probably know what to do with it. In fact, if they ever did detain any number of ID, they wouldn't live long enough to realize their folly. Individuals would get bitten and turn, eventually overrunning the enemy before they would figure out what they were dealing with."

Peter didn't care for the Major's snarky attitude or his glib approach to the apparent expendability of live human soldiers in relation to that of the apparently expensive ID.

Lockwood handed Peter the shotgun. "Would you like to give her a try?"

Peter nodded and accepted the shotgun and earmuffs to protect his ears. He placed them on and followed Lockwood to a booth in the shooting range.

Lockwood pressed a button on a control panel, and a cardboard cutout of a man holding a gun popped up. Peter squeezed the trigger, taking off its head.

Lockwood gave him the thumbs up and began to press multiple buttons. Multiple cutouts popped up, and Peter squeezed and squeezed and squeezed, pop, pop, pop.

He was surprised at the rate he could fire off rounds, particularly for a shotgun. Lockwood showed him how to pop out the tube of expended ammo and insert the next.

"This *will* come in handy in a swarm situation," Peter said barely hiding the delight in his voice. He was like a kid on Christmas morning.

"Here," Lockwood handed Peter a pistol and took the shotgun. "Try this."

Peter received it rather enthusiastically, took aim out at the range, and smirked. "Pull."

Lockwood pressed some more buttons, and Peter fired rapid rounds into the cutouts. He took off the earmuffs and handed them to Lockwood. "Show me more."

Lockwood gestured to follow him, and Major Lewis brought up the rear, smiling, rather satisfied with his choice of Lieutenant Birdsall.

Lockwood took him over to a rather elaborate-looking dummy. He handed him a small black cylinder.

Peter flicked his wrist smartly, extending the baton. "It feels so light."

"But it packs quite a punch," Lockwood added. "This dummy has a simulated skull with artificial brain matter inside. Go ahead and give it a whack."

Peter smiled at Major Lewis, raised his right hand above his head, and brought the baton down in a crushing blow, breaching the skull rather easily.

He was sprayed with artificial brain matter. He looked comical, standing there with baton in hand, grinning through what looked like strawberry jam splattered all over his face.

Lockwood continued his instruction. "The retractable batons will be helpful if it were to become necessary to engage in close hand-to-hand combat. Of course, such a scenario should only occur as a last resort. Use of the baton will only be effective when facing one or two ID. If there were three or more, hand-to-hand combat would prove extremely dangerous if not futile."

"Will we be wearing any protective head gear?" Peter asked.

"In the field, your helmet will be provided with protective goggles," said Lockwood. "You won't want to get any of their brain tissue or blood in your eyes. You'll want to keep your mouth closed as well."

"Well that's interesting," remarked Peter. "What *are* the rules anyway?"

Major Lewis looked confused. "The rules? What rules?"

"You know, every zombie movie has rules. How you kill them, how to get infected…you know, the rules."

Lockwood stepped in. "The only way to put them down is with a headshot. Don't get bitten or get their blood in your mouth, eyes, or any of your orifices. If someone is bitten, the time it takes for them to die is variable, but re-animation occurs within five minutes of time of death."

He reached back and put the baton back on the table. He picked up a book and handed it to Peter. "The Tactical and Intructional Manual for Wrangling Insidious Drones."

"You've gotta be kidding me," Peter said rhetorically.

"Actually we're not," said Lockwood. "It's incomplete. We were hoping that you could help us finish it, fill in the details, plan for every possible scenario we can anticipate."

Peter looked up at Lockwood in disbelief.

"Well, Lieutenant, we've run some preliminary training exercises, but it's all still very sloppy. We were hoping you could help us tighten things up to meet the standards for a mission."

"And I'm sure you have some ideas for the Navajas," Major Lewis coaxed.

Peter was overwhelmed. This was all so sudden and strange. "I'll do my best, sir. When do I start?"

"You'll start tomorrow. First, you'll meet your platoon, and then you'll begin rudimentary exercises and eventually training simulations. But for today, I've scheduled a session with Captain London."

Peter's expression changed, and the enthusiasm faded. He felt his cheeks flush as he recalled the night at Frisky's and being seen with the brunette bimbo.

Major Lewis sensed his reticence. "Lieutenant Birdsall, it is crucial that you continue your relationship with her during your participation in the program. It is in your best interest and the best interest of your platoon to keep a level head. The long-term psychological effects of working with the ID have not been assessed."

"I understand, sir."

"Your appointment is at 15:00."

"Yes, sir."

"Dismissed."

Peter saluted and returned to the barracks.

***

"So, how was your first day in the ID Program?"

Peter sat in his chair staring at Captain London. It was as if he was just realizing how truly attractive she was, but he was not sure why. She was pretty, blonde, athletic, smart—but he did not know why now.

"It's all so...overwhelming. I mean, you see stuff like this in the movies, but you'd never think it was real."

"Or that the army was working with it no less," she added.

"But it all makes perfect sense," he said. "They're just low-maintenance, relentless killing machines that swarm their targets."

"Speaking of which, do you have any worries about working with them?"

He paused thoughtfully. "When I was a kid, I used to play with scorpions and rattle snakes. I even used to work on a ranch. I would imagine it's similar."

"The herding part and the prospect of being bitten by things that can kill you, yes. But did you ever herd cattle into a building to kill someone?"

"No, of course not."

"How do you feel about that?"

"Well, the targets would be cartel or terrorist."

"What about civilians? What if they got in the way of your ID and the targets?"

"Well, I guess I haven't thought about that."

"Peter, in the first decade of this century, Presidents George W. Bush and Barack Obama were criticized for their aggressive use of drones in the border of Pakistan—too many civilians killed."

"But that's the nature of using drones, isn't it? Collateral damage."

"Well, Peter, does the end justify the means?"

"I'm not sure what you mean."

"I mean how many civilian deaths are acceptable during a mission? A few, several, fifty?"

"I-I don't know, exactly. I guess the same that was acceptable under Presidents Bush and Obama."

"But that's the point, Peter. The military thought they were doing the right thing, that the 'collateral damage' was minimal. But the press thought otherwise."

"But the press is not the first consideration in any of our exercises. Besides, it sounds like we'll be storming caves. Isn't that the intended application of the ID? To go where live soldiers cannot normally go. I doubt there'll be many civilians in the caves."

"What about the 'neutralization,' Peter? Can you handle the targets being eaten alive? Even terrorists?"

Peter hesitated, digesting the question and its implications. "I guess water boarding was once considered excessive prior to 2024. Even with September 11th. But there have been so many more terrorist attacks throughout the world, and they're now providing security for the Mexican cartels to flood our country with drugs."

"So that warrants the use of ID?"

"Well, doesn't it?"

"I'm asking you, Peter. My opinion doesn't matter. I'm only asking these questions…"

"Yes, as an exercise. I know."

He thought about her question. "We cannot catch these terrorists, and the cartels are almost equally elusive. I guess it would be for the greater good."

"You guess?"

"I don't know. I would be following orders from men who have given this a lot more thought."

"So you're just another blunt instrument? Like an ID?"

"No, of course not."

"Really? They don't question orders. They're just pointed in a direction, and they achieve the objective. Then they're rounded up and returned to await the next combat scenario."

Peter was becoming frustrated with her line of questioning. "Yes, but they can't think."

"Ah-ha. So there is a difference. *You*, Peter, can think. I want you to remember that, not just during the training exercises, but when you unleash the ID out on the world that you are supposedly protecting."

Peter's brain hurt. It must have been evident by the expression on his face.

"Look, Peter. It is my job to make sure that you keep your head on straight during this whole thing. Working with the ID can be dangerous, not just physically but psychologically. You can lose your humanity after a while. And once you lose yourself, your judgment follows and people can get hurt."

"Oh, for a minute I thought you actually cared about *me*."

"I do, Peter. But remember, these sessions are not just about you."

He remembered…Apone.

Captain London shifted topics. "So, how's your scruffy little brother? Does he still want to be all he can be?"

Peter laughed. "It's quieted down for now. My mother must've gotten to him."

"Oh, that's a shame. He would've made an excellent soldier."

"*My* brother? Really? Why's that?"

"Well, he's intelligent, brave…"

"Brave?"

"He approached me in a bar and struck up a conversation out of thin air, clumsily but effectively. You just stammered when I approached you."

Peter was embarrassed. His face felt hot, and he again began to stammer. He never stammered when talking to women. "I-I-I was just surprised to see you there. That's all."

"He also seems to feel that he doesn't fit in anywhere."

"Well, that's always been true."

"He's looking to belong. With his intellect, I think he's definitely officer material."

Peter's face was so hot, you could've fried an egg on it. She definitely triggered his competitive nature, but was he…jealous? And if so, of what?

"Well, if you talk to him, tell him I said hi."

"Yes, ma'am."

"Same time next week?"

"Yes, ma'am."

"See you then. Call me if you need me."

"Will do."

Peter was thankful to end the session at that point and did not hesitate to leave Captain London's office.

***

Peter was lying in his bunk reading the manual that Lockwood had given him. He flipped through the various chapters on hand-to-hand defense, ID battle formations, roundup and cleanup.

This whole thing was so surreal. Apone would've shit his pants from laughter if he found out about any of this. Or would he have been horrified?

As a matter of fact, Peter was hit with all of this so quickly, he was not sure about his own feelings. The idea of being around even one of those ID gave him the willies, particularly after his experience with the one in the Labyrinth. He pitied anyone designated as a target.

But he and his men would supposedly be protected. There were the suits, the guns, and the MRI devices. It all seemed to make sense. Plus, the idea of getting those chicken-shit terrorists hiding in those caves made him salivate. He mused that maybe he wasn't so different from the ID after all.

The Navajas had something wicked coming their way. They were in for a rude awakening, and he would be leading the charge.

Just then the monitor of his communicator was flashing. It was a call from home. He accepted.

His father and mother's faces popped up on the LED screen.

"Hi, Mom. Hi, Dad."

"Hi, Pete."

"Is everything okay?"

"Yes, everything's fine," Peter's father said.

"We talked Carl out of enlisting," his mother beamed.

"Well, that's great, Mom."

"Yes, I've managed to get him a job in the mall at the coffee boutique."

"And he's okay with that, Dad?"

"No, you know your brother. But maybe if he can prove himself, corporate will notice and he can move up."

The notion was ridiculous. The job market was flooded with college graduates who couldn't find work. He would just get lost in the white noise.

"That's great, Dad. I'm sure he will. He's smart, smarter than me."

His father waved a dismissive hand. "We're very proud of you, son."

But his mother was frowning, voting against her husband's remark with her silence.

"Thanks, Dad."

He heard Carl's voice in the background.

"Oh, yes," his father added. "Carl wants to know if Captain London asked about him."

"What? Dad, I have to go."

His father nodded his understanding, and Peter heard Carl's protests in the background as he terminated the call.

He picked the manual back up and read on about dividing platoons into four squads of ten, using two SWEEPERS (field engineers) with portable Magnetic Resonance Imaging (dubbed MR.UD) and coordinating sixty Insidious Drones.

He imagined sixty of those things lumbering around in all directions as his platoon herded them along. Kluver-Bucy, his ass. He had never heard of such a thing. And where did they get sixty zombies from? Were there more? There had to be.

Peter put down the book, his head spinning, and got ready to go to the mess hall. His stomach was rumbling terribly, and as he got up to leave, he wondered if the ID felt hunger the way he did.

Part II
The Rise of Carl

Chapter 5

Carl was sitting on his couch reading a book about nanotechnology when his father entered the room. He had his mini tablet laptop on, running a scan, and downloading updates.

He had been online in the middle of a session on Popularity.soc (.soc was reserved for social networking websites), checking to see how many people were looking for him today. It was in the middle of tabulating his "Curiosity Count" and determining his place on the leader boards, when his computer detected new updates as it did every few minutes.

"Carl, can you pick up your mother. She went to have her hair done, and it should be 'did' by now."

"Yeah, no problem, Dad."

Carl put his book down on the coffee table and absent-mindedly turned off the television in the middle of a report on poor air quality due to high ozone concentration and pollen count.

He grabbed his coat out of the closet by the front door and a black umbrella with one broken spoke. He opened the door and ran outside into the driving rain.

He opened the car door and flung himself into the driver's seat, retracting the umbrella and tossing it on the floor of the passenger side. He activated the ignition with his Mini-com and pulled out of the driveway.

The heavy raindrops pelted the roof of his car like bullets, nearly drowning out the Christmas songs on the radio.

Now 10 minutes of music every hour on WTHZ FM, your official Christmas music station, WTHZ, Texas, that's WTHZ, WTHZ FM…

Carl detested Christmas, but it was his father's car and the stations were preset. It was one of the many inconveniences of sharing one car, but given the economy and their finances, they had no choice. Besides, his parents got a 10G tax bonus every year that they used only one car.

Carl remembered when his mother used to drive Pete and him to the mall, but in those days, the mall was a very different kind of place. There used to be stores.

However, with advances in technology, internet commerce, and the increasingly unnecessary overhead of maintaining storefronts, the stores began to disappear. It began with bookstores. Print on demand replaced costly mass printings. Then clothing followed suit. Then electronics and appliances, and eventually even groceries. Everything was ordered online and shipped to your front door.

At about the same time, air quality had begun to steadily decline. People no longer looked to venture out of their houses, except for work. Telecommuting had become commonplace for many jobs. The interesting thing about the decline in air quality was that its origin was surprising, ironic even. In the 1980's, there was a lot of fuss about the ozone layer. In the 1990's, the environmentalist movement gained momentum.

At the turn of the millennium, the Democratic Party gave it legitimacy, and policy was drawn to reduce pollution from industry. Green was good, and everyone thought they were doing their part to help the environment. But the world, like anything else, appeared to swing on a great big pendulum.

After decades of pollutants and smog being released into the environment, the air was significantly clearer. The vegetation subjugated by industry for so long, eventually rebounded, and with a vengeance. There was a steady increase in pollen count from all types of flora to the point that it was saturating the air. There was an epidemic of asthma, allergies, and a plethora of respiratory problems. People were actually choking on their fresh air.

So when commerce went digital, it was no longer necessary to go out and shop. The economy was adversely affected. The disappearance of storefronts and the automation of exchanges meant fewer and fewer jobs. Fewer and fewer jobs meant less spending, which meant less commerce and fewer and fewer jobs.

Malls had become venues for the only part of commerce that could not be executed on the internet—services. Car mechanics, doctors, hair stylists, and the DMV, were all now housed in these malls. Carl's mother had gone for her usual Christmas Eve hair appointment. Her family was due this evening at the homestead, and she wanted to look her best.

Carl pulled into the parking lot, and his Space Finder function popped up as a holograph on his windshield. He hated driving out to the mall on Christmas Eve because of the crowds, and there was never enough parking. A vacant space icon flashed red. He made it to the spot and pulled in as another spot poacher was coming down the row.

The man in the blue car glared at him as he passed, and Carl thumbed his nose at him. The man's expression was humorless.

He turned off the ignition, grabbed his broken umbrella, braced himself for the deluge, and flung himself out of the car. He hastily made his way up the aisle as his face was spattered with rain. The umbrella offered little respite. As he crossed over onto the wide sidewalk in front of the mall, a car stopped short of hitting him.

"Why don't you be more careful?"

The man just glared at him over the steering wheel. He was a scruffy-looking man with an olive complexion and dark eyes. He looked foreign, Mediterranean perhaps. For a moment, they stared each other down in the driving rain. At this point, Carl's umbrella was serving no purpose whatsoever as he stood there in the pouring rain looking rather stern and rather ridiculous.

At last, the man in the blue car pulled around Carl and drove off in search of another parking spot.

"Some people have no sense of humor," Carl muttered to no one in particular.

He stepped onto the wide patio area in front of the entrance to the mall, looked up, and saw his mother exiting the hair salon through the glass doors of the mall entrance. He waved to her, but she didn't see him. He walked toward the front doors, tossing his lame umbrella into a garbage bin on the way. As he entered through the glass doors, the high-powered blowers did a good job of drying him as he passed through.

He strode past the gaudy fountain by the entrance where a mother was changing her infant's diaper on a bench, and he put himself in his mother's line of sight. It took only a moment for her to see him, and then another to recognize him. They met in front of a doctor's office.

"So, your father saw it fit to send you out in this rain."

"I wasn't doing anything anyway, Mom. Your hair looks great."

She coifed her hair gently in the hood of her coat. "Yeah, well not when the rain gets through with it."

"Why didn't you cancel the appointment?"

"Carl, do you have any idea how difficult it is to get an appointment this time of year between Christmas and New Year's? Besides…"

"I know. It's tradition."

"You know I always get my hair done for Christmas Eve."

At that moment, Carl felt bad for his mother. She used to manage a whole team of employees, and now all she had to manage was her Christmas Eve hair appointment. "Well, you look great."

He glanced over her shoulder at the army recruitment center. Every mall in America had one. His mother's expression soured when she detected his not so furtive glance.

"Don't even think about it, Carl."

"What, Mom? Think about what?"

"I saw you look over at that army recruitment station."

"I just looked…"

"I thought we discussed this."

"We did. You forbade me from even thinking about enlisting."

"And yet here you are thinking about it, right in front of me no less."

"Listen…" Passersby were looking at the escalating conversation. Carl took a moment to maintain the conversational volume of his voice while conveying his annoyance. "Do we have to discuss this here?"

She paused, looking him up and down, sizing him up. After a moment, she had apparently decided that the mall was not the time or place to have this discussion. Some of her friends might be there and overhear them. "No, I suppose we don't. Let's just leave."

"I'll pull the car up so you won't have far to go in the rain. But first, I just have to use the restroom."

"Oh, okay," she huffed, "I'll wait by the fountain." She stomped off to stand by the water fountain.

"Okay," he muttered behind her.

Carl stalked over to the men's room and relieved his almost bursting bladder. As he washed his hands, he appraised himself in the mirror. He knew he was going to hear more about the army recruitment center in the car. It was going to be a long ride home.

He detested unemployment and living with his parents. He felt so helpless. It was humiliating, even if the vast majority of his cohort was in the very same position. Here he stood, a grown intelligent man, and he was afraid of his mommy. Afraid to be a man and choose his own destiny, even if it was in the army.

He left the restroom and walked towards the water fountain. His mother stood there glaring at the glass doors to the parking lot. As he approached her, he was not sure if she was still annoyed with him or if she was annoyed at the rain for threatening her newly done hair.

"I'm going to get the car and pull around."

She only glared in response.

He stepped through the glass doors and into the deluge, but his face was hot from the exchange with his mother and his own humiliation, so he didn't feel the drops assaulting his face.

He looked down at his Mini-com and activated the Car-search function. It began to beep and flash arrows directing him to his father's car. He stepped into the parking lot and briskly walked down his aisle. He flung the door open to his car and jumped into the driver's seat.

He turned on the car and blasted the heat. The Christmas station immediately began to blare, but this time Carl turned it off. Enough noise for one day. He looked behind him and backed out into the aisle. A woman in another car quickly took his place. Carl wondered if the woman would jump into his grave so quickly.

He pulled up to the front of the mall and stopped off to the side. He was looking in and saw his mother looking down at her Mini-com. He honked the horn, but to no avail.

In the parking lot behind him, some impatient jerk was revving his engine. Boy did Carl hate Christmas.

His mother looked up and saw him. She waved.

But Carl heard tires screech and an engine gunning. He turned around in time to see a car careening right towards the front of the mall…

…and he was right in its path.

Carl took a split second to assess the unbelievable nature of the scenario unfolding before him, and realizing that the driver intended to drive right through the glass doors and into the mall, he backed up just in time as it flew past him.

It was a knee-jerk reaction for self-preservation, and he was in that instant unaware that his removal of himself from the car's path opened another path into the mall entrance…

…right into his mother.

In the seconds that passed, Carl registered that it was that jerk in the blue car. The car jumped the curb, slid through the entrance on its own momentum, and there was a great flash of light.

Suddenly Carl felt like he was punched in the face, he was upside down and his ears were ringing. His head was throbbing from the cacophonous blast and the car was sliding into the parking lot on its roof.

He felt the sting of broken glass and nitrogen from his deployed air bag, and he heard the muffled sounds of people screaming. After some undetermined period of time that felt like several minutes, some man had opened the door to his car, disengaged the seat belt, and pulled him out.

He got to his feet, and the man was shouting something to him, but he could not make out what it was. People were standing in the parking lot in the rain staring at a rather gaping hole in the front of the mall where the elegant glass entrance had once been.

Smoke was billowing out of the yawning gap, and the uneven concrete around the opening was black. It took Carl a moment to get his bearings, when he remembered his mother. He began to walk towards the smoking mall. A few other onlookers passed him, brushing his shoulders as they ran up to the scene.

Where was his mother? He thought back to before the blast. Was she standing by the glass doors when the blue car drove through? Did she get out of the way?

It was impossible to see through the gray smoke pouring out of the mall. There was a hysterical woman crying and tugging on his arm. She might have been shouting at him, or shouting at no one in particular and simply hysterical, but he did not hear her words.

He choked on the smoke and dust that filled the air as he strained to look for his mother. It appeared that only the entrance had been hit. The bulk of the mall appeared to be unaffected, and Carl foolishly hoped that his mother was somewhere in the recesses of the structure, scared out of her wits.

He heard on-lookers calling various names into the smoke—husbands, wives, brothers, and sisters. However, at the moment, he only cared about one. So he joined the panicked chorus.

"Mom. MOOOOOM. MARLA. MAAAARLAAAA."

Ash wafted in the air like snowflakes drowning out the rain all around them.

"MAAAARLAAAAA!"

His eyes welled up with hot tears as he choked back a horrible inevitability that he did not want to accept.

To add insult to injury, part of the roof collapsed, sending the onlookers reeling back towards the parking lot. Concrete and steel crashed down into the smoke and on top of the bodies of those whose names were being called out.

There was more screaming and sobbing as the smoke reflected flashing red and blue lights. The first responders had arrived. Police officers pulled people back away from the mall as firefighters rushed into the smoke and disappeared, consumed in clouds of gray and black.

A police officer, around his age, pulled Carl back. He was a man in his early twenties with a buzz cut and a frightened expression on his face. He was led into the arms of a paramedic who wrapped a blanked around him and led him over to an ambulance.

Carl gazed in horror as police officers set up a perimeter and firefighters fought the blaze. The interior of the mall was still obscured by smoke, dust, and debris.

A paramedic was talking to him, but to Carl it sounded like they were underwater. The man checked the cuts on his face from broken glass as more ambulances piled into the parking lot, which had become quite the scene. The press arrived only moments later. The whole scene had become some kind of circus.

A police officer came over. "Are you alright, sir?"

That was not why he came over. "Yes, I'm okay."

"Did you see anything?"

Ah, there it was. "There was a man in a blue car."

"A man in a blue car?"

Carl's Mini-com was vibrating. It was his father. "Yes, a blue car. Hold on a moment…" He answered the phone. "Hello…hello?"

He couldn't hear his father over the phone. The ringing in his ears was too loud. He passed the phone over to the officer.

The officer took it. "Yes…yes…hold on, sir…" He looked at Carl. "Are you Carl?"

Carl nodded. The officer spoke into the phone. "Yes…yes, sir…he's okay…what…who…" The officer put down the phone. "Where's your mother?"

Carl pointed at the mall.

The officer turned his back on Carl and said something low into the phone. After a brief exchange, the officer hung up the phone and handed it back to Carl. "That was your father."

"I know."

"So you said you saw a blue car?"

Back to business. "Yeah. I pulled up to the front of the mall to pick up my mother when I heard a car gunning toward the mall. I backed out of the way as the blue car crashed right into the entrance and exploded."

"And your mother was by the entrance?"

Carl nodded, choking back a sob, and he began to shake.

The officer knew when enough was enough. "Thank you, sir. If we find anything out about your mother, we'll let you know." The officer walked off into the mayhem.

Carl sat there in the back of the ambulance trying to process what had just happened, because none of it seemed real at the moment. Maybe it was his mind defending itself against the horror of the reality of what had just occurred.

It was a terrorist attack.

The news had been warning of communications intercepted by government agencies about possible attacks. The targets were supposedly "soft" targets—malls, restaurants, and movie theaters.

Apparently, the terrorists were no longer going for the large symbolic targets and the grand spectacles.

He looked the bastard right in the eye.

Suddenly waves of guilt began to pound the shores of his rational mind. What if he hadn't glanced at the army recruitment station? What if he hadn't gotten into that argument with his mom? What if he didn't use the damned restroom? They would have left sooner and missed the explosion, that's what.

It was his fault. Now here he sat in the back of an ambulance while his poor mother...

Why a freaking mall? Of all the places. In Texas no less. It was as if they were attacking the last semblance of capitalism. Americans were agoraphobic as is. Now they really wouldn't leave the house.

The terrorists had tried to attack the internet, as it had become the last bastion of the free market. However, what prevented the government from regulating it had also prevented the terrorists from attacking it.

The internet was not just some collection of servers. It was something much bigger than that. The total had become much greater than the sum of its parts. The internet was arguably one of the great wonders of the world. It was intangible. It was a construct, an idea. It was the Wild West in digital form. One could knock out servers and nodes, but others would spring up.

It couldn't be destroyed. It had become too damned big, too complex. It took on a life of its own, and its life consisted of millions of users around the globe. It *was* the free world.

So all that was left was to attack malls. They were some of the last public gathering places left in American society. The fact that they attacked one in a Texas suburb meant that no place was safe.

Homeland Security now couldn't just focus on New York, Chicago, and the big cities, the obvious targets. There was no way they could protect every city and every little town across America.

Those bastards had learned to do what they did in their own back yards. In Afghanistan, Iraq, and Pakistan, it was not unusual for some suicide bomber to wander into a public place and blow himself up.

However, Carl never thought that one of them would come all the way to the United States to blow his poor mother up.

***

First Lieutenant Peter Birdsall stood at the ready with a platoon in reverse Vee formation, awaiting the release of the ID into the hangar. After a few rudimentary exercises, they had progressed to funneling the ID towards and into the Labyrinth, which was supposed to simulate a cave system.

The targets were three pigs at the end. Peter was glad that he did not actually have to enter the Labyrinth with them. No, this time he would remain outside.

They were using live rounds, and two field techs would sweep the building with the MR.UD's to confirm that the targets had been neutralized. Peter had his finger on the Amygdala Inhibitor master switch, and they would lure the ID back out with more pigs and the retrieval frequency to funnel them back into their container.

Peter nodded to Sergeant Lorenzo, who in turn ordered the release of the ID. Electric nodes from the back of the container prompted the lethargic ID to leave, and they came stumbling out looking for food.

They passed the soldiers in the widened entrance of the Vee without incident, the suits doing their jobs in masking the soldiers' presence to the ID. The ID funneled down and the flanks moved with them, their guns trained for headshots. Those at the widest ends of the Vee kept watch for insurgents, covering the rest of the platoon. The narrowed front covered the target structure, suppressing enemy fire. This was Peter's design.

There were forty ID in this exercise, and all appeared to be running smoothly as they approached the Labyrinth.

But suddenly, at the mouth of the Vee, several ID turned on each other and began piling up. Within minutes, there was a heap of Insidious Drones humping each other as the rest of the mass stumbled around them.

Sergeant Lorenzo looked to Peter, who signaled for them to continue their advance. Lorenzo nodded and passed along Peter's orders to continue.

This phenomenon was a regular nuisance in these exercises, but it was better than the ID turning on the men. That hadn't happened in several exercises, and Peter kept his fingers nervously crossed over the AI kill switch.

The mass of ID that were not engaged in the humping suddenly came alive—so to speak—as they must have picked up the scent of the three pigs at the end of the Labyrinth. One soldier at the front of the formation breached the door and quickly got out of the way, as dozens of eager ID funneled into the front door.

The formation had accommodated the ancillary mass of humpers by flanking them and stopping the right flank at the location of the orgy. The left flank had advanced a bit further, skewing the Vee, but the formation was effectively maintained.

As the last of the ID filtered into the Labyrinth, Peter signaled to Lorenzo, who signaled to the two SWEEPERS to mobilize. They made their way down the reverse Vee and began to sweep the sides of the building under the cover of two separate squads.

Peter checked his watch and waited patiently. The two SWEEPERS were following the meandering mass of red ID from the sides of the building as the covering squads cleared the windows and flanks.

The ID were still minutes away from reaching the targets, which still registered as blue on the MR.UD's. The pigs began to squeal and pace nervously in their back room, as if they knew what was coming for them.

The SWEEPERS saw the ID close the gap on their monitors, and dozens of red ID flooded the room as the pigs squealed in terror. The squeals turned into what one could only call screams, as their blue indicators faded out and vanished from the MR.UD monitors.

The SWEEPERS then radioed to Lorenzo, who in turn signaled to Peter that the neutralization of the targets had been confirmed. Peter then hit the AI kill switch, and the dozens of ID roaming the rooms of the Labyrinth, as well as the heap of amorous ID, became immobilized.

Normally they would set up more pigs and lure them out of the building, but the heaping pile of humpers would be behind the pigs, and they would have ID coming from two directions.

Peter needed to figure out a way to deal with the humpers before luring the other ID out of the building. "Lorenzo, how many humpers?"

Lorenzo ran up to the immobilized pile and began to count. He signaled ten.

This was a decision point. Peter could designate a few men to pull the heap apart, one-by-one, and drag them back to the container. However, this would cost them time and weaken the flanks. He had to account for an insurgent attack at any moment.

He could use one of the pigs to lure the humpers, while using the other two to lure the rest out of the Labyrinth in a kind of staggered extraction. But that would mean that the platoon would have to account for two groups of ID instead of one, and in this game, complexity equaled accidents.

Another option would be to neutralize the humpers with headshots and then bring out the rest, but one of their directives was to minimize waste of ID soldiers. God forbid.

Peter had an idea. He called Lorenzo over. "Listen, we need to push the humpers back to the front door and then lure them all back into the funnel towards the container together."

"So they'll all move as one group," Lorenzo finished. "We can set up a wall of fire for stopping power."

"Make it so," Peter commanded.

Lorenzo nodded and ran off to bark the orders. Several soldiers at the front of the Vee were instructed to back away and fire body shots at the humpers as they rose. The three pigs were set up about thirty feet in front of the humpers.

Lorenzo nodded to Peter, who then flipped the AI kill switch off. The humpers slowly began to move and look around. Then, catching the scent of the bait, they pushed themselves up and off each other and began to lurch towards the pigs.

Lorenzo ordered suppressive fire, and the small squad in front began to shoot the ID in the torsos, sending them staggering back against each other.

The SWEEPERS on either side of the building were indicating that the ID inside were just meandering around, bumping into one another, but they were not moving out of the structure.

Lorenzo relayed this info to Peter.

"Shit," Peter snapped, "the bait isn't close enough. They can't smell it from in the building. And they're not responding to the retrieval frequency."

Just then, cardboard cutouts were popping up on either side of the formation, and the flanks began to open fire.

"Bring one of the pigs here," Peter ordered.

The bait handler brought one over. Peter picked up the pig and shoved a grenade in its mouth. He waddled up to the humpers—who were now pushed back towards the front door—pulled the pin, and flung the pig with all of his might at the ID.

They stooped down and seized the pig as it exploded, raining flesh, blood, and guts all over them. They stood there, dazed for a moment.

The SWEEPERS on the sides of the building signaled movement out of the Labyrinth. Apparently, they caught the scent of pig blood and innards in the air.

Peter yelled, "Okay, boys, follow the leader."

The humpers had regained their composure and started after the remaining two pigs. They followed them back up the funnel as the ID in the Labyrinth poured out and followed the scent of pig guts on the humpers.

As they passed, one ID turned towards Peter and reached out for him. He had the smell of pig on him. He fired a body shot at close range, pushing it back into the throng, and backed further away from the flank.

With the distance Peter put between them, the drone had apparently lost the scent or lost focus. It continued moving forward with the throng towards the other pigs.

The ID followed the pigs into the large shipping container, and when the last of them were in, the reinforced door was closed.

Peter checked his watch. "TIME."

Lorenzo walked up to Peter. "How'd we do?"

"Not our best time, but we circumvented the humper situation without any loss of ID or human soldier."

"All of the insurgent attackers were neutralized," Lorenzo added.

"Not bad, but this time they were only cutouts. We have to do something about those damned humpers. There's always some in every batch, and one way or another, they're going to get us killed. We'll discuss it in debriefing."

Lorenzo nodded and rounded up the men.

Peter and Lorenzo stepped into the debriefing room. Lieutenant Farrow was already seated. Major Lewis was at the front of the room. Peter and Lorenzo saluted the Major and took their seats. Lockwood entered the room last, saluted the Major, and took his seat.

"What went wrong out there?" Major Lewis accused more than asked.

Peter was confused by the remark. "Well, given the circumstances, I think we did pretty well, sir."

"We didn't lose any soldiers or ID, and it wasn't our slowest time, sir," Sergeant Lorenzo added.

Peter turned to Lieutenant Farrow. "We need to do something about those humpers."

"We're trying to suppress the sexual behavior."

"That's not what I'm talking about. The problem is the Amygdala Inhibitors. The kill switch is all-or-nothing. What if we break the ID down into squads and there are separate AI switches."

"Yes, but you're assuming they'll break down into squads to hump. What if pieces of multiple squads break off and hump? Then you'll be deactivating entire squads, some who won't be humping."

"But it'll be better than deactivating all of them."

"It's still too sloppy," Major Lewis said dismissively.

What the hell were they supposed to do? It was as if he expected perfection.

"I have an idea," said Lorenzo.

They all turned their gazes to Lorenzo, who continued, "I used to work on my father's ranch, and we used to herd sheep with dogs."

Major Lewis could not believe the suggestion. "Dogs?"

"Yeah, dogs. The sheep responded to them. I know it sounds low-tech."

"But what if the ID try to eat the dogs?" Farrow asked.

"Exactly! Then they'll follow the dogs. We can train the dogs to corral them. Like intelligent bait."

"Great, just great," said Major Lewis sarcastically. "Pigs, dogs…why don't we have a whole goddamned zoo out there?"

"No, that actually makes sense," Peter said with no small measure of epiphany. "We've been using pigs, but the pigs are too passive, and they're afraid of the ID. But dogs, we can train them to run in the buildings after them and lure them back out, herding them like sheep. No more pigs."

"It'll be a lot more efficient," Lorenzo added. "We won't have to keep buying pigs."

"I see," said Major Lewis contemplatively. "We'll discuss this *dog* idea. In the meantime, get cleaned up and get some rest. Dismissed."

They all stood, saluted, and left the debriefing room.

In the hallway, Peter joked with Lorenzo. "Dogs, huh? It almost makes sense."

"Yeah, it worked on the ranch. And it's been done since the Wild West."

"I guess that makes us cowboys, don't it," Peter jested.

"Yeah, I guess it does."

Peter liked Lorenzo. He, too, was a native Texan. He reminded Peter of someone he would've hung out with in high school. They were about the same age. Lorenzo didn't have a family of his own yet either. So when they went out on pass, they were great wingmen for one another, two tomcats on the prowl. They had a simpatico from day one.

Just like with Apone. The connection stung Peter. He didn't want to get too attached. Not like last time. But Captain London would tell him that avoidance wasn't the answer.

Speaking of Captain London, it was almost time for their next session. Sessions were often scheduled after training exercises.

"I'll see you later," he said to Lorenzo. "Got a date with the doctor."

Lorenzo flashed him a *you sly dog* look and made for the barracks.

***

Peter stepped into Captain London's office. He took his headgear off and saluted, and she gestured for him to sit.

However, this time there was something different about the office. It looked like an office. There was no holographic ambiance reflecting his childhood home. Was it broken?

"Peter, have you received a call from your brother, Carl?"

Peter looked perplexed at the question. "No, why?"

"Perhaps you should access your messages here."

"Oh. Okay. Why the urgency?"

"I think you should hear it for yourself."

Now Peter was concerned. What on earth was she talking about? He stepped around to the back of her desk, and she got up and gestured for him to sit in her chair. "Peter, if you want me to leave the room for a moment…"

"Don't be silly. You're my therapist. Whatever it is, I'm sure it'll be grist for the mill."

She nodded in grave support.

Peter entered his username and password, and the com unit indicated that he had three messages. He pressed a button, and the first message began to play. It was Carl. It looked as if he had been crying.

Hi Pete. I'm calling because…well, I don't know how to say it…there's been an accident. It's Mom. She's…she's dead, Pete.

Peter was stunned into silence. His mother, dead? How? Why?

I was picking her up at a mall. She was getting her usual Christmas Eve hairdo.

Carl's voice began to waiver.

There was this creepy guy in the parking lot…nearly ran me over…I told Mom to wait…I needed to use the bathroom…

Carl paused as if he was choking on the next words to come out of his mouth.

The guy drove his car into the mall and blew it up. Mom was right by the front entrance waiting for me to pull the car up. It was raining and I…

Peter was no longer listening to what Carl had to say. First Apone and his squad, and now his own mother? He could understand his squad; it was an occupational hazard, but his mother was supposed to be safe back in the States. She was supposed to play cards with her friends and go out to eat with his father. He was supposed to be the one throwing himself in harm's way for her…for everyone.

"Son of a bitch."

"Now, Peter, let's talk about this. That's why you're here."

"That's why I'm here? That's why I'm here? I thought I was here to keep my head straight in the Insidious Drone Program, not to discuss my mother being blown up to kingdom come!"

"I understand how you feel, Peter."

He looked at her with such bile. What a ridiculous statement.

"You? You understand how I feel? You're a goddamned noncombatant."

"I've had friends, comrades die in the call of duty…"

"Friends. Comrades. My poor damned mother, also a noncombatant, was just blown up."

"Peter…"

"We're supposed to be OUT THERE so the enemy doesn't come HERE."

"Peter, this could've been a domestic terrorist. There's been a real rash of them lately."

"And what the hell are we doing about it? The army has me dicking around with dead heads in the airfield, while terrorists are blowing up malls!"

"But that's why you are doing what you are doing."

"The progress is too slow. We still don't know how to handle the humpers. We're miles away from training with live enemies; instead, we are using cardboard cutouts. The AI kill switch is too general."

"All of this will work out in time. What you need to do is take some time off and be with your family. Your father and brother need you."

Peter was practically foaming at the mouth. He wanted to cry, and he wanted to tear apart Captain London's office, but he didn't know which to do first.

Then he thought of his father. The poor man must've been beside himself. He was thankful that Carl was there. "You're right. I have to go home to be with my family. To say goodbye to my mother."

Captain London's fingers took furiously to her Cybernetic Digital Organizer. She pressed a final button. "There. I just wrote you a pass. Major Lewis will more than understand. You are on leave effective immediately."

Peter looked at Captain London. He looked exhausted, physically and emotionally. "Thank you, Fiona."

She smiled warmly. "Go. And tell your brother I said hi. Give him my condolences."

"Will do."

Peter got up and left the office.

Captain London dialed Major Lewis.

"Hello, Captain London."

"Hello, Major. I'm calling about Lieutenant Birdsall."

"Is something wrong?"

"His mother was killed today. That terrorist attack in Aurora."

"Is he okay?"

"Well, he's understandably sad and angry. He's experienced a great deal of loss, sir."

"Is he compromised?"

"Pardon, sir?"

"Is he fit for duty?"

"I granted him leave time to be with his family. I think he'll be okay when he returns."

"Yes, his family, good. He needs to be there."

"Yes, sir. That's what I figured."

"Keep me posted when he returns."

"Yes, sir. I always do."

***

Peter stood outside the funeral home in full uniform. He dreaded going inside. It wasn't the body. It would be closed casket.

It was the finality of it all. It was the closure. He would never see his mother again, and he felt that if he didn't step into that funeral home, he would see her at home cooking one of her tour de force meals in the kitchen.

They would drink eggnog by the Christmas tree, and she would watch him open presents with the same excitement as when he was a small child. His father would be sitting on the couch watching the news, or reading the newspaper.

But he knew this to be only a fantasy, and he secretly chastised himself for letting his mind wander in that direction. It was juvenile.

He took a deep breath and walked into the funeral home. He passed through the mirrored greeting room with its plush couches and plastic plants, soft music playing. It looked as artificial as a made up corpse. He made his way down the hallway past one of the showing rooms until he saw the sign: Birdsall.

He took off his headgear and stepped into the showing room. It was a small room with antiquated wallpaper, more plastic vegetation, and several rows of cushioned chairs. He knew the scene all too well.

There were aunts, uncles, and cousins, friends (some who he knew, many he didn't). He walked the gauntlet of relatives exchanging token phrases of condolence.

When he made it to the front of the room, his father broke away from his brothers and threw his arms around Peter. He was crying.

"She's gone, Peter," he cried into Peter's shoulder.

"I know, Dad. I'm so sorry."

After a long embrace, Peter's father pulled away and let Carl step in. Carl hugged him.

"Hi, Pete."

"I'm so sorry, Carl."

"They gave you some time off?"

Peter nodded. Of course they did. Carl was just making uncomfortable small talk. It's funny how two boys can grow up together and be so close, yet at a time like this, not know what to say to one another.

Peter walked up to the closed casket and kneeled on the cushion. He closed his eyes so that it would look like he was praying, but words escaped him at the moment. He wondered how he was supposed to pray to a God who allowed the slaughter of so many innocents and took so many people he loved out of his life.

He wanted to cry, but he could not. He felt a kind of clinical detachment creep in, robbing him of his ability to mourn. He cursed himself. Was this what his training afforded him?

Callousness so profound that he was unable to cry at his own mother's funeral?

After what would have seemed like an acceptable amount of prayer time, Peter made the sign of the cross and stood up. He walked back over to Carl and his father, but was intercepted en route by his mother's younger sister, Aunt Cecelia.

She was sobbing and hugged him tightly. When she pulled herself away, she gripped him by the shoulders and forced words through the sobs like someone trying to talk through their teeth while trying not to vomit.

"The army, they're doing something about this, right?"

There was impatience in her voice, as if she was expecting a particular answer. Peter just looked at her. He didn't know what to say. She squeezed his shoulders tighter.

"*You* are doing something about it, aren't you, Peter." She was telling him, not asking him.

Peter's father saw the exchange and rushed over to Peter's aid. He put his arm around Cecilia. "My dear, Peter told me that the authorities are looking into it aggressively as we speak."

She wiped her nose with a very used tissue and nodded hysterically. "Yes, yes, the authorities. They're looking into it."

Peter's father guided Aunt Cecelia away from Peter, looking over his shoulder at his son. Peter flashed him a look of gratitude.

"You know she's right, Pete."

Peter was still looking at his aunt who was nowhere near calming down. "About what, Carl?"

"Someone does have to do something about this?"

Peter now looked at Carl. "What are you talking about?"

"I mean enlisting, Pete."

Peter could not believe what he was hearing, and apparently, he showed it in his face, because Carl continued. "I'm tired of sitting at home mooching off my parents and dodging college loans, Pete. I want to do something. I want to help."

Peter put his arm around Carl and led him out of the showing room. "Let's not talk about this here, Carl."

Carl nodded and allowed his brother to lead him out. They stepped into the men's restroom. It was empty.

Carl walked in first and turned around to face his brother. "Pete, I want to…"

But Peter grabbed Carl by his suit lapels and pushed him over the sink and into the large vanity mirror so hard that it cracked.

Peter drew so close to Carl's face that he was dousing him with spittle as he spoke. Carl was so shocked that he just stared at his brother in horror.

"Listen, you little shit. I have lost enough people in my life that I care about. I don't need you to die too. Dad doesn't need you to die either. You need to stop thinking about yourself for a change."

Carl was terrified of his brother, not just by the sudden act of violence, but his eyes. Peter looked like he was trying to burn a hole through Carl's skull with his glare. In all of the years they grew up together, Carl never saw Peter like this.

"What's wrong, Pete?" His voice sounded embarrassingly small.

Just then, their cousin Tommy walked into the men's room, but he stopped short at the sight of Peter in uniform holding Carl up against the cracked mirror. "Wh-what are you guys doing?"

Peter turned his fiery gaze to Tommy. "We're having a conversation."

Tommy put his hands up apologetically and backed out of the men's room.

"You scared Tommy, Pete. Shit, you're scaring me."

Peter turned back on his brother, his voice unnatural. "I want to scare you, Carl. You think this is a game."

"I don't think it's a game, Pete. Quite the opposite, I take this very seriously."

Exasperated, Peter loosened his hold on Carl, and Carl got off the sink. He attempted to straighten his torn lapels in an act of futility.

Their father barged in. He had a worried expression on his face. He looked at the cracked mirror above the sink and then at his boys.

"What the hell is going on in here?"

Carl answered first. "Nothing, Dad. We were just…," he looked at his brother sardonically, "…having a conversation."

Their father looked around the bathroom and then at Peter. Peter was looking at his shoes.

"Well…alright. Don't stay in here all night now."

Carl smiled. "We won't, Dad."

Their father stood there for a moment, wondering if he could leave the two of them alone. Then he left the men's room.

"Pete, Mom was here in the States and she was killed. What makes you think I'm any safer here? Besides, I'd be helping to protect Dad. He's all we've got left now."

Peter was still looking down at his shoes. He found it really difficult to look his brother in the eye. He wondered what Carl would say if he found out Peter was not fighting terrorists in the Middle East. He wondered what he'd say if he found out his big brother had been in Mexico fighting the war against the cartels. Now he was playing around with zombies in an airfield. Zombies and pigs. And soon dogs.

Maybe Major Lewis was right. Maybe it was all some big, ridiculous circus, or some kind of demented petting zoo.

Carl put his arm around his big brother. Peter looked up at him and smiled. They walked out together and re-entered the showing room. Their father looked relieved to see them walking in together.

Chapter 6

Peter was back in the hangar outside of the Labyrinth with his platoon. They were awaiting the signal for the beginning of the exercise. No live rounds this time—paintballs only.

This meant live "insurgents" attacking them. It also meant less protection against the ID. But their side arms had live ammunition, only for use against rogue ID. Just in case.

This was the first time they were using the shepherd dogs, and Peter was not quite sure it was going to work. It would be a shame for perfectly good shepherd dogs to be eaten by zombies.

Peter signaled to Lorenzo to release the ID. The shipping container was opened, and two dogs were released. This time the flanks of the reverse Vee gave the oncoming ID a wider berth, and each dog ran alongside of the ID driving them along.

To Peter's surprise and Lorenzo's delight, the dogs appeared to be doing their job. They had the effect of startling the ID, who then staggered after them. The effect was a tighter funnel, which allowed the flanks to focus on their surroundings.

Once again, a soldier at the narrow mouth of the Vee breached the door and backed away as the dogs led the ID up to the front door. When the mass of ID reached the front door, the dogs quickly veered off in each direction far and quickly enough away from the herd so that their scent was lost. The ID piled into the Labyrinth after the targets waiting in the back.

The two SWEEPERS moved along the sides of the building, tracking the red indicators on their screens. This time the pigs were separated in the maze, and they were moving through the rooms.

Lockwood wanted to see how the ID would hunt moving targets rather than keeping the pigs stationary. And once those pigs would get a whiff of those ID, boy would they run. Lockwood also had them greased—his own brand of humor that only Lorenzo seemed to get.

Despite multiple field exercises with incremental improvement, Peter felt off his game. But he did his best to get focused, because if he wasn't, people would get hurt.

As they waited for the ID to neutralize the targets, the reverse Vee was flanked by would be insurgents. The formation opened fire and was able to neutralize the insurgents without losing a single man.

Peter was starting to feel a little better about the way things were going, but he was a firm believer in Murphy's Law and did not want to celebrate prematurely.

They heard the terrified squeals of the targets inside the structure. Apparently, the ID were having some time getting hold of them. But within minutes, the squealing turned to desperate shrieks and then silence.

When the blue indicators had been extinguished, the SWEEPERS signaled to Lorenzo, who then gave Peter the thumbs up.

Peter hit the AI kill switch. "Okay, position the dogs!"

The handler signaled the dogs to wait by the front door, and then Peter cut the Amygdala Inhibitors. The ID sprung to undead life and began to make their way to the front door after the dogs. Sensing this, the dogs began to run up the inside of the reverse Vee funnel.

The ID piled out in predictable fashion. As they shambled down the funnel after the dogs, a group of insurgents attacked the right flank but was dealt with effectively. But, with their backs turned, a small faction of ID broke off and began to pile up.

"We've got humpers!" Lorenzo shouted.

"Dogs!" Peter responded.

The dogs came around and began nipping at the amorous separatists. As a result, they began to disperse and chase the dogs back into the funnel.

On the way, one ID grabbed a flank member and, not recognizing him as food thanks to the suit, began to hump the poor bastard.

Lorenzo ordered a couple of nearby soldiers to assist, but Peter sent in the dogs so as not to waste a single soldier. After all, the poor soldier was in no apparent danger of being eaten, just humped to death.

The dogs were all over the amorous ID soldier, and sensing the commotion and absence of the dogs' guidance, the shambling mass of ID began to fall into disarray, coming dangerously close to the soldiers in the flanks of the funnel.

If order was not going to be restored in minutes, they would have to be put down. Major Lewis would not be pleased.

Peter let out a string of obscenities and pressed the AI kill switch, thus ending the exercise. "Goddammit!"

Lorenzo ran up to Peter confused. "Lieutenant, why did you…"

Peter threw down the AI controller and stomped on it. "Goddamned humpers! Ruined a perfectly good exercise."

"But Lieutenant, we could have…"

Peter put up his hand to silence Lorenzo, and Lorenzo knew better than to continue his line of questioning. There would be plenty of opportunity for discussion during debriefing.

Peter walked up to the humper, which was now standing immobilized, and he pushed the victimized live soldier aside. He then hit the humper in the face with the stock of his shotgun. "Lousy son-of-a-bitch."

The thoroughly humped soldier stood aside and watched with wide eyes. The humper did not move or register pain.

Lorenzo walked up behind Peter, and the soldier standing aside flashed him a look of concern.

"Freaking moron…," Peter continued, insulting the ID.

Peter hit the humper in the gut, doubling it over from the force of the impact rather than pain, and then he brought the stock down on to the back of its head.

"Lieutenant…," Lorenzo put a hand on Peter's shoulder.

Peter shrugged it off impatiently and pushed the doubled over ID to the ground. "There's a few of you in every goddamned batch…"

Peter began to kick it in the ribs. The whole time it never responded. It only laid there like a crash test dummy.

Lockwood had run out into the field. "Lieutenant Birdsall, stand down."

Peter ignored him and kept kicking the sprawled out ID.

"LIEUTENANT BIRDSALL, STAND DOWN."

Peter kept kicking it in the ribs and the head, unfazed by the crowd that had gathered around him staring in shock as he, their commanding officer, lost his cool.

Peter jumped out of his skin at the sound of Lockwood's pistol shot up into the air. He stood there foaming at the mouth and panting heavily.

Lockwood holstered his sidearm. "Birdsall and Lorenzo, debriefing, NOW."

Peter took off his helmet and hunched over the downed ID, collecting himself. Lorenzo shot him a look of stern disapproval and headed for the debriefing room.

Peter looked around at his platoon. They were all looking at him with a mixture of concern and fear.

"Yeah," was all he said, and he walked off to the debriefing room.

This time only Lorenzo and Lockwood were in the debriefing room. Lorenzo was seated, and Lockwood was standing at the front of the room. Peter took his seat next to Lorenzo, who sat irritated in silence.

Major Lewis then stormed into the room, passed up his seat at the desk in front, and stood directly in front of them. "Jesus tap dancing Christ. What the hell just happened out there?"

Lorenzo sat in silence, waiting for Peter to offer up his explanation. Peter knew he had to be the one to explain.

"Sir, as the ID were leaving the structure and following the dogs down the funnel, a small group of five ID split off and began humping. Sergeant Lorenzo wanted to allocate two men from the flank to address the ID, which in hindsight was probably the best solution."

"But…"

"But I did not want to detract from the protective flank, in case any more insurgents were going to attack, and I didn't want any of the humpers wasted, so I sent in the dogs. The dogs broke up the pile, but one ID began to hump a soldier on the flank."

Peter cleared his throat awkwardly and continued.

"The dogs responded on my command, resulting in a loss of control of the remaining ID in the funnel. So, I saw it fit to hit the Amygdala Inhibitor kill switch and end the exercise."

"Is that how it happened, Sergeant Lorenzo?"

"Yes, sir, exactly as Lieutenant Birdsall said."

"Do you disagree with his call to terminate the exercise?"

"Well, sir, I-I…"

"Spit it out, son."

"I believe that we could've sent the dogs back out to regain control of the remaining ID, and we could have dealt with the one humper, sir. It wouldn't have been our smoothest execution, but we would have completed the exercise."

Major Lewis was glaring at Peter during Lorenzo's report. "Lieutenant Birdsall, explain to me what happened after the exercise terminated."

Peter gulped and again cleared his throat. His mouth was dry as a bone. "I-I kind of lost it, sir."

"Lost it? You assaulted one of the ID."

"Pardon, sir, ' assaulted'?"

Peter regretted his question as soon as it escaped his lips.

Major Lewis bore down on him like a parent reprimanding a recalcitrant child.

"You struck the ID soldier with the stock of your shotgun repeatedly, threw him to the ground, and proceeded to kick him while he was down. That's assault in my book."

Against his better judgment, Peter challenged the Major. "But who exactly did I assault? It's not like it was a person."

Major Lewis rested both palms on Peter's desk and leaned in.

"You assaulted an Insidious Drone soldier, a member of the United States Army, an egregious breach of decorum during a combat exercise."

"I beg your pardon, sir…"

Lorenzo shook his head in exasperation at Peter's stubbornness as he looked down at his desk.

Peter continued. "But the ID are instruments, like jeeps or tanks. Can one assault equipment?"

"Lieutenant, if I were to witness you kicking a jeep repeatedly during a combat exercise, I'd send you for psychological evaluation. Speaking of which, after you change, I want you to report straight to Captain London. I'll inform her of what happened and tell her you're coming. Am I clear?"

"Yes, sir. Crystal."

"Dismissed."

Peter and Lorenzo were changing in the locker room. Lorenzo was silent and doing his best not to look at Peter.

Peter broke the silence. "I'm sorry about what happened out there today."

Lorenzo finished pulling a fresh shirt over his head. He paused, choosing his words carefully. "It's not just the dogs and terminating the exercise, Pete. You shouldn't have done that to the humper."

Peter snickered at the remark. "It's not like it felt anything."

"Pete, it's still not right."

"It's not human, Mike."

"Well it was at one time."

"But it's not now. It's only a corpse. A walking corpse. It has no thoughts or feelings. It has no soul."

"That doesn't give you a right to beat on them. They're not slaves."

Peter could not believe what he was hearing. "Slaves? They're objects, Mike."

"They're Americans...or at least they once were. They deserve better."

"What are you talking about? They deserve better? We're sending them after greased pigs. We're training them to go into caves to be shot at."

"It still doesn't give you the right to beat on them." Lorenzo closed his locker. "Perhaps you should discuss this with Captain London."

"I'm sorry, Mike."

Lorenzo sighed. "I know, Pete. Just get your head screwed back on right. Okay?"

Peter nodded. Lorenzo slapped him on the shoulder and left the locker room.

On the way to Captain London's office, Peter wondered what Apone would've thought about his treatment of the ID. Would he have seen him as a cruel master beating on his slaves?

Peter knew that slaves were human and they had rights, and that slavery was wrong and constituted an ugly chapter in American history. The whole concept was so primitive.

But was that what the use of ID was? Was this slavery? He had so many questions, and he was actually glad he was having a session with Captain London.

When he entered her office and sat down in his usual seat, he hit the ground running. "So I assume Major Lewis…"

"Yes, he did. Do you want to explain what happened?"

So Peter launched into his report, consistent with what he told Major Lewis during debriefing. She listened patiently, her poker face devoid of judgment which made it that much easier for Peter to relate.

When he finished, he waited for her response, but she only looked at him expectantly. He was anxious to hear her feedback. "Well…"

She just looked at him. She did not appear angry like Major Lewis, nor did she appear shocked like Sergeant Lorenzo. She just waited.

"So you're not going to answer me?"

"You haven't told me everything yet."

"What else is there to tell?"

"I don't know. You tell me."

Damn she was good. "All right. My brother Carl enlisted last week."

She smiled wryly. "Ah, so that's what this is all about."

"No—kind of—yeah, I guess so."

"You seem angry, Peter."

"I-I just wanted better for him. I want him to be safe."

"Peter, he's his own man, capable of making his own decisions. He chose a path, a path that was good enough for you."

"But he can do better."

"Really? Peter, I'm a little insulted."

"Insulted?"

"You heard me. What is better than sacrificing to serve your country, to protect your loved ones?"

Peter was a bit embarrassed. "I-I didn't mean…"

"Peter, you can't protect Carl anymore. He needs to look after himself. Besides, he might surprise you."

Peter's anger seemed to melt away with this newfound insight. His anger was a way to take charge and protect his brother, but they weren't little kids anymore. He no longer needed protecting.

"Okay, but getting back to what happened during the training exercise today…I'm a little weirded out by Lorenzo's reaction."

"Not Major Lewis?"

"No, I get his point. It was a total breach of etiquette during a combat exercise. But Lorenzo appeared to…"

"Feel bad for the ID you beat up?"

"Yeah. Should I have felt bad? I mean, he said I beat it as if it was a slave."

"Is that what you feel it was like?"

"No…but I'm not so sure. I don't believe in slavery, but that ID is not human. It has no rights."

"So it's just a tool?"

"Yeah. I guess so. Something like that. So why do you think Lorenzo was so upset, Doc?"

"Perhaps to him it was a matter of decency."

Peter couldn't believe it. Not her, too. "Decency. *Decency*. What is so freaking decent about a zombie anyway? In fact, it is the complete opposite of decent. It's unholy."

Captain London sat back in apparent satisfaction with his statement. "Ah, at last we came to this point. I thought you'd never get around to it."

"What point? That the ID are unholy?"

"Is that how you view it?"

"Can you please stop answering my questions with other questions? It's getting on my nerves."

"Peter, you are going to have to come to terms with what you are doing in this program. Is it unholy? Is it an abomination? Or is it technological application?"

"I don't know anymore. I've never really given it this much thought."

"Too preoccupied with thoughts of revenge that you never stopped for a moment to consider, really consider, exactly what it was you were doing."

"Help me, Doc. I don't know what to make of any of this."

"Well, let's start with what your views on death are."

"Well, I'm not religious. You know that."

"So, you still must have some idea about death."

"Well, I don't know if I believe in a heaven or hell."

"So what do you think happens?"

"I don't know. Maybe we just cease to exist."

"Okay. Snuffed out like a light. What about a soul?"

"I don't know. Maybe."

"And what would happen to the soul?"

"Maybe it gets reabsorbed into the universe."

"Good. So what of the body left behind?"

"I-maybe it rots in the ground."

"What about cremation?"

"Makes no difference to me. I won't care if I'm dead."

"So what's the quandary about using bodies to hunt terrorists?"

"Lorenzo thinks it's indecent."

"Well, what about organ donors? What if you needed a kidney and someone was good enough to kick the bucket and give you one? Would it be indecent for you to accept it?"

"No, of course not. But we're not sending the kidney into caves to get shot by terrorists."

"Really? That kidney goes wherever you are, does it not?"

"Yes."

"Well, don't we send you into situations where you are shot at?"

"I guess."

"Peter, so what if the ID are, for all intents and purposes, the ultimate organ donors, as in they donate all of themselves?"

"I-I guess...but is that what happens? Do these people give permission?"

"Does it matter? As you said, it really doesn't matter what happens to the body after death."

Peter thought about his mother and his friend Delroy Apone. "Well, I'm not sure I'd completely agree with that."

She gave a wry smile again. "Oh, so we're back to decency again."

Peter huffed in exasperation. "Are you enjoying this? Because I hope you are. Somebody has to be enjoying this, because I'm not."

Captain London chuckled.

"Go ahead, laugh at me, Doc. Do you torture all of your patients this way with your circular arguments?"

"No, just you, Peter. And those are your own arguments. I'm just helping you see your own arguments."

"So I'm supposed to figure this out on my own. Is that it?"

"Actually, the fact of the matter is that the army sees it fit to use reanimated, soulless bodies to hunt and kill terrorists. And that should be good enough for you."

"And what happened today?"

"You obviously don't feel right about what you did. Don't damage army property."

"So now they're property?"

"Yes."

"Nothing more?"

"What more you ascribe to the ID is based on your value system. Just remember that they belong to the army and are to be respected, if only for that purpose. If you want to apply decency to the scenario, then do so, but don't go to the other extreme and wind up getting attached to any of them. They're not pets."

Peter put his hands up. "Oh, I know that. I'm not that confused."

"All right. Something to think about."

"Yes, ma'am."

"Dismissed."

Peter stood up, saluted, replaced his headgear, and left the office.

As he strolled back to the barracks, his head swam with questions, hypotheses, and possibilities. He was not only beginning to sort out his feelings about the ID; he was sorting them out about death as well.

He thought about his mother and Delroy Apone, and where they were. He hoped there was something better for them than this world. If life did indeed cease at death, at least they felt nothing. At least he hoped so.

He wondered how he would feel if the reanimated corpses of his mother and Delroy Apone served as ID. The notion worked on an intellectual level, but the decency of such a thing gnawed away at his conscience.

He went to sleep that night unsettled, and he consequently had a fitful slumber with visions of his mother, his friend, and zombies and terrorists dancing in his head. He soaked his sheets with sweat as he tossed and turned, struggling against frightening apparitions and their wrath for letting them die.

When he woke sometime around 03:00, he sat there and shivered in the dark, alone with his guilt as the early hours of morning wound down at a slow, cruel pace.

Chapter 7

Fort Leonard Wood
Missouri

Carl was exhausted, but then again, more had happened to him in the last few days than most of his life in total.

At the start of basic training, Carl felt like a freshman on the first day of high school. A very rigorous high school. He was out of his element, he didn't know anyone, and he felt the first twinge of doubt about his decision to enlist.

But every new job had its orientation, right? There were forms to fill out, videos to watch. One had to figure out where the bathroom and the cafeteria were.

A few days ago, his head was shaved, he submitted to a physical examination, and received inoculations. He was handed his uniform, duffel bag, and mouth guard. He wondered why he needed a mouth guard.

The physical assessment test at Reception Battalion was brutal. They expected him to do seventeen sit-ups within one minute, thirteen push-ups within one minute, and run one mile in eight-and-a-half minutes.

He was able to manage, but several recruits in the initial group were not. Consequently, they were sent to what the drill sergeant, Sergeant Maddox, called "Fat Camp." Carl was not sure what happened there, but he was glad he passed the physical assessment.

Now he was in day three of Basic Combat Training, which was to run for ten weeks. He was in what Maddox referred to as the Patriot Phase. This apparently meant that the drill sergeant followed them around everywhere, correcting them on their posture, how to salute a superior properly, how to maintain a clean area in their barracks...you name it.

At first, Carl found the attention to every detail to be amusing, but before long, he found it exhausting. But he understood the purpose. They were soft from civilian living. He was soft from sitting on his parents' couch, dodging student loan companies demanding their pound of flesh.

He knew that as recruits, they had to be broken down to be built back up. However, an intellectual acceptance of this reality did not ease the pain of Maddox's constant correction. It was supposedly army policy that the drill sergeant did not correct recruits using physical violence of any kind. Instead, they were supposed to use Corrective Action: Physical Exercise (CAPE)—push-ups, laps, and such.

Well, let's just say that Sergeant Maddox utilized both, depending on the recruit, his feelings towards him, and his mood at that particular moment in time.

On the first day, after cursory introductions in the company area and what only Sergeant Maddox would perceive to be a pep talk, he had them engage in this ridiculous exercise called the bag drill. All of the recruits were instructed to make a large pile of their duffel bags and then back away. Sergeant Maddox then told them they would have two full minutes each to find their bag.

The time limit was ridiculous, but the whole point of the exercise was to ensure failure. After endless iterations, Maddox, in his infinitely delicate and supportive manner, suggested that they work together rather than every man for himself.

After successfully completing the drill, the recruits were then all broken up into platoons. Towards the end of the week, Carl was issued a "rubber duck"—a fake rifle—and was taught how to stand at attention, face, and stand at ease. This went on ad nauseum for several hours a day.

The recruits, however, were given a chance to handle a real, functional M16 to become familiar with it. Carl found that interesting and almost worth the monotony of the Drill and Ceremony training.

The classroom exercises were like school all over again, with a dash of a draconian version of the Boy Scouts. They learned the "Army Core Values"—loyalty, duty, respect, etc.

At 17:00, the recruits gathered in the mess hall for dinner. In the beginning, Carl sat by himself. After a couple of days, a table of guys that were just like him adopted him.

There was Gary Koontz from Brownsville, Texas, once a college student like Carl. He, too, could no longer afford it. He was a tall, thin man with a baby face. Then there was Mark Fromm from Aberdeen, Idaho, a twenty-three-year-old mountain of a man who worked in construction in the private sector and was laid off, another casualty of the economy.

Nolan Kettle from Blue River, Colorado, was the wise ass. Every group had one. He was a real clown, and he would entertain the group by imitating Sergeant Maddox in less than flattering ways. Sergeant Maddox had apparently picked up on this. Either that or he just had a natural dislike for the kid, as Nolan was frequently the recipient of Maddox's sadism.

Then there was Ricky Cartieras from Cave Creek, Arizona, who Nolan called "Silent But Deadly." He didn't say much, but he always sat at Carl's table.

"Who do you think the platoon's going to choose for GFT tomorrow morning?" Kettle instigated.

GFT—Ground Fighting Technique—was hand-to-hand combat training. The training was nearing its completion, and as per custom, one recruit was selected from each platoon to duke it out in a competition.

"God, I hope it's not me," gasped Koontz.

"Well, I'm too pretty to get my face busted in," joked Kettle. "Hey, maybe it'll be Cartieras."

"SILENT BUT DEADLY" everyone chimed in simultaneously. Cartieras only regarded them with a half-smile.

"I think Fromm stands the best chance," Carl declared.

Fromm shot Carl an unappreciative look.

"What?" Carl said defensively. "It's true."

"What about you, science boy?" Fromm retorted.

"Hey," Kettle needled, "Birdsall is one vicious nerd."

"Screw you, Kettle," Carl replied. "Maddox hates you, so maybe it'll be you and he'll get to sit back and enjoy watching you get your ass kicked."

"Oh, he'd love to see that," Fromm chimed in. "To see someone else do what he's wanted to do since we got here."

"Hey, hey, hey. Easy, guys. Basic Training would be boring without my sophomoric antics," Kettle reminded.

"It's probably going to be none of us. In all likelihood, we're going to get to sit back and watch someone else do it," reasoned Carl.

The rest of the meal Carl suffered more macho teasing, dirty jokes, and Maddox impersonations, but the whole mess hall was buzzing with anticipation as to who was going to be voted to participate in the competition tomorrow.

Carl wasn't worried as he was mediocre in relation to the rest of the group in GFT. He was certainly not the best, but he was also not the worst. He didn't stand out at all, which was the way he liked it. That was how one got along in Basic Training. One didn't stand out. One did his best to stay in the middle of the group. You didn't show the others up, and you didn't hold them back.

During personal time, following drill sergeant time, Carl attempted to raise Peter on his com unit in the dark, Spartan barracks, but Peter was not answering. He figured his brother was engaged in something important.

He felt a little guilty about his enlisting, but he now believed that he could relate to his big brother for the first time. They were both army. Now he knew what his brother went through, which gave him a newfound respect for the guy (not that he didn't respect him already).

That evening Carl was on Fire Guard with Cartieras, who was quiet as ever. So Carl was left to his own thoughts. He thought about home. He thought about his father and his mother.

He wondered if his mother was proud of him. More importantly, he thought he was finally proud of himself. He was no longer a part of the "Boomerang Generation" mooching off his parents. He was his own man, carrying his own weight, and performing a valuable duty to his country.

Was he scared? Hell yeah. But that was what made the sacrifice so important. Even in this age of rampant unemployment and idle youth, not everyone chose military service.

As they walked in between barracks scouring the grounds for recruits attempting to go AWOL, Carl tried his best to think of this new, strange environment as home. Not that it would be his home for long. When the ten weeks were up, he'd have another home, but he really wanted to embrace the whole experience as his future.

He was not used to the around the clock micromanaging, being told what to do and when to do it, particularly from a sadistic bastard like Sergeant Maddox. Nevertheless, he knew Maddox was doing it for their own good. He had to pummel their softness into hardened resolve. Basic Training was only the beginning. This was just the preparation. There were many wars being waged all around the world, and the list of enemies was growing.

Carl could not help but think of his great, great, grandfather, Lingus Enright, who fought in World War II. From the stories passed down to him, it seemed that in the 1940's, war permeated all of American life. Everyone was doing their part, and although they were all scared, they knew they were doing right. And they had quite the adventure travelling all over Europe and romancing European women.

Carl tried to think of this time in the same way. The Order for International Liberation was the modern day version of Nazis if one really thought about it, and America needed more soldiers to fight them.

Carl and Cartieras walked their patrol in silence, in Carl's view, as future heroes of democracy.

***

The next morning passed quickly, and there was a nervous anticipation about the Ground Fighting Technique competition between platoons. Over breakfast, there was much speculation as to who would be chosen. It was like the Super Bowl of Basic Training. Kettle was making the rounds from table to table, whispering in ears. The scoundrel was probably taking bets.

At 08:30, the platoons gathered in the company area by a large set of rubber mats, the likely arena for the competition. Carl knew these mats well. They were rubber, but they were by no means soft. He knew from firsthand experience.

Sergeant Maddox, master of ceremonies, strolled onto the mat, silencing the crowd of recruits. "Alright, fresh meat, listen up. This morning is a continuation of a long-observed tradition in Basic. It commemorates the completion of GFT training. Today, each platoon will select a combatant to represent it, to represent what it has learned. The selected combatants will fight on this mat."

Carl looked around anxiously. He looked at the recruits in other platoons, and he looked at those in his own. He looked at Fromm. He would vote for Fromm when the time came. Fromm stood the best chance as much as anyone Carl knew.

Maddox continued. "Your selections have been made, and now it is time to announce the lucky recruits."

What? The selections had already been made? When?

"Our first match will be from the First Infantry...Private Wilkinson."

Wilkinson stood up, passed through his ranks, saluted, and stood next to Maddox.

"And from the Second Infantry...Private Bates."

He too stood, saluted Maddox, and took his place on the other side of Maddox.

"Okay, men. Rules...no striking, that's no punching or kicking, no eye gouging, no fish hooking. You know the drill. First man to submit the other by tap out wins. Take your positions."

The two men went to the center of the mat and faced each other. They were both of comparable height and build. Carl did not estimate an advantage in either one's favor.

Maddox blew his whistle, and the two men began to grapple with each other. Carl found the sight to be odd, two men on the same side duking it out, but they were soldiers.

As the two recruits struggled together, Carl thought of tiger cubs he saw on a nature show play fighting. It was practice, and one day they would fight for real...for survival.

Bates put his foot behind Wilkinson's right leg and shoved hard. Wilkinson was thrown off balance, and Bates was right on top of him grabbing for an arm or a leg. Wilkinson did his best to avoid being caught, but once Bates was on top, it was only matter of time.

Bates eventually got his hands on Wilkinson's left arm and pulled an arm bar, stretching it out and bending it in a direction it was not meant to go. Wilkinson tapped out quickly and Maddox blew his whistle, and like that, the Second Infantry picked up its first victory.

"Very good, Private Bates. The match goes to the Second Infantry."

There were hoots and cheers from the Second Infantry. The two men shook hands and returned to their platoons.

"Remember, men, one mistake and you're toast. And now for the next match…from the Third Infantry…Private Cronos."

A rather large man from the Third Infantry stood, saluted Maddox, and took his place on the mat. Carl felt sorry for the poor slob fighting him. He looked over again at Fromm and thought he'd be a perfect match.

"And from the Fourth Infantry…"

That was Carl's regiment.

"…Private Birdsall."

Carl was stunned. He looked around, unsure if he heard correctly. Everyone was looking at him. It was as if someone read him his own obituary. He looked over at Kettle, who shrugged sheepishly. Asshole. That's why he was so busy making the rounds. They'd have words at dinner…if there was anything left of him.

Carl stood up, his pulse pounding in his ears, and he saluted Maddox, who remarked snidely at Carl's hesitation.

"So nice of you to join us, Nancy. Why don't you go take your place on the mat?"

Carl stepped through the crowd, hearing stifled snickers and feeling his regiment's gaze upon him. He stood on the mat in front of his monster of an opponent.

As Maddox reviewed the rules, Carl stood there in horror. He expected he'd have to fight sometime, but not against such a goliath. He had sparred many times in GFT. He won some and he lost some, but this was the game. What did he expect to do, use harsh language against terrorists?

Recognizing how ridiculous his terror was, and accepting that he was now indeed a combatant, he calmed down enough to focus on the match.

"…grappling and submissions only. Am I clear?"

"Sir, yes, sir," Carl and Private Cronos answered in unison.

"Face each other."

Maddox blew his whistle.

Cronos and Carl began to circle each other on the mat. Although Cronos was twice Carl's size and build, he was hesitant, as if he was sizing Carl up.

"Are you two going to dance all day? This ain't the prom, sweethearts. Engage."

This tentativeness emboldened Carl and none too soon, because Cronos rushed him. They locked arms.

Cronos was bigger, so Carl attempted to swivel and throw the larger man off balance. To his as well as Cronos' surprise, it worked, and Cronos fell face first down on the mat.

Seizing the opportunity and feeling increasingly more confident, Carl jumped on his back and sunk a hook under Cronos' neck while wrapping his legs around his massive torso.

Giving up his back to Carl was a critical error, but Cronos used his size and strength to flip over out of Carl's grip and land on his back with his legs wrapped around Carl's waist, restraining him.

Carl was powerless to prevent the transition, and he pressed down as hard as he could to get to Cronos. But Cronos kept him at bay between his legs, holding him away from his body.

Carl knew that it was only a matter of time before Cronos would gain enough strength to turn the tables on him. He tried to pass Cronos' guard, but Cronos kept him in place.

He was trying to get a hold of one of Carl's arms. Carl did not want to get caught in an arm bar, so he slipped out of Cronos' grip time and again. But Cronos was very strong, and he got a hold of Carl's right arm. Carl struggled to pull it away, but Cronos was shifting his legs to go for the arm bar.

In desperation, Carl rolled to one side of Cronos, but ended up sliding on top of him and giving up his back.

It didn't take long for Cronos to wrap one of his massive tree trunk arms around Carl's throat, pressing down on Carl's head with the other hand, cutting off his windpipe.

It was now only a matter of time. Carl felt his vision blur, and his head swam. He did not want to tap out. He was pissed off at his error and decided to go down with the ship.

Suddenly, a memory from childhood entered his faltering brain. He and Peter were wrestling in their living room as kids. Peter, the older brother, was bigger and stronger, and he put Carl in a headlock. Although they were only play fighting, Peter was getting a little rough, but Carl didn't want to submit. He held on, pushing with all of his might against his brother, but his mother walked into the room and broke the two of them up.

The memory faded as a sound brought him back to the real world. Sergeant Maddox was saying something to him, but he couldn't make it out.

Then, just like that, Private Carl Birdsall went to sleep.

***

Carl found himself in "Fat Camp"—formally known as the Fitness Training Company—which also happened to be where injured recruits went for rehabilitation. Since the match, Kettle had been poking around, feeling guilty about his little stunt. Carl had refused to talk to him.

Kettle came in bearing a sanctioned magazine as an olive branch. "Hey, Carl."

Carl ignored him.

Kettle put the magazine by Carl's side. "I thought you might need some entertainment."

Carl could no longer remain silent. "Why, Nolan? Why did you do it?"

"Honestly?"

Carl nodded impatiently.

"Because you're tough in a way that most people don't see. You look like a nerd, but there's this...intensity about you."

Carl looked at him incredulously.

"If it makes you feel any better, my bet was on you."

"Ah, the truth. You wanted to bet for the underdog. You figured no one else would bet on me. Nice odds, I guess."

"Yeah, well, thanks to you, I lost," Kettle joked. "Are we still friends?"

Carl glared at him.

"I said I was sorry."

"We'll see."

Like all good comedians, Kettle knew when to end on a high note. Encouraged, he smiled and began to back out of the room.

"Thanks, buddy. I knew you'd come around."

"Get lost, Nolan."

"I'll see you later." Kettle ducked out before Carl could say anything else.

Carl shook his head and picked up the magazine. It was some tabloid rag about the sex lives of celebrities, something a girl or housewife would read. He opened the front cover…

Inside was a Penthouse Magazine.

Carl smiled to himself. "Always the scoundrel."

Chapter 8

Captain Fiona London was sitting in her office listening to the complaints of yet another soldier in the ID Program. His name was Sergeant Michael Lorenzo. He reported directly to Lieutenant Birdsall.

"Captain…"

"Fiona."

"Sorry. Fiona, I just don't know how I feel about this anymore. I mean, something about it just feels wrong, using dead bodies like this."

The truth was that she was not quite sure how she felt about it herself, but as a psychologist, her values were unimportant. It was essential that she help her patients sort through their values in an objective and supportive manner.

"I mean, it feels like slavery. I know they're not alive, and they don't have any souls, but it still feels wrong. I mean, where do we get these bodies from anyway?"

The honest truth was that she did not know herself. Not specifically, anyway. "Michael, just think of them as total organ donors."

"Yeah, but organ donors choose to donate their organs. Did these folks even have a choice?"

"I'm not privy to that information."

"Well then, who the hell is? I'm getting nightmares, real nasty ones."

"Can you describe some of them?"

"Well, where do I start? There's this one where I'm at a funeral, and right in the middle of the mass in the church for all to see, the body pushes the coffin open, sits up, climbs out, and staggers over to me."

"And then what happens?"

"It stops right in front of me. And everyone in the church is staring at me, even the priest."

"Whose funeral is it?"

"I don't know. Somebody's. You can't tell in the dream."

"Okay, so it stops right in front of you. Then what?"

"It salutes me."

"It salutes you."

"Yeah, and then I wake up."

"There's definitely an element of embarrassment or shame. That's why everyone's looking at you, and it's making you uncomfortable in the dream."

"There are other dreams, too. There's one where I'm in combat, and a couple of comrades are shot next to me. As I'm shooting at the enemy, they rise up and attack me."

"Really."

"And that's not the worst one. There's one I get every once in a while where I'm holding this baby, and it's crying in my arms. There are monsters all around us trying to get at the baby. But there's a staircase in the middle of nowhere, so I climb the stairs and take the baby away from the monsters."

"Is the baby safe?"

"Yes."

"Well, that doesn't sound so bad."

"But that's not all. Here's the kicker. I walk down the steps and start walking amongst the monsters. Only, they don't bother me. It's like they recognize me."

"And you find that disturbing."

"Yes, I do. What does it all mean?"

"I think that you are very conflicted about what you are doing. Part of you is very ashamed about it. You definitely don't trust the ID, as you shouldn't. To them, we are all just food. But there's a positive."

"Really? And what would that be?"

"The baby. It represents life. You place life above all of this death, hence you placing the baby up above the monsters."

"Yeah, I guess. But it really bothers me that when I come down the stairs in the dream, they don't attack me. I'm walking with them."

"You are afraid you have become one of them—a monster."

"Yeah. It's freaking me out."

"This is all like the stem cell debates at the turn of the millennium. Everyone knew that stem cells held tremendous, even miraculous potential to cure disease, correct injuries and deformities, so on and so forth."

"Yeah, that's a no brainer."

"Well, it wasn't back then. The application of stem cells was not what was being questioned. It was the source. In the beginning, a significant portion of stem cells were coming from aborted fetuses, and some found this to be morally reprehensible and any positive outcomes to be tainted."

"So what happened? I mean, we obviously use stem cells today."

"Well, there was much debate. The scientific and medical community thought the benefits outweighed any moral questions about where the stem cells came from. To them, their capabilities to heal were everything. Then there were others who thought that if any amount were harvested from aborted fetuses, they should not be used at all. The scientists believed that they were throwing out the baby with the bathwater."

"I see. So although I recognize that the use of ID is perfect for hunting terrorists in inaccessible landscapes, like in Afghanistan…"

"And their use would save the lives of American soldiers," Captain London added.

"…yeah…I'm questioning the source. So am I throwing out the baby with the bathwater?"

Fiona hesitated, allowing Lorenzo to draw his own conclusion.

Lorenzo hesitated, mulling it over. "I would like to smoke those bastards out of the caves."

"Michael, they've been hiding, using the terrain, for decades, popping out momentarily to cause trouble, staging attacks in the West. Until now, we've been unable to get to them. For the first time, we have a chance to hunt them down and eliminate them."

Lorenzo nodded uncertainly like a child complying with a parent without yet fully grasping the parent's rationale. She continued.

"Think of the lives that will be saved. The lives of our soldiers who won't have to be sent into foreign cave systems and mountains. Think of the victims that will be spared random terrorist attacks."

"I guess it's better than nukes. In this politically correct world, we would never be allowed to use nukes," he mused.

"Nukes would prevent reconstruction," Fiona added, "because the land will be rendered useless. But with the ID, once the targets are eliminated, we can begin to rebuild. We can instill democracy in a chaotic world."

"And profit off the reconstruction," he added cynically.

"That, of course, is part of it. These wars don't pay for themselves."

"Thanks, Fiona. I think I'll be alright."

She smiled at him. "I think so, too. I mean, really, it's like stem cell research. In the beginning, it was thought by some to be morbid and unnatural. But we use it all the time now, and even the religious groups and Conservatives now recognize its value. Imagine if we let our squeamishness get the better of us back then."

"I guess you're right."

Captain London looked at her desk clock. "Same time next week?"

Lorenzo nodded.

"Great. See you then."

Lorenzo stood up, put on his headgear, and saluted. Then he left.

As Captain London activated her Cybernetic Digital Organizer to enter the session note, she became lost in thought. She was sure she believed in the Insidious Drone technology.

At one point, stem cells were just considered discarded tissue, not just aborted fetus tissue. At one time, placental tissue was considered the body's detritus, jettisoned as waste. Boy was that view wrong.

However, the greater American public was still unaware of the existence of the Insidious Drones. The technology was still being developed, and it had not yet been applied in an actual combat situation.

The public didn't hear much about a drug until it had passed clinical trials and obtained FDA approval. Until then it was rumor at the most. She figured this was no different. Or was that just a rationalization?

Captain London had her hands full. It was a full-time job to manage the soldiers' doubts and anxieties. A few had washed out entirely from abject terror. After sorting those with weak constitutions out, the remaining crew was solid.

However, they needed her help, even more than Major Lewis comprehended. She sometimes thought his expectations for the men were too high and his timelines for results too ambitious. She would do her balancing act of running interference for the men while keeping them sane enough to meet Major Lewis' objectives.

She touched the screen of her Cybernetic Digital Organizer and began her entry on Sergeant Michael Lorenzo.

***

Carl Birdsall found himself fifty feet above the ground clinging on for dear life as he climbed rope ladders and traversed rope bridges in an exercise called Victory Tower.

He had not realized how afraid he was of heights until this moment, but Sergeant Maddox didn't tolerate any lollygagging. As a result, Carl and the rest of his squad careened over the heads of the rest of his platoon to reach the end.

The rest would have their turn at it squad by squad. But at the moment, he was just trying not to fall to his death.

A private in front of him stumbled on the bridge and fell through, his groin stopping him from total free fall. In the process, he shook the whole bridge, causing Carl and the three men behind him to fall off the side.

They all held on.

Carl struggled to regain footing, but the recruit in front of him kept shaking the whole bridge. Carl called out to him. "Mendoza."

The terrified recruit was not listening. He clung to the rope, frozen.

"MENDOZA."

He looked at Carl, eyes wide as platters. The other recruits were cursing at him for shaking the bridge.

"Mendoza, look at me. Don't listen to them."

Mendoza just stared at Carl in horror. Then he nodded like a terrified child to a parent trying to explain that there is nothing to fear in the dark.

"Mendoza, you're okay. You're not going to fall."

"He's going to make us all fall," Koontz shouted from behind Carl.

Carl looked over his shoulder. "Shut up, Koontz. You're not helping." Then he turned back to Mendoza. "Mendoza, just look at me. You're fine."

Mendoza nodded. "I can't move, Carl."

"Listen, Jeremy," Carl used his first name, "I want you to pull yourself up with your arms, slowly."

Mendoza nodded and began to pull himself up slowly.

"Great," Carl coached, "now swing your leg around and put your foot against the rope."

Mendoza did as Carl said and then awaited further instructions.

"Great. Now pull yourself up to a kneeling position and wait for me."

Mendoza pulled himself up and knelt, clinging to the rope railing of the bridge, but he was still shaking, preventing the others from regaining their footing.

"Mendoza, keep looking at me, and stay still. I'm coming to get you."

Mendoza stared at Carl so intensely that he almost forgot to blink. Carl pulled himself up and regained his footing. The others behind him followed suit.

Carl began to inch his way, hand-over-hand, to where Mendoza was clinging to the railing. "Okay, Jeremy. I want you to stand up slowly and hold onto me."

"Just pass him, Birdsall. We don't have time," Koontz jeered.

"Goddammit, shut up, Koontz," Carl reprimanded, "or I'll knock you off the bridge myself." He turned back to Mendoza. "Okay, Jeremy. I got you."

Mendoza pulled himself up slowly, grabbing onto Carl. Carl tensed his body so that they wouldn't rock the rope bridge.

"Okay, now I'll be right behind you. We have to make it to the zip line."

Mendoza's voice was trembling. "I can't…"

"I'm right behind you, Jeremy. Now MOVE."

He jabbed Mendoza in the ribs with his index and middle finger together, and Mendoza sprung forward. Carl made sure he was right behind him, jabbing him and speaking tough encouragement in his ear.

They made it to the zip line.

"Okay, Jeremy. Grab the handles."

Mendoza was feeling better now that he was off the rope bridge.

"You can do it, Jeremy, just grab the handles."

Mendoza nodded, his face screwed up in determination. He grabbed the handles, and Carl pushed him off the platform.

Carl watched him slide down, legs dangling, and then took the handlebars on the zip chord to the left. He pushed off the platform and sailed above the rest of his platoon and Sergeant Maddox.

He met Mendoza on the platform on the other side. They were at the worst part. They had to repel down a fifty-foot wall backwards.

"Okay, Jeremy. We'll do it together."

Mendoza nodded.

They each grabbed the thick rope in their hands and turned, putting their backs to the drop.

Carl braced himself. "MOVE IT, MENDOZA."

They both pushed off backwards. Carl landed with his feet to the wall. Mendoza was not so graceful. He slammed his body against the wall, but he regained his composure and pressed his feet against the wall. Carl nodded and they repelled down together, swinging out almost in unison until they reached the ground. Carl slapped Mendoza on the back supportively, and they backed away allowing the rest of their squad to follow.

When the last of their squad, Fromm, hit the ground, Maddox clicked his stopwatch. "God almighty that was the worst time I've ever seen. You ladies move slower than a group of pregnant cows."

He looked at Carl. "Birdsall, step forward."

Carl did as he was told.

"Explain to me what went wrong up there."

Carl cleared his throat. "One of the squad lost his footing on the bridge, sir. We couldn't pass until we helped him back up."

"You could've passed him at any time."

"Yes, sir, I suppose we could have."

Maddox got right in Carl's face. "So you're telling me that you let one soldier interfere with your mission? Is that what you're telling me, Birdsall?"

"I'm saying we leave no man behind, sir. And we completed the mission."

Maddox smiled venomously in Carl's face. Then he whirled around and addressed the rest of the platoon. "Do you see what we have here? Do you know what this is called?"

They all stared at Maddox silently, knowing the question was rhetorical. Carl swallowed hard. His throat was dry as a bone.

"This is called leadership. I expect this out of each and every one of you."

Maddox then turned to Carl's squad. "Fifty laps around the airfield. Now."

They groaned from exhaustion, but they started to jog off.

"Not you, Birdsall."

Carl turned around. "Pardon me, sir, but I believe my place is with my squad."

Maddox smiled widely. "Good man, Birdsall. Good man."

He nodded, and Carl ran off to catch up with his squad. He was weary from the exercise, but he felt good doing laps with his squad.

It just felt right. As they ran, Koontz glanced over at him. Carl expected some kind of wisecrack, but Koontz only smiled. Mendoza flashed him a brief look of gratitude.

They completed their laps together, as a unit, feeding off each other's strength and company. Carl was beginning to understand what Basic Training was all about.

***

Peter was jogging along with his platoon in reverse Vee formation as thunder rumbled in the distance. The airfield was dark from cloud cover, and the air was damp.

Lockwood arranged an obstacle course with barriers of varying heights. Their objective was to corral the ID through the course. It was supposed to simulate difficult terrain.

The ID were not known for their speed or their agility, but they had to coax them through the course, improving on the time from previous iterations.

The dogs raced along the insides of the V, prodding the ID along while managing to stay out of arms reach. As they hit each obstacle, the ID in front tripped and fell, and the ones behind piled on top and crawled over.

It was messy and barely coordinated, but that was the nature of the ID. They progressed through the course slowly but surely, surmounting obstacle after obstacle. A few ID began to pile on and hump in front of a particularly tall obstacle, but Peter waited as the others climbed over them and over the obstacle.

When all the ID made it over, Peter sent the dogs back to coax the humpers apart. After a few minutes, when he saw they were ignoring the dogs, Peter signaled to Lorenzo to send the dogs back up with the other ID to keep them moving forward.

When the dogs were clear, he triggered the Amygdala Inhibitors for the humpers. As a result, two of the three were immobilized. The one that was apparently not a member of the deactivated squad kept going.

Peter signaled Lorenzo to continue with the group, and Peter shot the remaining humper in the head. He then left the other two immobilized and rejoined the formation.

They progressed through the course, losing one or two ID who had to be put down while immobilizing a couple of more squads. When they reached the end of the course, Peter immobilized the rest and they waited while Lockwood counted the ID that made it through.

"Eighty-four percent."

Major Lewis strode up to address Peter and Lorenzo. "We need to do better."

Peter nodded.

They had broken the ID into squads, and each squad now had their own Amygdala Inhibitor switch. But the humpers didn't necessarily break down by squad.

It was an improvement, but far from perfect. Not only did they have to plug a few in the head, but they also had to immobilize several others, thus eliminating them from the exercise.

They were now fighting attrition, and something had to be done about the humpers. It was the rare exercise where there weren't any, and it was holding them back from reaching what Major Lewis considered acceptable levels of attrition.

In debriefing, Peter voiced his frustration. "Permission to speak freely, sir."

Major Lewis nodded.

"We need to do something about these humpers."

"Well, I thought the squad specific Amygdala Inhibitors would help."

"They do, sir," Lorenzo said, "but there's still an ID or two that need to be put down."

Major Lewis put up his hands in exasperation. "Well, any ideas?"

"What about electromagnets? Opposite polarities would force them apart," Peter suggested.

"No," Farrow responded, "it won't work. Some ID would repel each other, but others would be attracted, making matters worse."

"What about electroshock as a deterrent?" Lorenzo speculated.

"No, that won't work either," said Farrow. "They don't feel pain."

Peter remembered the ID he struck repeatedly and how it just stood there taking each blow. It didn't even flinch.

"The dogs didn't even have an effect on the humpers," Peter added.

They all sat there thinking of a way around the problem. Finally, Peter's eyes lit up with epiphany. "What if we hit the AI kill switch and then immediately restarted them."

"You mean like a reset?" Farrow asked.

"Yeah, like hitting the reset button. All this time, we assumed that once we hit the kill switch, those AI were out of the exercise," Peter said excitedly.

"And because we'll only be switching them off and then on again, any of those with the main group who are affected will only be halted for a brief moment," Farrow added in understanding.

"This just might work," said Lorenzo, obviously impressed by the suggestion.

"It's definitely worth a shot," Peter coaxed.

Major Lewis was all poker face as usual. "Okay, we'll try it next exercise. Lieutenant Farrow, make it so."

"Yes, sir. I'll get right on it."

"In the meantime," Lewis continued, "you're all due for a pass. Take some R&R and report back in three days."

This was music to everyone's ears. Major Lewis sensed that the men were burning out. They were working hard, and if he pushed them too much, it would be counterproductive.

They were dismissed from debriefing, and Lorenzo approached Peter in the locker room. "Hey, Pete, what are you gonna do with your pass?"

Peter was putting on deodorant. "I was actually going to go home and check in on my dad. Why?"

"Well, I've got no plans as of now. I was wondering if I could tag along."

Peter and Mike had become friends since the ID outfit was put together. Mike, like Peter, was young and unattached.

"You don't want to visit your family?" Peter asked.

"They're on a cruise somewhere in the Caribbean."

"Poor them. Sure, you can tag along."

Lorenzo closed his locker. "Great. When do we leave?"

"As soon as we get back to the barracks. We'll pack and go."

"Awesome. It'll be great to see where the fearless Lieutenant Peter Birdsall grew up."

"It's a simple place, Mike. Nothing too impressive. I think you'll be disappointed."

Lorenzo put his hand on Peter's shoulder. "Beats the hell out of Fort Bliss."

"Amen to that."

Peter and Mike were packing a few changes of clothes into their duffel bags. Peter turned on his com unit and called Carl. Carl picked up.

"Oh, hey, Pete."

"Carl, you look exhausted. Rough day in Basic?"

"Two words: Victory Tower."

Peter couldn't help but smile. "Ah, yes, the Victory Tower. I remember that. How'd you do?"

"I did fine. One of the other recruits lost it on the rope bridge and almost took the rest of us with him. But I was able to talk him through it."

"Was the drill sergeant impressed?"

"Yeah, and I got fifty laps out of it."

"Yeah, sounds like Basic. No good deed goes unpunished. But it all makes you tougher."

"I know, Pete. How are things with you?"

"Got a pass for three days. I'm going home to visit Dad, see how he's doing."

"That's good. I wish I could be there."

"Eight more weeks, Carl."

"I know. I know."

"I warned you it wouldn't be easy."

"Hey, did I say I was quitting?"

Carl sounded defensive. Peter always enjoyed getting a rise out of him. What were big brothers for?

"Relax, bro. I wasn't saying you couldn't hack it."

"Well, it sure sounded like it."

Peter changed the subject. "Your girlfriend was asking about you the other day."

Carl's face lit up on the monitor, but he played dumb. "My girlfriend? Who?"

"Oh come off it, Carl. Captain London."

"Really? She asked about me?"

"No, but look how excited you got."

"Screw you, Pete."

"Good bye, Carl."

"Say hi to Dad. And don't tell him I'm screwing up or anything. He's got enough to worry about."

"Okay, Carl. Take care."

Carl hung up.

"Pete, you ready to go?" Lorenzo was standing behind him.

Peter turned around. "Yeah, just gave my little brother a call."

"He doesn't look so little anymore."

Peter laughed at this. He noticed it too. Carl was toughening up. It was only a couple of weeks, but Basic changes a man. It makes him hard.

"Let's get out of here."

Peter and Mike Lorenzo left the barracks to catch their ride to Peter's homestead.

Chapter 9

Peter was startled when his dad answered the front door. He looked tired and haggard. His mother's death definitely took its toll on him.

"Hey, Dad."

"Peter. Come in."

They stepped into the living room. The house was dark.

"Who's your friend?"

"Dad, this is Mike Lorenzo."

Peter's father offered his hand, "Barry Birdsall," and Mike took it.

"Pleased to meet you, sir."

Peter's father stood there, not knowing what to say next.

"Dad, you should turn on some lights. It's no good to stay in the dark like this."

Peter flipped on the light and was startled by what he saw. There were dirty laundry, used paper plates, and organofoam cups everywhere. Part of a pizza still in the box was on the floor and half-under the couch. His father stood there with his hands in his pockets looking sheepish.

"Jesus, Dad. What a mess."

He was embarrassed in front of Lorenzo, but most of all he felt bad for his father. Peter walked past him and into the kitchen. He turned on the light and found a mountain of dirty dishes piled up in the sink, more fast food detritus covering the kitchen table and some of the chairs, and the toilet off the kitchen was running.

Lorenzo stood next to him. "Need some help?"

"Mike, no. I'll…"

"Pete, I invited myself here. The least I can do is help."

Peter's father shuffled into the kitchen. "You don't have to do anything guys, really."

"Dad, I can't just let this happen. Mike, you know how to work a grill?"

"I'm from Texas, Pete. What do you think?"

Peter opened up the refrigerator. "We can cook up some steaks or something."

However, the refrigerator was practically empty, save some half-empty bottles of various condiments, a six-pack of beer, and a full bottle of cola. There were food stains all over the inside of the fridge.

Mike looked over Peter's shoulder and into the fridge. "Take out?"

Peter closed the door. "Take out." He turned on the com unit. "Pizza?"

Peter's dad smiled. "Pepperoni would hit the spot."

"Sounds good to me," Lorenzo added.

"Pepperoni it is," Peter confirmed.

He dialed a local pizzeria and ordered two large pies with extra pepperoni. He grabbed a large garbage bag and took to the living room, picking up garbage and dirty laundry. Mike took the kitchen, where he began to load the dishwasher.

When the doorbell rang, Peter dropped what he was doing and answered the door. He paid the deliveryman sixty dollars, and he brought the boxes into the kitchen.

Mike had cleared off the kitchen table. Peter put down the boxes. A holographic advertisement for Joe's Pizza flashed on the top box cover.

"Peter, let me pay you for that."

"Don't worry about it, Dad. It's no problem. Sit down."

They all sat down at the table and consumed pizza. In between bites, Peter's father regaled Lorenzo with embarrassing stories from Peter's childhood.

"We were at this barbecue at a neighbor's house…"

"Oh, Dad, no. Not that story."

"And Peter was playing catch with his brother and some of the neighborhood kids. He was ten years old, I think."

"Oh boy, here it comes."

Peter was laying it on thick, faking obligatory protest to egg his father on. This was their routine whenever his father told stories.

He knew his father loved it, and he felt it might pick up his spirits, at least during dinner.

His father continued. "And a yellow jacket flew right up his shorts and stung him in the groin."

Lorenzo, in the middle of chewing, grimaced and elbowed Peter. "Holy cow. That must've hurt."

"Like you wouldn't believe, man."

"He was crying and crying," Peter's dad continued. "All of the other kids just stared at him in disbelief."

"And then there was the time he had his brother Carl convinced that he had a magic force field around him. He used to drag his feet on the carpet and dare Carl to touch him. When Carl touched him and got shocked, he really freaked out."

"Yeah, Dad, but you put a quick end to that. You explained to him what static electricity was. But it was a fun afternoon."

They all laughed as they ate their pizza and drank their cola. When they finished, Barry was banished to the den to watch television with a glass of scotch while Peter and Lorenzo finished cleaning up.

Peter wiped his brow as he dragged several bloated garbage bags out to the shed in back. When he returned, Lorenzo was nursing a beer and leaning against the kitchen counter.

"Hey, Mike. Thanks for helping out. You didn't have to."

Mike took a gulp of beer. "No problem, Pete. I'm paying myself in beer."

"Hey, not here. When my dad goes to sleep, we're going out. I'm buying. There's this local watering hole—a real shithole—but it's close, it's cheap, and the local girls love military men."

Lorenzo perked up. "Oh, really. Sounds like fun."

They kept Peter's father company until he dozed off in his armchair. Then they crept quietly out of the house and walked to Frisky's.

***

Peter and Lorenzo sat at the bar. They ordered two beers, and Lorenzo took in the atmosphere. "So this is the old stomping grounds of the mighty Lieutenant Birdsall."

Peter smirked. "Aren't you just overwhelmed with its awesomeness?"

Lorenzo had already made eye contact with a beautiful brunette across the bar through the smoke. The scent of sweat and sex saturated the air. "The local tail ain't bad."

Peter laughed. Lorenzo was a player, and apparently, he moved quickly. Peter guessed that he was able to walk the walk, making him a good wingman. "Do you have any places like this where you're from?"

The beers came. Lorenzo took a swig before answering. "None this sleazy."

Peter punched him in the shoulder. "Hey, thanks again."

"For what, Pete?"

"For helping me with my dad."

"No problem. He's great. I wish I had a nice father like that."

Peter gulped some beer, wiping suds from his mouth. "You two don't get along?"

"Nope. Never did, Pete. He always had a problem with me."

"What do you mean?"

"When I was little, I was too hyper or too messy or I was a cry baby. When I was older, I was too lazy or too stupid."

"I'm sorry to hear that, man."

"Yeah, well, I got out of that house any chance I got. I ran with other boys like me. We began to do things. You know, vandalism, stealing cars and taking them for joyrides."

Peter put down his glass a little too hard on the bar, an indication of his surprise. "You? Really?"

"The local cops were cool about it. They'd always take me home. I begged them to lock me up, but I never escaped the beatings."

"So why did you do those things?"

Lorenzo took a thoughtful sip of his beer. "To piss him off, I guess. It was worth the beatings."

"He never got tired?"

Lorenzo was staring directly ahead of him at nothing at all. It was as if he was replaying his childhood like an old movie in his head. "Oh, he got tired. One day he told me that I was to join the army or he would throw me out of the house, and if I ended up in jail, I was on my own."

"So that's when you enlisted?"

"He took me to the enlistment center himself and watched me sign my life away."

Peter downed the rest of his glass. "Shit, that's heavy."

"Oh, I was more than happy to leave that house. His years of criticism and abuse made Basic a breeze. You might say I was used to it."

Peter called over the bartender. "Two whiskey shots, black label."

Lorenzo nodded his approval.

"So, do you have any regrets?" Peter asked.

"No. I'm a different person now. The army taught me self-reliance...yet, I finally feel like I'm a part of something."

Peter stared forward. "Yeah, I guess that's what we all want."

The shots came. They each picked up a shot glass.

"To belonging to something," Lorenzo toasted.

"Bottoms up," Peter responded.

They downed their whiskey.

"Smooth," Peter commented, and then to the bartender, "Two more beers."

"So why did you join, Pete?"

Peter had plenty of time to mull this question over given his brother's recent decision to enlist.

"I was never a good student. I did okay, but let's just say I wasn't doctor or lawyer material."

"Not that there's any jobs for doctors or lawyers," Lorenzo added.

"I don't know. It just seemed right. Some people become cops, some people become firefighters, and some join the army."

The two beers came.

"Yeah, I guess they're all dangerous," Lorenzo said.

"Exactly. Why don't people ever see that? Especially a cop. A cop can be shot or stabbed at any time. But for some reason, it's more acceptable than joining the army."

Lorenzo was making eyes with the brunette again. She was whispering to her friend, who was now casting sultry glances. He elbowed Peter in the middle of sipping his beer, causing him to spill a little in his lap.

"What the hell?"

"Hey, Pete, enough about the army. Those two ladies have been eyeing us since we came in."

Peter looked over, and the girls met his gaze. He felt the electricity from across the room. "Like shooting fish in a barrel."

"Amen, brother. Why don't we go over and introduce ourselves."

They stood up. Peter stepped back and gestured for Lorenzo to go first. He wanted to see the man in action. "After you. I'll cover you."

Lorenzo grabbed his beer off the bar and sauntered over with Peter, where they were received quite warmly.

Chapter 10

16 Weeks Later

Carl had completed Basic Training. He sailed through weapons training using the M16, M4 carbine, grenade launchers, and various automatic weapons. He mastered drill and ceremony training, and he struggled through special tactical Field Training Exercises where as a platoon, the recruits practiced decision-making on the battlefield.

He graduated to Advanced Individual Training (AIT) where he would be trained in his Military Occupational Specialty (MOS). Having two years of classes in engineering under his belt, he applied to Fort Leonard Wood in Missouri and was accepted. However, because he did not complete four years of college, he was not accepted into the engineering program.

This disappointed Carl greatly. He was, however, accepted into the field technician program and received his training at the Edwin R. Bradley Radiological Teaching Laboratories, one of the few actually licensed by the Department of Defense.

Being a natural student, Carl passed his classes with flying colors. After the physical rigor of Basic, he felt like he was back in his element.

He was graduating in a week from the program and faced assignment. It was evening, and he just returned to the barracks from the mess hall. He threw himself on his bed and picked up his textbook on subatomic particles when his com unit flashed that he had an incoming call. He put down his book and touched the screen. It was Peter.

"Hey, Pete."

"Hey, Carl. How's it going?"

"Okay. I was just reading about quarks."

His big brother's quizzical expression amused him. "It's a subatomic particle, Pete. I have one last exam tomorrow."

"You excited about graduation?"

"Yeah, I guess. But I'm a little worried about where I'm going to be assigned."

"I'm sure you'll be useful wherever you go."

"Well, I'm worried about Dad. I'd like to be close to him if possible."

"Carl, when you enlisted you cut the apron strings. There's no going back."

"I know. I know. I just worry about him."

Peter hesitated. Carl knew that the only time Peter shut up was when he had something important to say.

"What is it, Pete? I have to get back to studying."

"Well, I was thinking that if you were interested...I could maybe pull some strings and get you assigned to Fort Bliss here in Texas. They need some good techs. There's a lot of interesting R&D going on here."

Carl sat up. "Really? What kind of R&D?"

"Classified, bro. But it won't be if I can get you an assignment."

"Really? You can do that?"

"I have some connections."

"That would be great. We'd be on the same base, and close to Dad."

Peter smiled wryly. He figured he'd torture his little brother a little. "Are you sure you're not sick of Texas? Maybe you want to see other places."

Carl took the bait, amusing his brother. "No, no. Fort Bliss would be fantastic."

Peter hesitated, watching Carl squirm. "Okay. Okay. I'll see what I can do. In the meantime, you get back to studying. I won't be able to do squat if you fail your last final exam."

"Thanks, Pete."

"Don't mention it."

Peter terminated the call. He sat up in his bunk. He had an appointment with Captain London in a few minutes, and wanted to discuss the prospect of bringing Carl into the ID Program.

He stood up, straightened out his uniform, and put on his headgear.

***

"You want to do what?" Captain London asked, the disapproval obvious in the tone of her voice.

"Hey, I think the ID Program Radiology Department could use him. He's very smart, you know."

"You just want to keep an eye on him. You know Major Lewis will never allow it. It's policy. He can't be in the same unit as you."

"Major Lewis owes me."

Captain London sat forward in her chair. She couldn't believe what she was hearing. "Major Lewis doesn't *owe* you anything. You follow his orders and army policy. Period. There are no favors, Peter."

"Tijuana. Major Lewis sent me into a death trap. I joined his precious ID Program and developed it into what it is today. We're on the verge of being fully operational."

"Peter, did you ever think that you'd be dragging Carl into dangerous combat scenarios with you? You're going to be engaging Mexican cartels…with dangerous undead drones no less."

Peter shook his head impatiently. "He would be a SWEEPER. They don't directly engage the enemy."

"And you could keep an eye on him."

Peter played dumb, but she wasn't buying it. "Well, now that you mention it, Doc, I guess that is also true."

"Oh, come off it, Peter. This request is very inappropriate."

"Frankly Doc, it's not your call to make. So why don't we just let Major Lewis make the call."

She glared at him, frustrated. "Requesting this of him is not a good idea. If I were you, I'd just drop it."

"Is that your clinical opinion, Doctor?"

She didn't like him mocking her, but he continued anyway. "I thought you of all people would be happy to see him."

She glared at him. "And just what's that supposed to mean?"

"You know, Frisky's…"

"And?"

"You thought he was cute."

She sat back and put her palm to her forehead. "I knew I shouldn't have said that."

"Why?"

"Peter, you should've seen him trying to hit on me. It was clumsy and pathetic, but I felt bad for him. I wanted to boost his confidence."

"So you're saying you don't think Carl is cute?"

Her voice, for the first time since he met Captain London, now carried an authoritative tone. "This conversation is heading in an inappropriate direction."

Peter realized he crossed a line. He couldn't tell if he struck a nerve or she really regretted calling Carl cute, but either way he had to back off.

"Sorry, Doc."

She regained her composure. "It's okay. You were frustrated and were lashing out. Listen, if you want to make that request with Major Lewis, I can't stop you. It's your funeral."

"Thank you."

"In the meantime, you need to focus on your duties, soldier, and not concoct fantasies about what I or any other officer find attractive."

"Yes, ma'am."

That was the first time she referred to herself as an officer in session.

"Now get out of here."

"Yes, ma'am. And I really am sorry."

She nodded and gestured for him to leave. "Go."

Peter heard the door close behind him. He would meet with Major Lewis tomorrow after debriefing. Surely, he would at least have to consider Peter's request. At least Peter believed he should.

However, even he knew that what he believed and what Major Lewis would do were two very different things.

***

The next day Peter's unit assembled into the hangar outside the Labyrinth. Major Lewis had wanted them to practice extraction from a confined area, as their first mission might involve neutralizing cartel members in cenotes.

Peter awaited the signal from Sergeant Lockwood for the beginning of the exercise, and then he signaled the release of the ID.

They staggered out, as usual, into the funnel of the reverse Vee formation, the dogs running alongside of them. Peter scanned the flanks for insurgents.

A private at the mouth of the funnel breached the front door and stepped back into formation. The ID piled into the Labyrinth as they had practiced so many times before.

There was inevitably a small faction of humpers, but Peter identified the squads involved and hit the AI kill switch. He counted to five and reactivated the humpers, and they rose and rejoined the group. His idea four months ago about "resetting" the humpers had worked.

The SWEEPERS ran along the side of the structure, their squads covering them, tracking the ID. The interior walls inside had been removed to simulate a cenote. A crane held a shipping crate aloft, simulating a helicopter.

After the ID were in and the front door was locked to contain them, Peter hit the AI kill switch disabling the ID in the Labyrinth. He then signaled to Sergeant Lorenzo, who was standing on top of the crate.

Lorenzo signaled to the crane operator, who began to lower the crate into the Labyrinth. When the crate was just twenty or so feet above the frozen ID, Lorenzo signaled for the crane operator to stop.

He then repelled down into the Labyrinth and moved ID that were in the way aside. When he signaled the crane operator, the operator lowered the crate until it rested on the floor inside.

Lorenzo opened the crate and climbed back on top, holding on to the tow cable. He signaled to Peter, who reactivated the ID. The two pigs inside the crate began to squeal as hungry ID piled into the crate. It appeared they still had use for pigs after all. When the last ID was in, Lorenzo closed the crate doors from on top and signaled to Peter.

Peter hit the AI kill switch again, immobilizing the entire ID platoon. Lorenzo signaled to the crane operator to take them up. When the crate reached its zenith, Lockwood called time and the exercise was over.

Flawless.

Peter ran over to Lockwood and slapped him proudly on the back. "See you in debriefing, Sergeant."

Lockwood nodded. "Well done, Lieutenant."

Peter sauntered into the debriefing room. Farrow was already seated. They waited for Lockwood, Lorenzo, and then Major Lewis.

Major Lewis addressed the group. "Well done. Flawless execution. Your months of training have paid off. The ID Program is nearly operational."

There were congratulatory comments. Then they were silent, as Major Lewis was not yet finished.

"But the true test will be in an actual combat situation. Mark my words; there will be no paintballs, cardboard cutouts, or second chances. There will only be your training."

They all nodded solemnly. They had spent so many months working on these exercises, wrangling the ID that it almost seemed like a game. But this was no rodeo. They were training for a purpose, and they would be tested soon enough.

After a review of some of the finer details of the exercise, they were dismissed. Lockwood strode off, and Lorenzo waited for Peter, but Peter was waiting for Major Lewis.

"You coming, Lieutenant?"

"No, you go ahead. I'll catch up with you later."

Lorenzo looked at him uncertainly, as if he wasn't sure what he was up to.

"Good job, Sergeant. I'll see you later."

Lorenzo smiled uneasily and walked off in the direction of the barracks.

Major Lewis stepped out of the debriefing room and practically ran into Peter.

"Excuse me, sir."

Major Lewis addressed him tersely. "Something I can do for you, Lieutenant?"

"I would like to speak with you privately, sir."

Major Lewis appraised him rather obviously. "Yes, of course. In my office."

He walked off toward his office. Peter followed like a smaller, yippy dog following a larger dog. The irony was that Peter was taller and broader than Major Lewis was.

When they reached his office, Major Lewis rounded his desk and stood waiting for the formality before sitting. Peter removed his headgear and saluted. Major Lewis returned the salute and planted himself behind his desk. Peter sat as well.

"What can I do for you, Lieutenant Birdsall?"

"I would like to make a request, sir."

"Oh, and what would that be?" He sounded disinterested, almost sarcastic.

"I have a younger brother, sir, and he just graduated AIT..."

"Oh? In what MOS?"

"He's a field technician, sir."

Peter waited for some kind of comment, but Major Lewis just looked at him creating an awkward silence. Peter took this as a cue to continue.

"And, well, I was wondering if it was possible if it could be arranged for him to be assigned to Fort Bliss, sir."

Major Lewis looked him in the eye, considering the request. "Well, I suppose something could be arranged..."

"To the ID Program, sir."

Major Lewis' expression soured instantly. "Now you know darn well that such a request cannot be granted."

"Why?"

Major Lewis raised an eyebrow at the question. "Are you questioning a superior officer?"

Peter sat up as straight as he could in his chair. "Permission to speak freely, sir."

Major Lewis paused, eyebrow still raised, and then nodded once.

"I have done everything you've asked me to do. I joined the ID Program, I've developed it for you, I've contributed every step of the way, and I believe the results speak for themselves."

Major Lewis sat listening with his right index finger pressed thoughtfully to his lips.

"Lieutenant Birdsall, I can certainly consider your request to have your brother assigned to Fort Bliss. But you know that the military has a policy about siblings serving in the same unit ever since World War II when the Sullivan brothers all died together on the same ship."

"But, sir," Peter retorted as firmly but respectfully as he could, "there is no actual 'Sullivan Act' present in navy or army policy prohibiting siblings from serving together. It's a myth."

Major Lewis glowered at Peter. Peter was stunned into a rather uncomfortable silence. "Technically you are right, Lieutenant. But nevertheless…"

"Please, sir. We could use another SWEEPER."

"Why?"

"Pardon, sir?"

"Why do you want him assigned to the ID Program so badly?"

"Because I don't want to see his talents wasted elsewhere, sir."

"And it would have nothing to do with you wanting to watch over him."

Peter had to stop himself from rolling his eyes. "Sir, Captain London is mistaken."

"Captain London? Mistaken about what?"

Peter was not sure if this was some kind of test. "Surely she's spoken to you…"

"Actually she has not."

Peter knew he was caught. It was a guilty response on his part.

Major Lewis sat behind his desk scowling. He folded his hands and looked down at them for a moment. Peter swallowed hard. His palms were sweaty as he realized he was gripping the armrests of his chair.

"Okay."

Peter did not believe what he was hearing. "Really?"

"Did I stutter, Lieutenant?"

Peter tried his best to sound contrite. "No, sir. You were crystal clear."

"But if I find his presence is undermining your effectiveness, I'm transferring him out immediately. Am I clear?"

"Yes, sir."

Major Lewis put on his glasses and began to sort through things on his desk as if Peter wasn't there. When Peter didn't move, he looked up over the tops of his glasses.

"Will that be all?"

Peter knew when to exit on a high note. "Yes, sir. Thank you, sir."

Peter stood up and saluted the Major, who did not look up. Peter slipped out of the office and practically ran back to the barracks.

Once again, big brother came through.

It was time for dinner, but Peter ran back to his bunk and called Carl on the com unit. Carl didn't pick up, as he was likely at the mess hall himself.

Peter left a simple message: "You're coming to Fort Bliss."

Then he hung up and walked briskly to the mess hall. He found Lorenzo eating with the men. He grabbed a tray, made his way through the line, and once his tray was full, he joined his men.

"I did it, Mike."

"Did what, Pete?"

"I was able to get my brother assigned to Fort Bliss..."

"Really? That's great, Pete."

"To the ID Program."

Lorenzo put down his fork. "Do you think that's such a good idea, Pete?"

"Why?"

"Isn't there a policy..."

"No Sullivan Act. I looked it up."

"And Major Lewis approved it?"

"It took some coaxing."

"Holy shit. What'll he be doing? I thought he was some kind of egg head."

Peter scooped up what was supposed to be mashed potatoes and shoved the load into his mouth. "Field technician. He can be a SWEEPER."

Lorenzo nodded with approval, picked up his fork, and stabbed his chicken as if it wasn't already dead.

Peter devoured his meal in earnest. He was looking forward to serving with his brother. For once, they had something in common. Peter would be his commanding officer, but he was his big brother his whole life. To Peter there was no real difference. It would be like old times.

"Well I'll be damned," Lorenzo said, "another Birdsall. This'll be interesting."

***

Private Carl Birdsall reported to the El Paso Intelligence Center at the Biggs Army Airfield, Fort Bliss. He was instructed to go to Hangar Four and report to a Sergeant Michael Lorenzo.

He passed some heavy security, which only intensified as he neared the hangar. This stoked his curiosity. He wondered what type of assignment he was receiving. Peter had alluded to some classified R&D.

He entered the hangar and was instructed to wait in a debriefing room. He was in there for around twenty minutes waiting, and just as he was about to get up, Lorenzo walked in.

Carl stood up and saluted. "Private Carl Birdsall, reporting for duty, sir."

Lorenzo saluted and stroked his chin thoughtfully. "Birdsall...you wouldn't be related to Lieutenant Peter Birdsall, would you?"

"Yes, sir. I'm his brother."

"Oh, I see. Be seated, Private."

Carl sat.

"Private Birdsall, you have been assigned to a very special anti-terrorist program using the latest in drone technology. I hear you're quite sharp."

"I do my best, sir."

"Any college?"

"Two years of engineering, sir."

"I see. And you don't have to keep calling me sir every time you speak."

"Yes, sir."

Lorenzo shot him a look.

"Sorry."

"So why aren't you in the engineering core?"

"Because the army didn't see it fit to place me there with only two years of college. And they needed field technicians."

"Well, we could sure use you in the ID Program, Private."

"What is the ID Program, sir?"

Lorenzo smiled easily. "Well, I'm glad you asked that. Because the ID Program is not something that can easily be explained. It's something that is best demonstrated."

Carl waited expectantly.

"Come with me, Private."

Lorenzo opened the door and exited the debriefing room. Carl followed. They walked a short distance to a large structure with a front door and no roof.

Lockwood was waiting by the front door. Carl saluted him enthusiastically.

"Who do we have here, Sergeant Lorenzo?"

"Sergeant Lockwood, this is Private Carl Birdsall, field technician and Lieutenant Peter Birdsall's brother."

Lockwood nodded. "Private."

"Sergeant Lockwood here is in charge of overseeing the training exercises in the ID Program."

Lockwood gave Lorenzo a knowing look. "I'll leave you two to the…orientation." He walked away.

Lorenzo opened the door to the Labyrinth and stepped aside. "Private Birdsall, please step inside."

Carl was taken off guard. In there? He wondered what was going to happen in there, but he stepped in as instructed.

"Private Birdsall, your objective in this little demonstration is to try to make it to the other side."

"Yes, sir."

"Oh, and you'll be pursued. Don't get caught."

"Yes, sir."

Lorenzo began to close the front door, but he stopped and offered one last remark. "Oh, do be careful."

Carl did not quite know how to respond to that, but he didn't get the chance as Lorenzo quickly closed the door. Carl heard the digi-lock engage.

It was dark in the room he was standing in. There were three doorways all around him. He chose the one in the middle. He did not have to wander long to realize that he was in some kind of a maze. He was confident in his visual-spatial abilities, so he cognitively began to map the maze as he traversed the rooms. He hit a few dead ends and had to retrace his steps on a few occasions, but overall he felt he was making progress.

Then he heard the footsteps.

They were a few rooms away but closing in. Carl remembered his training in Basic. His instinct was to move in the opposite direction of the footsteps, but he knew that would only get him lost and caught.

He kept his cool and tried to analyze the pattern of the layout of the rooms. He began to realize that there was indeed a pattern. It reminded him of his study of fractals.

He began to cross from room to room, making fewer errors in direction and encountering fewer dead ends. He was excited with his progress and almost didn't realize that he no longer heard the footsteps.

He was preoccupied with the layout of the maze when he ran right into someone who was apparently just standing there in the middle of a room.

He looked up. The face was hidden in shadow from the dim lighting, but the silhouette was unmistakably a woman.

"Pardon me, ma'am."

The woman sounded like she was wheezing.

"Are-are you alright?"

She stepped forward and reached out for him, her breath cold and putrid. Her grip on his shoulders was vice-like.

"Ma'am, please."

He tried to step back, but she pulled herself forward exposing her face. Carl gasped as a blue-green face with dark circles under the eyes pulled close to his. She appeared young. Her eyes were milky white, her hair was like straw, and the stench was overwhelming.

"Ma'am…HEY."

She opened her mouth.

He pulled away, and she pulled with him. He stumbled backward and fell, and she landed on top of him.

"What the hell's wrong with you?"

She had fallen in such a way that their bodies were askew. Her face was above his head, and her bosom was in his face. He heard her wheezing loudly.

"Ma'am, get off me."

He rolled out from under her, got to his feet, and backed away.

"Jesus. What is this?"

She turned around and snarled at him, jaws snapping. She pushed herself up onto her hands and knees and began to crawl after him.

Carl looked around quickly. He ran toward her, stepped up onto her back, and he jumped up against the wall, grabbing onto the top edge with his fingers.

She was beginning to stand up as he, hanging by his fingertips, inched over to a corner in the room hanging above the floor. She crossed the room, reaching out for him as he pulled himself up and propped himself on top of the intersecting walls.

He was able to steady himself as he rested on the top of the crisscrossing walls. She was snarling and reaching for him.

He took the time to look around, and he saw the layout of the maze. He saw that he was closer to the right side of the maze than the end.

He gave one final look to the crazed woman hissing and spitting at him, and he began to balance himself with his feet one behind the other.

He walked the wall like a tightrope and bid a fond farewell to his grotesque pursuer. It was just like Victory Tower. Only instead of being fifty feet up in the air with the clock chasing him, he had a crazed woman chasing him.

He kept his cool and made his way over to the right side of the Labyrinth, the woman wheezing after him through the rooms, and he jumped off the outer wall.

He landed on his side but rolled into a crouching position. As he stood up, he looked into an exterior window as the woman threw herself against it, smearing blood and saliva on the glass with her face.

"What the…"

He saw Sergeant Lorenzo running down the side of the maze toward him. "Private Birdsall, are you all right?"

"Yes, sir. What was…"

"Meet me in the debriefing room."

"Sir, excuse me…"

"In the debriefing room. That's an order, Private."

Carl stood up straight. "Yes, sir. Right away."

He walked off towards the debriefing room. The whole time he wondered if this was some kind of joke. Was that woman in makeup? Was this a psychological experiment? Did she have some kind of a disease?

He reached the debriefing room, and Lockwood was already seated. Carl saluted and took a seat. Lockwood was silent.

Moments later Lorenzo barged in. Carl looked at him expectantly.

"We're waiting for my commanding officer, the leader of the ID Program."

Carl waited. He wasn't sure if he succeeded in the exercise or he did something wrong. Then someone else barged in…

"Pete?"

Peter was laughing. Lorenzo also looked amused. Lockwood was still wearing his stoic expression.

"With all due respect, does somebody want to tell me what the hell is going on?"

Peter put his arms out, and Carl stood up. Peter hugged him. "Hello, Carl."

Lorenzo gestured with his hand toward Peter. "May I introduce Lieutenant Peter Birdsall, leader of the Insidious Drone Program?"

Carl was confused. He was surprised to see Peter, and he sure as shit wasn't sure if he just heard what Lorenzo said correctly. The Insidious Drone Program?

"I-I don't understand."

"Holy shit, Carl. We've never seen anyone handle the orientation exercise in quite that way."

"You said he was sharp, Lieutenant," Lorenzo said.

"Wh-what orientation exercise? What was that?"

"That, Carl, was an ID, or an Insidious Drone, an undead soldier," Peter announced with no small amount of pride.

"Un…dead? Like a zombie?"

"Yes, Carl. Exactly like a zombie."

Carl looked around and wondered if he was on the set of a reality show. "This is a joke…right?"

"No joke, Carl. This is the latest in drone technology."

"Drone? That was a drone?"

"Yes. It's a long story. It's a virus that causes the reanimation of dead cells. The result is a condition called Kluver-Bucy Syndrome."

"Kluver…"

"Bucy. It's caused by lesions in the amygdala that cause hyper aggression and sexuality."

"Hyper…"

"The girl was my touch," Lorenzo chimed in. "The Lieutenant told me you were afraid of women."

"I-I'm not afraid of women."

Peter put his hand on Carl's shoulder. "Carl, they are the perfect soldiers. They don't have to be fed, there's no dehydration, and they're relentless. All you have to do is drop several dozen of these suckers into a cave and they'll swarm any terrorist hideout."

Carl sat back down in his seat. He wasn't sure if he was dreaming. This was all a little too much.

"So you're telling me that the United States Army is using zombies to smoke terrorists out of caves? It sounds like a bad sci-fi movie."

"What gave you the idea to cross the maze on top?"

Carl wasn't sure who asked the question. It was Lockwood. In fact, it was the first thing the man said since they entered the debriefing room.

"Pete and I used to go to these corn mazes every autumn growing up. One we went to had two crosswalks overlooking the maze, giving you a chance to get your bearings and figure out the pattern. In this case, I figured out in the maze that it was a fractal pattern. But when I got up top, I saw I was close enough to the edge of the maze, so I hopped over."

Lockwood's stoic expression gave way to something else. If Carl wasn't mistaken, he would've sworn the man was impressed.

Peter smiled in recognition. "Yeah, I remember that maze. Good thinking, bro. See, I told you guys he was smart."

The rest of the day Carl was given a full tour of the program. He was introduced to Farrow, who demonstrated the technology and the role of a SWEEPER. Lockwood then introduced him to the weapons.

They returned to the debriefing room where the rest of the program was explained to him. They described the discoveries and progress made over months of training exercises: the ID squads and multiple AI kill switches, the pigs, the dogs, formations, extraction, and the humpers.

The next day Carl was integrated into his first training exercise. He swung along the side of the target structure scanning the inside and tracking the ID, confirming the neutralization of targets.

He was a quick learner and fell right into where the platoon was at in their progress. His role was simple but crucial, and he was thankful that he never had to get too close to any of the ID.

They gave him the creeps, but that was the point. It wasn't just their heartiness and their ability to swarm the enemy. They induced terror, which was intended to disorient the targets making them easier to catch. The neutralization wasn't very humane, but then again, they were terrorists.

Nevertheless, Carl was happy to be with his brother, and he was quite fascinated with the technology. He meshed well with Farrow and fed him plenty of ideas, many of which were utilized. He felt part of an important effort in combating terrorists.

After what they did to his poor mother, he welcomed any new application that would allow them to reach the terrorists sitting snugly in the depths of their hiding spots, confident that authorities would never reach them. He relished the prospect of testing the ID out.

He was introduced to Major Lewis, who only regarded him tangentially, and of course, Captain London.

"I believe you two have already met," Peter teased.

Captain London shot Peter a dirty look. "Hello, Carl."

Carl's heart was in his throat.

"Say hello, Carl," Peter needled.

"Hello, C-Captain London."

She was even more beautiful than he remembered. Maybe it was the uniform.

"Please, everyone calls me Fiona or Doc. I'm available for a session any time you want to talk. Most of the soldiers in the ID Program come to visit at some point."

"I can see why."

Captain London blushed at the comment as Peter stood by grinning like a wise ass.

"Oh, no, I mean because of the zombies," Carl recovered.

"The ID," she corrected.

"Yes, the ID."

"Your brother has sessions regularly."

"I'm not surprised. I think he was dropped on his head as a baby. Repeatedly."

She barely acknowledged the joke. It was if she was trying too hard to be professional. Peter noticed.

To be honest, Carl was different from what she remembered. He was more filled out, and he carried himself a little more confidently, even if he was still bashful.

"Well, welcome to Fort Bliss, Carl."

"Thanks, Fiona."

She shot Peter some daggers as she walked away. Peter stood next to Carl. "Hate to see her go, but you love to watch her leave."

Carl shoved him and walked in the other direction towards the barracks.

Peter enjoyed having his brother there. Both had gone through an awful lot, and they needed each other. Besides, he could keep an eye on him, but he would never admit that to anyone who asked.

Chapter 11

August 23
18:00

Peter's com unit was flashing. He touched the screen and Major Lewis' face appeared on screen. His expression had more gravity than usual, which was saying a lot.

"Lieutenant, you and Sergeant Lorenzo report to the debriefing room on the airfield immediately."

"Yes, sir."

Peter put on his headgear and went to find Lorenzo, but Lorenzo found him first.

"You get the message, Lieutenant?"

Peter nodded. They left the barracks in a hurry.

Carl took notice of their abrupt exit. Something was up. Peter and Lorenzo were leaving without the platoon.

When Peter and Lorenzo reached the debriefing room, Major Lewis was seated at his desk, and Lockwood was already seated. They saluted the Major and took their seats.

Major Lewis touched the screen on his Cybernetic Digital Organizer clipboard, and it lit up.

"Our forces have pursued the Navajas into Xcaret, Mexico, where it is believed that they are operating out of a rather large cenote on the outskirts of a popular tourist area."

He touched the screen of his clipboard and a map of Xcaret projected on the screen behind him.

"As you can see, the location of the cenote is in immediate proximity to three hotels and a wildlife park, which is why our forces cannot engage in traditional fashion. The Navajas have rendezvoused with Order for International Liberation, who is believed to be serving as security detail for the operation."

He touched the screen again and several satellite photos of Navajas and O.I.L. flashed up on the wall behind him.

"They are unaware that we have located their position, so we have the element of surprise. All the more reason why your detail is perfect for this operation. Minimum gunfire. Just let the ID do what they do best."

"What about the Mexican government?" Peter asked. "If they could evacuate the nearby hotels, it would free us up."

"Too risky," Major Lewis stated. "An evacuation of the three hotels would likely tip off the Navajas that their location has been compromised."

Peter nodded his understanding. Major Lewis continued. "You will take your platoon in with four Black Hawks. You'll be armed with a combination of the electronic ignition shotguns and automatic weapons to cover the ID and address any flank attacks."

He touched his clipboard screen again and coordinates appeared on the map.

"You will be dropped here under the cover of night, on the outskirts of the tourist area. You will make your way to the drop site here…"

He cued up more coordinates.

"…where three Chinooks will deliver three standard forty-foot shipping crates filled with a total of ninety ID, thirty per crate."

He pointed on the screen behind him.

"You will cross the terrain with the ID and locate the cenote. You will then funnel the ID into the cenote, and they will neutralize the targets. A small fleet of Blackhawks with smaller crates as sling load will lower the crates into the cenote, and you will begin extraction."

Peter looked at Lorenzo excitedly. This was the first mission of the Insidious Drone platoon. They had been training for this very moment for months.

"There's one complication…"

All attention was back on Major Lewis.

"In twenty-four hours, there's going to be a hurricane entering the region, a real nasty one. They're talking a possible category four. Drop-off, neutralization, and extraction have to occur well within this time window. If we wait till after the storm has passed, the Navajas and their O.I.L. escort will have likely relocated, slipping through our fingers."

"Why isn't the Mexican government evacuating the hotels?" Peter asked.

"They've evacuated Cancun, but they figure the elevation and topography of Xcaret will mitigate any threats from the storm. Each hotel has a concrete convention center where guests will be moved to for shelter-in-place."

Major Lewis turned off his clipboard.

"This will be the first mission of the ID Program. This is what you've been training for. Sergeant Lockwood will accompany you as an observer. Any questions?"

Peter and Lorenzo shook their heads.

"Assemble the platoon in Hangar Two. You mobilize in one hour. Good luck, gentleman."

Peter, Lorenzo, and Lockwood stepped smartly out of the debriefing room to assemble the men.

"Shit, Pete. This is it," Lorenzo said excitedly.

"I know. Hard to believe, but this day had to come sometime. And Navajas and Order for International Liberation in the same location. It's like Christmas in August."

"We do this right and we'll change the face of the war on terror," Lockwood said with no small degree of import.

***

20:00

The whirring of the blades spun by twin GE T700-GE-701C engines chopping through the night air had a calming effect on Peter, like white noise.

They were almost at the drop-off point, and he was going over all of his training in his head. It was like the locker room right before the championship game, and he was reviewing all of their plays.

He wondered how Carl was doing in another Black Hawk with the two other SWEEPERS and two squads. He was proud that he was able to arrange his brother's assignment to this unit.

It sure beat urban combat in Pakistan or Afghanistan. All Carl had to do was track the ID from above the cenote under the cover of his own squad.

Peter thought of his friend, Delroy Apone and his men that were slaughtered at the hands of the ruthless Navajas. He wondered what Apone would have thought about the ID and their first mission.

He knew he would make Apone proud. He wished he could have told Molly. He wished he could have told her that he was going to hunt down and kill the sons-of-bitches who murdered her husband in cold blood.

However, the mission and all of the activities of the ID Program were strictly classified. Cold, undead justice was coming to those Navajas bastards, and for the moment, that was enough.

Carl sat next to the other two SWEEPERS in his Black Hawk. He was admiring the instruments of the gun ship: the threat warning system, the infrared jammers, and the radar warning receiver.

He never thought he would one day be sitting in a Black Hawk helicopter on the way to Mexico. His parents never went anywhere exotic. Who could afford it in this economy?

His thoughts predictably and invariably drifted to his mother. His poor mother. Although he knew she'd disapprove, he was proud that he was going to neutralize a security detail of O.I.L. He didn't have to wait for the Middle East after all. Those bastards came to him and he had something for them.

He thought back to his second day at Fort Bliss. He and his brother were in the barracks talking. Peter had told him about Tijuana.

'Carl, somebody tipped the Navajas off that we were coming.'

'What happened, Pete?'

'We stormed a storefront at dawn. It was a damned trap. Snipers drove us into the store. They bottlenecked us inside using the aisles. There were a few of us left. I did what I could to stall for time. They took us to the outskirts and they executed my men in front of me. My friend, Delroy Apone, they shot him in the head like he was nothing.'

'How did you get out?'

'I was lucky, Carl. Very lucky. I managed to fight off the Navajas. I crossed into town, and they pursued me. I stumbled into an alley, and a prostitute took me in. A prostitute of all people. I don't know why, but she protected me. Her name was Lucita.'

'And that's why you joined the ID Program?'

'Major Lewis and Captain London thought I should get back on the horse. That I would be no good at all if I didn't get back in the game.'

Carl remembered the conversation. He saw the look in his big brother's eye. He knew how he felt. They both had vengeance on their mind, and if all went well, they would get it.

The helicopters stopped in a clearing and the platoon hopped out. The copters quickly flew away, and Peter looked at his watch. They had a little less than twenty-two hours.

He called Lorenzo over. "Vee formation. Tell the flanks to look alive. We make our way over to the ID drop coordinates."

Lorenzo nodded. He turned to the men and barked the orders. They got into formation, the SWEEPERS in the rear, and they began to make their way to the ID drop coordinates.

They crossed the terrain, cutting through dense vegetation. It was around eighty degrees, but there was a breeze. The suits functioned well to keep them cool, but the air was humid and electric with the approach of the massive hurricane careening in their direction.

They crept through the lush flora at a steady pace. Deer lurked stealthily, and iguanas rested under rocks absorbing the heat from the day as they slumbered.

Large trees with tangles of exposed roots like thick fingers probing the soil loomed over them, as palms gently brushed their arms and shins.

Peter halted by a pile of limestone and put up a closed fist, signaling for the platoon to halt. He consulted his Multi-tasker, which indicated that they were right by the drop zone.

It was almost dawn, and in the near distance, the hum of the Chinooks came. But to Peter's surprise, they remained in the distance.

"What's wrong?" Lorenzo whispered to Peter.

Peter was looking at his Multi-tasker. "The drop coordinates changed."

"Why?"

"I don't know. But they were definitely modified."

The map on his Multi-tasker indicated that one shipping crate was deposited nearby, only a few clicks away, but the other two were dropped at quite a distance away.

"This drop site may have been compromised," Peter whispered. "Instruct the men to fall back."

Lorenzo ordered the men, and they receded back into the flora. Peter received satellite pictures on his Multi-tasker. There was a squad of O.I.L. patrolling in the vicinity.

Lorenzo saw the satellite maps and the location of the squad. Peter had to make a quick decision. He signaled to Lockwood to come over.

"Lockwood, take two squads and a SWEEPER to locate the most distant two crates. When you've located them, send the coordinates back to HQ for extraction. Then establish a perimeter and wait."

Lockwood nodded.

"We're only using one crate?" Lorenzo asked. "That's only thirty ID."

"There's no time," Peter stated. "The other two crates are too far away. The thirty ID will have to do. The targets are only a squad of O.I.L. and several Navajas."

Lorenzo nodded. As Lockwood took his squads and SWEEPER, Lorenzo ordered the troops into formation, and they made for the closest crate.

And just in time. The Order for International Liberation security detail passed close to the original drop coordinates, which would have ensured traditional engagement. The ruckus would have alerted the nearby Navajas, and they would have missed their opportunity.

Dawn broke and the temperature was beginning to rise. As they trekked silently toward the closest crate, Peter noticed the silence. It was as if the wildlife knew a storm was coming and had taken refuge. The dogs were even getting antsy.

The relocation of the drop coordinates and the separation of the drops cost them valuable time, as did their evasion of the roving security detail.

As they grew close to the coordinates of the new crate, Peter received regular updates on his Multi-tasker via satellite on the position of the squad of unfriendlies.

The SWEEPERS, being primarily field technicians, were in the center of the formation. Carl crept through the vegetation with his squad, feeling particularly vulnerable given his role.

He didn't expect to be running from the enemy. He was supposed to track them as they were being eaten to confirm the kills. However, it appeared that, for the moment, *they* were the ones being tracked.

There was no evidence that the enemy had detected their presence at all. Nevertheless, if they weren't careful in evading detection, the tables would be turned.

After some time they came upon the nearest crate. They cleared the area. Fortunately, the crate hadn't been discovered. They set up a reverse Vee formation in front of the crate doors.

Peter had to move fast, because the roving patrol was in the vicinity. This forced him to make another decision. If he pushed toward the cenote, the roving patrol might discover the crate and raise the alarm. But if he dealt with the patrol, it would likely involve combat, which would once again raise the alarm.

He called Lorenzo over.

"Yes, sir?"

"I'm concerned about this patrol."

"So what are we going to do?"

"I have an idea…"

The patrol came to the edge of a clearing and saw a large, rectangular metal crate sitting in the center. The leader radioed in what they found. They scanned the area and saw nothing. They spread out around the edge of the clearing, surrounding the metal box.

The leader gave a signal, and they closed in. The surrounding area was silent. The leader banged on the crate with the butt of his AK-47. It sounded somewhat hollow.

They spoke to each other, as if debating what to do. After some conversation, the leader opened up the doors of the crate.

They looked inside and raised their weapons. They shouted commands into the box. One of the men made a sour face.

Suddenly, from out of the surrounding brush came two dogs and they attacked the men. But before the men could defend themselves, people from within the box emerged and began to fall upon them, biting into them.

The assailed squad was torn between the dogs and the biters and fell into disorganization. In the scuffle, not one shot was fired.

As the men were overcome by the people from the box, the dogs backed off. The silence was interrupted by screams of terror and pain as flesh was torn from bone with jagged teeth.

Insidious Drones 1, Bad Guys 0.

In minutes, the screaming ceased and the ID finished their meal in savage bloodlust. Then Peter, a master of field craft, emerged from his camouflage with the environment and hit the Amygdala Inhibitor master kill switch.

The platoon reemerged and formed their reverse Vee formation, and Peter reactivated the ID. Having dealt with the patrol, they resumed their mission, making their way to the cenote unfettered.

The passage of time breathed down Peter's neck like an unrelenting predator. It was just past noon, and their little diversion cost them time. Besides, they didn't have much time before the Navajas realized that their scouts had not checked back in.

All they knew at the moment was that their scouts found an abandoned shipping crate in the middle of the wilderness. He prayed they didn't get spooked and run.

They traversed more difficult terrain, slowly but steadily, as the ID staggered through underbrush and over exposed roots, the dogs running alongside and nipping at their heels.

There were a couple of instances of humpers separating from the group, but Peter flicked the AI kill switches on and off by squads, and they reset and rejoined the group.

By 03:00, they reached the vicinity of the target cenote. Peter signaled for the platoon to halt, and he hit the AI kill switch. The ID were immobilized.

Peter consulted his Multi-tasker and received satellite pictures of the cenote. It was definitely occupied, probably being used as a relay station for cocaine from Columbia. What better place to hide it than a large hole in the ground in a protected nature preserve?

Peter scanned the immediate vicinity for some time. No other patrols emerged from the cenote, and none returned. Peter made the signal to resume their approach, and he reactivated the ID.

As the mouth of the funnel came within fifty feet of the cenote, they must have tripped an alarm, because shouts came from inside the cenote.

Peter signaled for them to move faster and the formation pushed up to the edge of the hole, which had to have been about 100 feet across.

The ID walked right up to the edge and dropped right in like paratroopers stepping out of a plane. They fell like lemmings, one after another, without any regard for their own safety. But that was, of course, unnecessary.

Lorenzo called for the SWEEPERS. Carl leapt forward with the other, and they each swept along the side of the hole. There were many red blips and about as many blue blips, but the blue blips were vanishing quickly.

Shrieks and panicked gunshots emanated from the cenote as the Insidious Drones took to their ghastly work. The flanks of the formation, without the ID right next to them, were able to focus entirely on their surroundings.

Peter couldn't believe it. It was all working exactly as they trained. And none of them had to venture into the cenote itself. No matter how far the Navajas receded into the limestone bowels, the ID would pursue them.

Carl watched the screen of his MR.UD as the blue blips vanished before his very eyes. After about twenty minutes, the last blue blip extinguished, and he gave the signal to Lorenzo. The other SWEEPER confirmed.

The hole was now silent, save the shuffling around of hungry ID crunching down on tibias and fibulas. Peter hit the master AI kill switch. The hole was still.

Mission accomplished. Everything had gone according to their training. Peter thought at that very moment that he should have felt relief, but instead he felt something else.

Suddenly an inexplicable wave of panic swept over him. Rationally, he knew such a feeling made no sense given the context, but he saw the same reaction in his men.

Carl felt a sudden, alien feeling of fear, and he looked down at the screen of his MR.UD. The screen was flickering.

As fast as the sensation came on, it was gone and Navajas came out of the woodwork, AK-47's trained on Peter's platoon, shouting at them to drop their weapons.

His men raised their weapons and pulled their triggers, but nothing happened.

Peter looked truly stunned. "What the hell just happened?"

"EMP," Carl yelled over to Peter.

"EMP? As in electromagnetic pulse?"

"Yeah, some kind of weaponized version," Carl explained.

"Perfect for frying our nice new electric guns," Peter hissed.

There was only one thing to do.

"Lower your weapons," he ordered.

It was like Tijuana all over again. Another trap. Someone ratted them out, again. These Navajas had a mole on the inside. That was the only way Peter figured they had managed to always be one step ahead.

Behind him he heard the ID stirring about, their AI chips fried from the EMP.

"Who's in charge?" Peter demanded.

None of the Navajas answered. They just waited.

"Why aren't they talking?" Peter asked Lorenzo.

Lorenzo dropped his rifle to his side and sighed. "That's because they're waiting for me to answer."

Chapter 12

Lorenzo stepped away from Peter and stood in front of the Navajas. Peter was now doubly stunned.

"Mike, what the hell are you doing?"

"Peter, you've come to a very important decision point, and I want you to consider your options carefully."

"What options? What are you talking about, Mike? These guys are with you? So who was in the hole we just cleared?"

"Our competition."

"What competition?"

"The O.I.L. security detail that the Navajas have been using…until now, that is."

"I still don't get it, Mike."

"It's not rocket science, Pete. Now we're the security."

Peter did not believe what he was hearing. Was Mike in league with the Navajas? This was the man he trained with for months, the man he had countless drinks with, the man he invited into his home.

"So what, you're in the security business now, and for these rat bastards no less?"

"Pete, you're so short sighted. But I'll forgive you since these 'rat bastards' killed your squad in Tijuana. The situation is so much more complex than that."

"Really? Explain it to me then."

"Pete, you make me sound like *I'm* some kind of bad guy now. We're using the ID in Mexico to take out O.I.L. We'll be protecting a pretty gaping border. You know how many terrorists have been slipping through? The war's not just in the Middle East, Pete."

"And why not make some money out of it? Is that right, Mike?"

"Oh, you have no idea. Not only are we providing security, we're also providing the perfect mules."

"Mules?"

"Think about it. The drug runners for the Navajas have to cross desert and mountain to cross the border. They lose most of them to dehydration and exhaustion. But the ID…"

Peter was beginning to understand. "They don't need water. And they never tire."

Lorenzo smiled. "See, I knew you'd get it."

"But where are you getting the ID from?"

"I provided the Navajas with our precise drop coordinates and the drop coordinates for the ID. Their presence in the area caused HQ to modify the drop coordinates."

A light went off in Peter's head. "The other two crates."

"Yes, the fact that two were dropped off away from the third crate was dumb luck."

"You can't just take ID, Mike."

"Can't I? I'll just report that the mission was a sterling success, but we lost the ID. Lewis will be pissed, but we have more."

Peter had wondered if Lewis was in on it. From Lorenzo's remark, he guessed not. "Lewis?"

Lorenzo waived his hand dismissively. "He's just an administrator, a paper-pushing moron. He'll never know the details. He deals in broad strokes. I expect that I'll receive a promotion and run this outfit as I see fit, killing terrorists and making money."

A promotion. Peter knew that would only happen upon his death. "And Lockwood?"

Lorenzo smiled wickedly. "Oh, he's just waiting for me to finish with you."

Hence the ride-along as an 'observer.'

"So it was you who tipped off the Navajas in Tijuana?"

"Actually that was Lockwood. But you can't be too hard on him, Pete. He didn't even know you yet."

"So you're a drug runner now, Mike."

"Oh, don't be so naïve, Pete. The army moved opium in Viet Nam while doing their sworn duty to fight communism. Besides, the Navajas are small potatoes. The Order for International Liberation's the big fish. They're the real threat."

"Mike, don't give me that end justifies the means bullshit."

"Pete, it's like the war on gangs. You've got to team up with the little gangs to nail the big ones. How do you think the FBI took down the mafia? Deals with the small fish, that's how."

"Spare me. You're just a sleazy opportunist, plain and simple."

"Which brings us to one all important question, Pete. When opportunity knocks, do you answer?"

"You've got be kidding me, Mike."

"Pete, remember when I went to your house? Remember we talked about belonging to something? Well, this is your chance to belong to something."

"You are so self-deluded."

"Pete, we're doing good. We'll cut you in. Your brother, too."

Peter felt his men get antsy. They noticed they weren't in the equation. Peter made a sweeping gesture with his hand.

"You're going to bribe the whole goddamned platoon, Mike?"

"They'll be unfortunate casualties on the maiden voyage of the Insidious Drones. Heroes, actually."

The men began to stir, and the Navajas inched in closer, guns trained with itchy trigger fingers.

"So what do you say, Pete?"

He would not be the lone survivor again. This time he would go down with his men. "Take my brother."

Carl looked alarmed. "Pete…no."

"And you, Pete?"

"I'll share my men's fate."

Lorenzo shook his head disappointed. "I thought you might say that. In fact, it'll be perfect. I'll just tell good ol' Major Lewis that you caved under the stress and went bonkers, killing your own men."

Peter looked around. "So what now, you're going to shoot us?"

Lorenzo put his finger thoughtfully to his lips. "No, then it wouldn't look like an accident. There'd be an investigation, ballistic reports. There can't be anything left to analyze."

Peter knew what that meant. The ID were stirring in the cenote, and they were hungry. They were always hungry.

"In the olden days, British naval officers punished their own by making them walk the plank," Lorenzo gloated.

Peter looked at him incredulous.

"Oh, come on, Pete," Lorenzo said in exasperation, "I don't have to sketch it out for you, do I?"

Peter reached down and grabbed his rifle. The Navajas brandished their weapons menacingly. Lorenzo put up a dismissive hand.

"It's okay, muchachos. The guns are useless anyway. It might buy them an extra few seconds as melee weapons." He looked right into Peter's eyes. "My gift to you, Pete."

Peter looked around at his men.

"We have to go in that hole, Pete, don't we" Carl asked, his pitch high. "I'm not going in that hole."

Lorenzo picked his teeth with his fingernail casually. "You all have until the count of three. Jump into the cenote, or I'll be forced to gun you down."

"But that wouldn't look like an accident, Mike," Peter retorted in a last ditch attempt.

Lorenzo shrugged. "You know what they say about best laid plans."

Peter heard the ID writhing around in the cenote behind him. In that brief moment, he weighed being shot against being torn apart.

"One..."

If shot, he'd be dead. If he dove into the cenote he'd have a chance. Not a good chance. Hell, not even a slim chance. But it was a chance.

"Two..."

He looked over at his brother.

"Jump, Carl."

"Pete, I can't..."

"THREE."

Pete turned and jumped into the pit. He heard gunfire from up above. He landed hard on a bunch of horizontal ID and was rolled off onto the rock floor. He was lucky. It was a pack of humpers who were too occupied with their necrophilia to notice him.

He heard several other people drop. Some were not so lucky. Undead hands reached out for them and held them fast as jaws of death clamped down on their flailing limbs.

He hit an ID in the face as one approached him. "CARL! CARL!"

He looked around frantically for his brother as the cave was filled with the echoes of screaming men. Some were screaming in pain, others in terror.

The ID were swarming everywhere, and it was difficult to see. There were clouds of white in the air. The ID had disturbed the cocaine being stored down there.

"Pete...PETE."

"Carl, go into the water!"

Peter waded backwards into the cool spring water as bats flapped their wings in protest at the ruckus below. A few ID followed him, reaching out for him. He felt necrotic fingertips brush the front of his suit, unable to grab hold.

Peter bashed another in the face with his rifle as he saw Carl wade into the water still clutching his MR.UD. When Carl caught up, they were waist deep. The water was frigid due to lack of direct sun exposure.

"What are we going to do, Pete?"

"We go deeper into the cave."

They waded in further. Within minutes, they were treading water as several ID stumbled in after them. Several other soldiers made it into the water.

"Pete, the ceiling is dropping."

The ceiling of the cave was sloping down to meet the water.

"Where are we going?"

Peter looked behind him. The top of his helmet was now scraping the rough ceiling. The water was up to their chins, and the bobbing motion of treading water caused the crisp water to enter their mouths.

The pursuing ID, not knowing how to swim, were at this point under the water. Peter imagined feeling cold, dead hands grabbing at his ankles.

"Carl, we need to dive down."

"But what's down there?"

"It might lead to another cave. Some of these cenotes are connected."

"And what if it doesn't lead anywhere, Pete?"

"Then I guess we'll die. But we'll definitely die if we let them catch up to us."

Carl looked at him wide-eyed and shivering, and not just from the temperature of the water.

This was it. Do or die.

"Just trust me, Carl. Follow me."

Carl nodded.

Peter took a deep breath and held it. He dipped under the surface of the water. Carl dipped down too.

Under the water, Peter shined his shoulder light. There was a small hole about twenty feet away. He began to swim for it. Carl followed.

Peter quickly passed his rifle through first and then squeezed through it, tearing his suit. God he hoped it led to another cave. Otherwise, they were trapped underneath and running out of air fast.

Carl passed his apparatus through and then began to squeeze. He felt some resistance, but it took him a moment to figure out that it was not the size of the hole.

Something had his left ankle.

He began to kick wildly, expending the breath that he was trying so hard to conserve for as long as he could.

Peter saw his brother struggling, but he was running out of breath. His only option was to find air and come back for his brother.

He looked up and only saw ceiling. His heart was beating faster, and that profound wave of panic was beginning to take over.

In the meantime, Carl had wriggled free. He passed Peter and continued down the narrow conduit. Peter followed behind him. Both pushed against the rock with hands and feet.

As their panic mounted and their bodies began to squirm involuntarily due to the panic of oxygen deprivation, they squeezed through as the walls became narrower and narrower.

Carl squeezed through and shot straight up without looking, praying not to hit rock ceiling. He breached the surface above and gasped loudly as his lungs soaked in sweet air.

Peter popped up next to him, gasping, choking, and clawing at Carl.

"P-Pete. We...did...it."

Pete held onto Carl as if his life depended on it. Carl backstroked over to rock, dragging his brother with him. They waited until they caught their breath, and then they pulled themselves and each other up onto the cold, jagged rock.

Peter put his head back on the rock while Carl looked around. "You were right, Pete. It's another cave."

Peter was panting, but he sat up and surveyed their surroundings. A few heads popped up in the water. Some others had made it through.

All in all, there were now eight of them left. The other SWEEPER had made it through with his apparatus too. It was their training. Army did not part easily with their equipment during combat. In total, there was Peter, Carl, Mirabella, Barnes, Munger, Hasbro, Smithe, and Longo.

Peter looked up and saw daylight. It was a way out. But this opening couldn't have been much farther away from the original cenote.

"Sir, what do we do now? The platoon's wiped out." Private Barnes asked.

But before Peter could answer, there was a loud boom that shook the cave.

"What the hell was that?" Carl shouted, his ears ringing.

"That's Lorenzo tying up loose ends," explained Peter. "We've got to get out of here before he figures out that he didn't get all of us."

"How would he know?" asked Private Mirabella, the other SWEEPER.

"Trust me, he's checking right now. We have to scale the sides." He pointed to the far right wall. "The wall is jagged. It should be easy to climb."

The other side was too smooth. There were a few jutting rocks, but none that formed a natural spelunking trail out of the cave.

Peter led the way, grabbing a hand and foothold and hoisting himself up. The others followed one at a time. All Carl could think of again was Victory Tower.

Lorenzo was peeking in the hole and counting silently with one finger. "Nope. I don't think that was all of them."

"Come on, senor," coaxed one of the Navajas, a short but stout man in beige pants and a sweat stained wife beater. "There's no way anyone could've made it out."

Lorenzo was about to give in to his compadre's wheedling when he caught movement in his peripheral vision. He looked over and saw eight men climbing out of an adjacent cenote.

"Well I'll be damned...PETER, I SWEAR YOU MUST HAVE NINE LIVES."

Peter looked over at Lorenzo startled.

"Okay, men. MOVE," he ordered.

They began to take off into the brush. They ran as fast as their weary legs would take them. They heard shouting in Spanish right at their backs and bullets flew over their shoulders as the wind picked up.

Peter looked down at his watch. The storm was coming. They didn't have much time.

"Pete...where are we...going?" Carl panted.

"There's three hotels...around here...I'm aiming for...the closest one. If we can...get shelter before the storm hits...it might buy us some time."

"Time...for what?"

"To formulate...a plan."

"But won't that...be putting civilians...in jeopardy, sir?" Mirabella ventured, running alongside.

"Do you have...another idea? Because I'd love...to hear it."

No one answered him. It was the best plan they had. Maybe the Navajas would not risk exposing themselves. But he wasn't so sure about Lorenzo.

Lorenzo ran behind the Navajas with the stout man.

"They're headed for one of the hotels," the stout man shouted.

Lorenzo picked up his Mini-com Muti-tasker. "Halt your men, Vargas."

Vargas looked at him questioningly.

"Do it."

Vargas whistled loudly and shouted for the men to stop.

"Lockwood, come in."

"Lockwood, here."

"We're coming to meet you. There's been a wrinkle."

"Copy that. Will await your arrival."

Vargas was glaring at Lorenzo. Lorenzo was growing tired of him. "Oh, what are you looking at me like that for?"

"We could have had them, you stupid gringo."

Lorenzo snapped. "In case you haven't noticed, there's a freaking category four hurricane ready to drop right on top of us. We'll never catch up to them in time."

"So what are we going to do?"

"The ID are going on their next mission."

Vargas' eyes grew wide, and he had an expression of disgust on his face. "There are tourists down there."

Lorenzo mocked him. "Why Vargas, it's not your reputation to be so squeamish. You don't want them getting away so they can rat out our whole operation, do you?"

Vargas just glared at him. "I am not squeamish, senor. It just seems very…messy."

"We don't have any other choice. This storm will wipe us off the face of the Yucatan. Besides, it's practice. Just think of it as another field test for the ID. Whatever is left when the ID are done, we'll deal with personally…*after the storm*. Comprende?"

Vargas shoved past him, bumping shoulders very pointedly, in a silent rage.

"Patience, my stupid friend," Lorenzo said to himself. "All good things come to those who wait."

Chapter 13

Peter and what was left of his platoon tore through the wilderness as the storm descended on Xcaret. The wind fought their efforts, slowing them down.

But, as Peter fathomed it, at least they had the Navajas off their backs. All they had to do was find a hotel. He consulted his Mutitasker, which showed the Yucatan Grande Resort to be only a few clicks away.

They were assailed with various indigenous debris—palm fronds, branches, even pebbles—as the winds picked up. If they didn't make it to the hotel, they were history.

They came upon a chain link, perimeter fence on the outer boundary of the resort. They scaled it in quick order, nearly being blown over at the top.

The grounds looked deserted. The winds were tearing apart the thatched roofs, and debris cracked exterior windows and glass sliding doors. The surface of a large, amoeba-shaped in-ground swimming pool was tossing and foaming like the great sea itself in miniature, and lawn chairs were thrown to and fro.

They crossed the grounds slowly, arms locked in a tight huddle, their course zig-zagged as the wind pushed them back and forth.

"They'll be holed up in the convention center," Peter shouted over the now roaring wind. "Look around for it. It should be a large, concrete structure."

They passed along side of an exterior fence adjoining a zoo and wildlife park. There were separate buildings with individual units for guests. They wandered into the center of the resort, in between buildings, which provided some small measure of shelter from the wind.

Carl was waving Peter over. He was standing by a sign. Peter shielded his face with his forearm and made his way over to where Carl was standing.

"Pete, it's a map of the grounds. The convention center is right through the atrium on the left."

Peter smiled at his brother, impressed. "Nice job, Private."

They made their way through the atrium quickly, the very large thatch roof covered an expansive outdoor bar area and was on its way down.

There it was on their left. A large square concrete structure, just as Peter pictured it. The main entrance was blocked by fallen beams and debris.

He gestured for the others to follow him around side. There were two steel doors on the side. Peter tried to open them, but they were locked from the inside. He took the butt of his rifle and began to bang on the door.

They waited as branches and dirt pelted them and the wind tossed them around like rag dolls.

"Maybe they're not in there," shouted Barnes.

"No, they're in there," replied Peter. "They have to be. It's locked from the inside, and where else would they be?"

He banged on the door again. Barnes helped.

Carl scanned the area nervously. He figured the Navajas would have to be crazy to pursue them in this storm. He prayed Peter was right and that they would at least have until the end of the hurricane.

Finally, the doors opened, slowly at first until the wind hijacked them. A terrified hotel staff person in a tacky pink outfit with a green vest gawked at them as if they were from another planet.

They pushed their way in, aided by the wind at their backs, and they helped two hotel staff push the doors back closed. The two men then rammed the bolts home.

Carl looked around and saw a crowded auditorium of scared tourists. He figured they must've looked like something out of a science fiction movie with their black suits and space age guns.

A small man in a green suit and a nametag approached them. He said something in Spanish. When he saw they didn't understand, he immediately switched to English.

"Pardon me, but who are you?"

Peter took the small man aside in confidence. He didn't want to alarm the auditorium full of tourists. A futile gesture.

"I'm Lieutenant Peter Birdsall of the United States Army, and these are my men."

"The United States? What are you doing here?"

"We…were sent down to provide relief."

The man wasn't buying it, so Peter shrugged and did his best to look sheepish. "Apparently we got caught in the storm ourselves, but we're glad we made it. Is there anything you need?"

The diminutive man still looked like he was having difficulty swallowing Peter's story. "You are cooperating with local authorities?"

"Just lending a helping hand."

After a moment, the man decided to answer Peter's question. "We have clean water and snacks for the guests, enough to last us until morning. But the bathrooms are backed up."

"Okay," Peter didn't know what to say, "it looks like you have the situation under control. The plumbing is unfortunate, but it can't be helped at the moment. We'll just stay out of your way and help keep order."

The man nodded uncertainly while nervously eyeing Peter's defunct rifle. "I'll have to announce your presence to the guests, so they don't panic."

Peter looked at the man's nametag. "Absolutely, Jorge. Good move. Smart. You go do that."

The man nodded dutifully and gathered his employees. He then got on the bullhorn and began to relay what had just happened and who their new guests were.

While this was going on, Peter got his men into a huddle. "Alright, I told them we're here for support. There's no reason to tell them that fully armed drug cartel members led by a couple of mercenaries are coming their way. We have the night to formulate a plan and either get them out of harm's way or lead the harm away from them. This obviously isn't a good place to make a stand."

"Do you think they'll come for us and involve all of these tourists?" Carl asked.

"They can't afford to let us live, knowing what we know," Peter explained. "Besides, tourists mean nothing to the Navajas. They are absolutely ruthless."

"And our weapons aren't even functioning," Barnes added.

"Yeah, but we don't want the people in here knowing that, Barnes," Peter said. "It won't inspire confidence. As long as we keep the illusion that nothing's wrong, they should behave and stay out of our way to let us do what we need to do."

Carl flipped on his MR.UD. It flickered, but it turned on. "Hey, my MR.UD is working."

Peter came over to look. "But how?"

"Only flimsier electronics are blown by EMP. Heartier equipment may be unaffected. I guess Farrow knew what he was doing when he made these things."

Peter nodded. "Good design. But these guns aren't worth a shit."

"Private vendor, lowest bidder," Carl reminded.

"Right. So how do we fight off an assault without any weapons?"

"Maybe the authorities will be here in the morning," Carl said. "They can help us."

Peter looked like he had seen a ghost.

"What, Pete? What's wrong?" Carl asked, perplexed by his brother's reaction.

"I think we may have less time than I thought," Peter said gravely.

"What do you mean?"

"You just said it yourself. Lorenzo won't have an opportunity tomorrow morning with the Mexican authorities around…"

Carl finished his brother's thought. "So it's coming tonight. But how? The storm…"

"Carl, they have two more crates of approximately sixty ID at their disposal."

"Oh, right."

"So you mean Lorenzo's going to use the ID against *us*?" Barnes asked incredulously.

"Makes sense, doesn't it?"

Barnes was silent, his mind running through various permutations of grisly demise.

"SWEEPERS," Peter ordered, "Sweep the walls of this convention center. Let me know if you pick anything up on the outside. Just keep going back and forth. Oh, and pretend like you're sweeping the crowd. Keep up the illusion."

Carl and Mirabella strode off to make their sweeps for marauding ID. Peter addressed the other five men. "Okay. We're in a pretty solid structure with no windows. The weakest point would be the inside doors."

"They're not bolted because they're not exterior doors," Barnes added.

"Right," said Peter, "so we need to focus on those doors. There are three sets of doors. If they make it into the building, they'll be banging on those."

"What if we just wait them out?" Private Hasbro asked. "When the authorities get here they can deal with them."

Peter considered the option. "Too complicated. And complicated means messy."

"Messy how?" Hasbro asked.

"Well, the Mexican authorities won't know what the ID are. After several of them are eaten, they'll fight back, but there'd be a learning curve. More would get eaten, some turned. By the time they'd figure out that they need to take head shots, it would be chaos. Not to mention that once they'd breach this structure, they'd be paranoid and trigger happy with hundreds of innocent tourists."

"We need to leave this convention center," concluded Barnes.

"Right," agreed Peter. "We can leave through the interior doors. The manager won't stop us. We can set up some kind of a perimeter…"

"We have no functioning weapons," Longo reminded.

Just then, Jorge, the manager walked over, which Peter found to be perfect timing, "What are they doing, Lieutenant?"

He was pointing to Carl and Mirabella.

"Oh, they're just making a sweep…for safety. By the way, where's your maintenance equipment stored?"

However, Jorge was not easily convinced. "Sweep for what, Lieutenant?"

"Oh, you know…seismic vibrations."

"Seismic…vibrations?"

"Yeah, this is a powerful storm. The…barometric pressure might…disturb some of the fault lines…"

"Fault lines?"

"Yes, fault lines. We are just making sure that the…structural integrity of the building has not been…compromised."

Jorge looked at Peter as if he was speaking Greek, but didn't trust that it was actually Greek. "There is a large maintenance shed behind Building H."

"So where exactly is Building H?"

"You're not going back outside in the storm, Lieutenant."

"Jorge, we need to take inventory of the maintenance equipment for the cleanup tomorrow morning."

"Excuse me, Lieutenant, but isn't that *our* problem?"

Peter felt the vein on his forehead pulse. This manager was making a royal nuisance of himself.

"Jorge, I'm just trying to do my job here. Just cut me some slack. Where's Building H?"

Jorge apparently felt he crossed some kind of line, and he shook his head embarrassed. "Sorry, Lieutenant. Of course. I want to cooperate."

"Building H?"

"Yes, if you leave out those interior doors and make a left, you'll pass through the Business Center and run into our steakhouse. Go through the steakhouse and out the other side. Make another left, and go around the swimming pool. The building on the left is Building H."

"Jesus. You get all that Barnes?"

Barnes nodded.

"Jorge, this is very important. Muy importante."

"Yes, Lieutenant."

"Once we leave, do not open the door for anyone until morning."

"I do not understand."

"You may hear some knocking or banging on the doors or walls. That's just us testing the structure. But do not, for any reason, open the doors again. That's a direct order. Comprende?"

Jorge nodded his head enthusiastically. Maybe he really did want to help. Or maybe he just wanted to be rid of them.

"Good. BIRDSALL, MIRABELLA, ARE WE CLEAR?"

They each gave a thumbs up.

Suddenly everything went dark.

"What was that?" Barnes asked.

"Oh, the authorities have just cut the power. We expected this," Jorge explained.

Peter nodded and humored him. Then, as Jorge went to deliver his update over the bullhorn, Peter gathered his men close.

"That wasn't the authorities. It was *them*. Hell's coming, and we've got to throw a welcome party."

The men nodded. They knew things were about to get hairy, and they knew they had to move.

"Okay guys, lets rock and roll."

***

Peter closed the doors outside of the auditorium. They were in a large hallway. He imagined that when there was power, there must have been dozens of holographic advertisements for their various business services, conferences, etc.

However, for the moment the whole place was eerily quiet.

"Find a map of the grounds, there has to be one around here."

They fanned out with their mini lights.

"Here's a map," shouted Mirabella.

Peter came over and scanned it with his Multi-tasker.

"Good. Now we have a map. I'm sending it to each of you...Building H is too far, and it's too dangerous to go outside. I was hoping to find some machetes, but that's not an option. SWEEPERS, sweep the walls and keep an eye on your monitors."

Carl and Mirebella split up and began their sweep. Peter addressed the rest of the group.

"Okay, according to the map, there's a gym right down that hall." He pointed at the short hallway opposite the Convention Center doors. "Maybe there are some things we can use."

"Like what, Lieutenant?" Barnes asked.

"I dunno. Maybe we can use the free weights as weapons, to crush their skulls. We have our batons, but we can use whatever we can get our hands on. Remember, headshots are the name of the game…"

Just then, they all heard the sounds of breaking glass. It came from the steakhouse. The SWEEPERS stopped their sweep and looked at Peter for direction.

Great, he thought to himself, *and we don't have any viable weapons yet.*

"It came from the steakhouse."

The men didn't know what to do. Their guns were useless. Peter watched as two men came running in, each carrying something.

"Hold it, they're not ID."

They were obviously human; maybe some stranded tourists or even a couple of locals. Then Peter saw the AK-47's.

He raised his weapon and trained it on them. They were arguing in some other language, but when they saw Peter, they raised their rifles. Peter's men aimed their defunct weaponry at the two visitors.

The two men were yelling at Peter. Peter took his left hand off his rifle and held his hand out, palm facing them, a gesture for them to calm down.

"Is-is that…" Barnes started.

"Yes," Peter said in horror. These were terrorists, Order for International Liberation that were still lingering.

They continued to yell at him and point their weapons. Peter and his men kept bluffing with theirs. Peter kept telling them to calm down.

Thankfully, no one had fired a shot, as it would only have been from the terrorists. Apparently Peter's bluff was working.

"Don't lower your weapons," he instructed to his men.

This was quite the delicate stalemate, and undoubtedly a diversion that they didn't need at the moment. Soon the ID would be upon them, and they needed to find something to fight with and a place to make their stand.

Carl stepped forward, holding his MR.UD down at his side and his other hand out, showing that it was empty. One of the men pointed his AK at him and yelled. The other kept his gun on Peter.

"Carl, what the hell are you doing?"

However, before Peter could say or do anything else, Carl held his arms out stiffly in front of him and began to walk funny, groaning and snapping his jaws.

The two men apparently forgot about Peter and the others for a moment and just gawked at this funny man walking like a mummy.

Carl stopped and said loudly, "Zom-bies. Zom-bies. Yes?"

One of the men said something in his language, and both began to nod emphatically. It seemed that they understood his pantomiming.

Carl then gestured with his free hand in a sweeping motion ending in his pointing at the ground. "They're coming...HERE. They will be here."

Then he pointed his MR.UD at the windows as if it was a rifle and mimicked shooting at the windows.

"Jesus Christ, Carl," Peter said, but he watched the two men closely. Maybe they understood.

"We have to fight to-ge-ther," Carl said. "To-ge-ther." He made a wide gesture encompassing everyone ending with his one hand shaking the other in pantomimed agreement.

The two men looked at each other and nodded, but they continued to train their AK's on Peter.

"I don't think it's working," Peter murmured to Carl out of the corner of his mouth.

Then the best thing that could've happened did. There were more sounds of broken glass, and several ID came stomping through the steakhouse and in their direction.

"Shit, they're already here," said Longo.

Chapter 14

"Fall back!" Peter ordered.

Their two guests had other ideas. They began to open fire at the approaching ID. The ID stumbled and staggered through the gunfire, but only one that had been hit in the head (probably accidentally) was stopped permanently.

Carl ran up to one of the men and tapped him on the shoulder. The man looked over at Carl angrily as he continued to fire into the closing ID.

Carl made a gun with his thumb and index finger and pantomimed shooting himself in the head. The man shot him a look that could only be construed as pure bile, and then he aimed his rifle higher.

He took out two of the closest ID with headshots, but both men's bursts were too erratic and uncontrolled. They'd be out of bullets before disposing of the ID.

"Carl!" Peter yelled. Carl turned back to look at Peter. Peter made a swirling motion with his finger and then gestured with all five fingers on a straightened hand to move into the gym.

Peter retreated into the hallway, and his men followed. During the brief pauses between gunfire, Peter heard the tourists on the other side of the convention doors yelling out.

Jorge, don't open those doors, whatever you do. He tried to open the glass doors to the gym, but they were locked. He smashed the glass with the butt of his rifle and breached the entrance.

All of the men filed into the gym. They began to look around for anything they could use.

Behind them, they heard one of the terrorists screaming and banging on the convention doors. It appeared the ID were doing their thing, and quite effectively from the sounds of it.

"Quick, grab some free weights," Peter ordered. He went and grabbed a straight bar lying on the floor without weights on it. He wielded it to get a feel for it, like a kid taking a practice swing on deck at a little league game. It was longer and heavier than the baton he carried.

Carl put down his MR.UD and was looking around. "Where're we making our stand, Lieutenant?"

Peter looked around the gym. There were two sets of stairs separated by a landing leading to the machines upstairs.

"We go up. We can barricade the top with the machines. As they make it up and over one or a couple at a time, we smash their skulls in."

"Wait," Carl pointed over to the benches. "Let's load up the bars with the weights on them and take them up. We can drop them from the top and take a bunch of them down at once."

"Good idea, Carl. Barnes, Longo, and Munger, help Carl. Mirabella, Hasbro, and Smithe, bring as many free weights as you can up the stairs."

The hallway was eerily quiet. The ID were feeding.

"Let's move it, men. We only have until when the ID have finished their snack."

Carl and Barnes loaded up one bar with heavy weights and each took a side. They walked quickly but carefully towards the stairs, grunting under the weight of their load. Longo and Munger loaded up their bar and were right behind them.

They started up the stairs and were nearly startled into dropping their loads as the back glass door cracked from the impact of a rather large ID. Outside they were being blown all over the place. But the large, glass windows of the modern gym might as well have been a supermarket window, and the ID were getting a good glimpse of the food running around inside.

They all saw Peter and his men, and they were all converging on the gym in their relentless way, persevering in the 175 mile per hour wind.

"Hurry up! We gotta move!" Pete yelled in encouragement. Carl, Barnes, Longo, and Munger just reached the top when the ID started barging into the gym on the other side from the hallway.

"The machines, move 'em!"

They took treadmills, elliptical machines, anything they could find, and they piled them in a heap at the top of the stairs, wedging them into the rails at the sides.

A few ID burst through the glass doors at the bottom of the stairs and began to make their clumsy ascent. But they were only functioning as they were supposed to. Peter knew this. And having been trained in using them, he had some idea about how to deal with them on the receiving end.

His men moved with a purpose, and so far, no one lost their cool. But the true test of their fortitude was about to begin. It wasn't just the ID's appearance that unnerved their prey. It was their slow, steady pursuit. They took just about whatever was thrown at them, and then they kept coming.

But Peter and his men knew how to slow them down, separate them, and dispatch them.

"Bring the first barbell."

Carl and Barnes lifted it slowly and put it down on the inside of their barricade. The ID made their way up slowly, wheezing and growling, their glassy eyes fixed on their imminent meal and jaws snapping in anticipation.

"Steady. Steady."

The group from outside rounded the landing and were beginning their ascent of the second staircase, and the group from the hallway crossed the floor with the blood and intestinal juices of the two terrorists smeared across their faces.

The group climbing the stairs was almost all the way up and was reaching for the barricade.

"Okay, NOW."

Carl and Barnes picked up each end of the barbell and hoisted it up above their heads. They leaned up against their side of the barricade.

"On three," Carl grunted. Barnes nodded. "One, two, THREE."

They tossed the barbell down on top of the approaching hoard, catching several of them and pulling them down to the landing.

There was the crunching of bones. A couple were silenced permanently, their heads crushed under the weight. The others kept coming, grabbing onto the overturned equipment.

Those maimed on the landing below were beginning to recover and pulled broken carcasses up the stairs with whatever limbs and appendages they had left.

At least they thinned the herd, and that was the exact effect Peter was looking for. A couple of ID were climbing over the barricade.

Peter brought down his straight bar on the head of the first. He finished the job with a second blow. The one behind it almost made it all the way over, but Longo brought a free weight down on the back of its head, caving in its skull. As it reached out for him he struck again, and then one last time. Blood and grey matter splattered everywhere.

"Don't get any on you," Peter warned.

Peter saw they had mere moments before the next wave began climbing the stairs. He handed Barnes his straight bar, and climbed over the barricade. Barnes reached over and handed the bar back to him.

He flew down the stairs, taking two at a time, and began whacking the heads of those ID dragging themselves up.

Carl saw that the next wave was making their way up and closing in on his brother. He climbed the barricade. "I'll be just a moment."

He extended his baton and descended the stairs, bringing it down on the skulls of crawling ID alongside his brother.

"Carl, what are you doing?"

"Helping my brother. Look."

Peter looked up in time to see more ID reaching the landing.

"Let's go," he said as he smashed one lying on its back in the face.

Carl brought his baton down on one that grabbed his ankle, and then struck two more times. Peter grabbed him and they both turned around as undead fingertips clawed at their black suits. All of their suits were torn from their fall into the cenote, and the ID tracked their cuts and sweat.

They climbed the stairs as fast as they could, the ID right on their heels, and began to climb the barricade. They were half-way over when the second wave reached the top.

Barnes and Munger reached out and, grabbing their hands, pulled Peter and Carl back over. Longo and Hasbro had the second barbell hoisted in the air.

"NOW," Peter yelled as he hit the ground on the safe side.

Longo and Hasbro tossed the next barbell over, sending several ID crashing down to the landing below. But this time there was more of them, and they were climbing over the barricade.

They fought some of them off, scoring deadly blows to heads with batons and free weights, but some made it over. Now the men were retreating.

A female ID had climbed on top of Mirabella, opening her mouth wide, flipping the top of her head like a candy dispenser. As she lunged for his face, he pulled out his rather large knife and placed it over his face pointing out.

She fell on the knife, pushing into it as if she was trying to swallow it whole, and the tip came out the back of her head. Viscous black liquid dribbled down the blade and onto his gloved hand and wrist.

He rolled her then motionless carcass over and pulled his knife out of her mouth. Carl pulled him away from the other ID stumbling off the barricade and dragged him back with the other soldiers.

Another young woman in her twenties was crawling over the top of the heap of exercise machines. She got her footing rather quickly and looked at Mirabella with imploring glassy eyes whitewashed with death, an uncanny smile on her face.

He found himself swimming in her lifeless pools gazing into him, unaware of Carl shouting for him to get up. He was tired, so tired, and she at that moment did not look so abhorrent.

He was jarred from his exhausted reverie as she sunk teeth into his upper thigh.

"NO!" Carl yelled as the company drew back. More ID began to climb the barricade and reach the other side. Some piled on Mirabella, ending him.

"Don't look at their eyes!" Peter shouted.

They had never been on the receiving end of the ID, other than the orientation in the Labyrinth, so this was their first uncontrolled experience with the psychological component of being hunted.

There was the visceral revulsion of encountering an undead drone; the phobias of disease, germs, and being eaten alive, but these drones were once human and still retained many human traits and expressions. It induced a kind of Stockholm Syndrome, where you were so tired of being pursued that you just as well joined them.

However, the ID did no recruiting, and they took no prisoners. When they finished with you, there was nothing left to reanimate. Reanimation only occurred when they were interrupted from completing their ghastly purpose.

Peter looked around frantically. There was a workout room behind them, glass walled and mirrored on the inside, likely a room for classes.

"Into that room," Peter ordered.

The men fell back, striking blows with whatever they had. Hasbro had misjudged a strike with a hefty free weight, placing his fist directly into a middle-aged Asian man's mouth. The ID chomped down on his hand as two others reached around and pulled him in, seizing his forearms in their jaws.

Longo lost it and ran to the railing. Before Peter could shout any protest, he flung himself off the second floor in a final act of desperation.

He hit the ground, legs first, shattering his knee joints. As he laid there wailing in pain, two teenage boys began to shuffle their way over to him. He pulled out his baton, but he couldn't see straight from the pain. The boys closed in on him, their faces wild with cannibalism.

Peter heard Longo's shrieks as he entered the mirrored room. Barnes, Carl, Munger, and Smithe filed in and Peter closed the glass door, locking it from the inside.

There were now only five of them left, and Peter could not believe how his platoon was being victimized rather effectively by their own training.

The psychological effects were gradually setting in, the effect amplified by the mirrored walls. As the ID pressed themselves up against the glass, the reflections in the mirrors made it appear as if they were surrounded on all four sides.

Their banging on the glass, the hisses, and the moans prevented Peter from thinking straight. His men looked to him for guidance, for the glass would not hold the ID back much longer.

Carl saw his brother's vexation, so he snatched Peter's metal bar from his hands and smashed the mirror behind them. Then he did the same with the mirror on the wall to the left, and then on the wall to the right.

The act of Carl shattering the glass and the relief from the hideous reflections allowed Peter to come to his senses again.

"We gotta get out of here, Lieutenant," Barnes pleaded, his face pale with terror.

If Peter didn't come up with something quick, his men would descend into madness and let the ID take them.

Carl scanned the room. Suddenly, he was reminded of his experience with the Labyrinth.

"Pete, look up there," he pointed to a rather large air conditioning vent.

Peter traced the likely path of the duct with his eyes, and saw that it stretched over the gym and out. "Barnes, give Carl a lift up to that vent."

Barnes nodded and gave Carl a boost up. Carl pulled off the screen and tossed it aside. He stuck his head inside the vent, looked around, and then he pulled it back out.

"We can fit," he shouted down, "but we should only go one at a time and space ourselves apart. The ventilation shaft won't hold the weight of too many of us."

"Carl, you first."

Carl nodded, and he climbed in. The shaft was wide enough for him to squeeze in with some room to spare. With the power off, it was hot and stuffy. But Carl's special suit helped, as it was designed to, and he began to commando crawl through.

"Smithe, you're next," Peter directed.

Barnes gave Smithe a boost, and Smithe peered into the shaft. He saw Carl crawling away. "He's outside, Lieutenant."

Peter looked outside into the gymnasium and above the heads of more than a dozen frenzying ID. He noticed a bulge in the ventilation moving slowly over the gym.

"Good boy, Carl," he said to himself. Then he nodded to Smithe. Smithe hoisted himself up and into the vent and began his commando crawl across.

The ID were pounding on the glass. Silent spider webs were beginning to form, the cracking of the glass drowned out by the growling of hungry undead and the dull roar of the hurricane outside.

"Munger, now you."

Carl barely heard the noises of the ID over his own echoed clamoring through the airshaft. The dust was tickling his nose, and he did his best to stifle a sneeze. But he heard several sneezes from someone a ways behind him. He wondered if the ID detected men climbing through the airshafts overhead.

Eventually he took a sharp right turn and a bit of a dip as he figured he likely cleared the gym and was somewhere in the hallway in front of the convention center.

He came to a fork, where a shaft went ninety degrees to the left. He figured that was the direction of those hundreds of terrified tourists, so he pushed on forward. He hoped he guessed correctly, as the space was too small to allow him to consult his Mini-com Multi-tasker, which was at the moment strapped to his leg.

Peter and Barnes were the only ones left. The ID had breached the glass, jutting arms and heads through the jagged holes, snapping their jaws while shredding themselves on the shards. However, they didn't register pain and apparently hadn't noticed the damage they were inflicting on themselves.

All they noticed was that their prey was thinning in numbers, an apparent realization that seemed to cause them to double their efforts.

"You next, Lieutenant," Barnes said.

"No, you first," Peter insisted.

Barnes wanted to argue, but the truth of the matter was that he was scared out of his mind and was relieved at Peter's insistence that he go first. Who was he to question a commanding officer?

Peter laced his fingers together, palms up, and gave the massive Barnes a boost up. Barnes peeked into the shaft. He didn't see anyone. He looked down at Peter.

"What about you?"

"I'm right behind you."

"But how are you…"

"I'm right behind you," Peter said, voice steady, tone insistent. "Get going. I have to wait until you get far enough away."

Barnes nodded his understanding rather emphatically and pulled himself into the shaft.

Peter knew he wasn't going to make it.

The ID were beginning to topple the glass wall entirely and push through the door. For once, he figured he wouldn't be the last one left. He saw that Carl made it up and out, and his little brother would have to work with the other men to survive the rest of the way.

Since Tijuana, Peter was resolved that he was going to die in action. It was the only decent way to go. To rejoin his old squad. To be with his friend, Apone. To silence his guilt.

Although he was tempted to take his own life on a few occasions, he knew fate would provide the proper venue for his ticket out of this world if he only waited.

No more nightmares. No more blame. Just peace.

Several ID made it fully into the room and began to close in on Peter. But just because he counted on dying, didn't mean that he had to go quietly. Oh, he planned to fight to the bitter end, exacting what hateful vengeance he had left on the drones right in front of him.

He picked up his metal bar and pounded it into the floor in front of him. "All right, you dead heads. Let's dance."

The few closest to him were more than happy to oblige, and he began swinging like Babe Ruth with a curious smile on his face.

Carl saw a grate in the floor of the shaft. He crawled his way over to it and peeked down.

The room below was dark and apparently empty. He saw the top feeders of what must have been copy machines. A long countertop wrapped around an area with printers and fax machines. It looked like the inside of the Business Center.

Carl decided to push the grate down. It fell and clanged on the countertop below. He waited for any kind of movement. After a few minutes of silence, he flicked on his shoulder light. Satisfied that the room was empty, he decided he would drop inside.

He lowered the upper half of his body down through the open grate and hung upside down bent at the waist. As the blood rushed to his head, he took stock of his surroundings.

He grabbed the edge of the opening and flipped slowly, controlling his movements, as he slid his lower body out and assumed a chin-up position.

His fingers gave way under the weight and the clumsy angle, and he fell, landing on the counter on his butt. It wasn't the most graceful of entrances, but it had to do.

He slid behind the counter for cover as he scanned the room for anything he could use. One-by-one the others would be coming and they'd regroup. Pete would have some kind of plan.

He heard shuffling from somewhere behind him, and he reeled around to see an ID stumbling around behind a large plastic ornamental tree.

Carl switched off his shoulder light, ducked behind the counter, and held his breath as he listened. He didn't think the ID saw him, but he couldn't be sure. He mustered up the courage to venture a look.

He slowly peeked above the countertop, and the ID had apparently won its wrestling match with the plastic tree. Free, it was wandering in Carl's direction. The ID was sniffling and wheezing, and Carl wondered if it had picked up on his scent.

Fortunately, Carl was enclosed in the work area by the counter. But as he traced the perimeter with his eyes, he saw an opening in the counter. If this ID made it around the counter, it would most likely find it, and in turn Carl.

Carl scanned the countertop. There were staplers, two computers, and a paper cutter…the paper cutter. He crawled over as silently as he could to the paper cutter. The wheezing seemed to follow him around.

He reached up and began to unscrew the hinge from which the large blade and wooden handle jutted out. It was one of those industrial strength paper cutters that could chop through a good batch of paper if the proper amount of force was applied.

As he loosened the screw it squeaked softly, and the ID seemed to grunt in response. Carl stopped, straining his ears. After a few heartbeats, the ID resumed its shuffling.

Carl removed the screw and reached up with both hands, cradling the large blade. He gently slid the blade off, making a small noise as metal scraped on metal at the joint.

The shuffling and gurgling was now past him and moving in the direction of the opening in the countertop. Carl crawled over towards the opening, dragging the large blade silently on the carpet beside him.

He got to his feet, but in a hunched position, and grabbed the blade's handle in his right hand. He waited, as the shuffling grew nearer. He prepared himself. His strike would have to be quick and accurate. He probably had only one shot to cleave this bastard's head open before it grabbed him.

The ID padded in front of the opening, and it looked like it was going to keep on going by. But it suddenly stopped, sniffing the air and wheezing like a set of old bagpipes.

Carl braced himself, hoping it would continue past. He would then run up behind the ID and strike his blow.

However, the ID looked in the gap and then down at Carl with those white eyes. The man looked like he must have been young, sturdy, and even handsome in his heyday.

Carl stood up and brought the blade back behind his head with both hands as the ID growled at him like a bobcat. Before it could reach out for him, Carl brought the blade down on its head.

But something went wrong. The ID staggered backward, losing its balance for a moment, but other than that, appeared undamaged.

Carl looked in his hands and saw that in his nervous haste, he brought down the dull end on the fiend's head. Cursing his carelessness, Carl spun the blade handle and leapt forward bringing the sharp end down on its skull.

The ID fell to the floor in a prone position, flailing about but still quite undead. Carl lined the blade up, drew it back over his head, and brought it down on the back of its neck. The blade sliced through half of its neck, and it flopped around on the floor at Carl's feet like a

flounder on the deck of a boat. Carl put his foot on its head to keep it still, and he brought the blade down two more times, severing the head from its body.

It lay there still as Carl caught his breath. He wheeled around as he heard a crash behind him, raising the blade above his head again.

Smithe stood up and rubbed his head sheepishly.

"Jesus, Smithe. What took you so long?"

Smithe looked down at the decapitated ID at Carl's feet. "Kick ass, Birdsall."

"Did Pete make it out?"

"I don't know. Someone's not too far behind me, but I'm not sure who." Smithe looked around. "So this is the Business Center. Nice. I have to have my next business conference here."

"The ID in the gym are going to figure out that their meal vamoosed, and they'll be searching for us. We don't have much time," Carl said with urgency.

"There's nowhere for us to go," Smithe said, "We can't go outside. It's too dangerous."

"How many you figure we got in the gym?"

Smithe looked like he was doing quick calculations in his head. "Several, I'd say. Maybe a dozen."

"Shit, there's more than several coming for us. We can't keep running around the Business Wing killing a few at a time. We need to find a way to take them out in bunches."

Munger poked his head through the vent. "Hey, guys."

He lowered himself down a little more gracefully than Smithe. He hit the countertop on his side and then swung himself over to the outside of the work area. He looked down at the decapitated ID.

"Christ."

"Birdsall's handiwork," Smithe announced proudly.

"Nice job, Birdsall," said Munger, obviously impressed. "Any others?"

"Yeah, but we saved 'em for you, Munger," Smithe said sarcastically.

"Screw you, Smithe."

"Good one. I think the ID have wittier comebacks," Smithe taunted.

Carl was walking around the Business Center while the other two were exchanging sophomoric insults. He peeked out the glass doors. The room in front of the convention center was empty…for the moment.

He reached out and tugged on the door handle. It opened a little. Carl closed it and looked down. There was a small bolt. He pushed it down with his foot, driving it home and locking the doors.

There was another crash behind them.

"GODDAMMIT."

It was Barnes. The mountain of a man had come crashing down behind the countertop. Smithe and Munger rushed around to the opening in the countertop.

Carl ran over. He heard Barnes gasping in pain. "You all right?"

Barnes tried to get up, but he winced in pain and fell back down. "I think my leg's broke."

"Great," Munger said, "now we have to drag his huge ass around while we run from the ID."

Munger was right. Barnes was a large man, an asset in hand-to-hand combat with the ID. However, with a broken leg, he became their biggest liability.

"Did Pete make it into the shaft?" Carl asked, hopeful.

Munger and Smithe helped Barnes up, who was balancing on his good leg. "I don't know. I told him to go first, but he insisted I go."

That was Peter. The hero. Everyone's big brother. Carl began to pace back and forth. Barnes sensed his anxiety.

"Your brother's a tough bastard, kid. I'm sure he made it." But Barnes' sentiment offered Carl no comfort.

"Birdsall was just saying that picking the ID off one-by-one won't work. We need to find a way to kill lots of them at once," Smithe said.

"He's right," said Barnes, "There's too many of them for this cat-and-mouse bullshit."

"What are we going to do? Kill them with paper clips and staples?" Munger remarked.

Carl was lost in his own thoughts.

"What are you thinking, kid?" Barnes asked.

"The steakhouse."

"What about the steakhouse?"

"Check it out. Birdsall's hungry," joked Smithe.

"There are steaks. Lots of meat."

"Yeah, so? What do you have in mind?" Barnes asked.

"We can put it all out in one pile. It would attract the ID. They'd smell it."

"But that would just buy us some time," said Munger.

"No, it would get them in one place," Barnes corrected. "But then what?"

"We blow the steakhouse," Carl said gravely.

"How," Munger began.

"The gas still works," Barnes said. "The power's out, but I bet the gas still works."

"But wouldn't the government have turned off the gas with the power?" Smithe reminded.

"The Lieutenant said it wasn't the government that cut the power, remember? It was Lorenzo." Barnes said.

Peter. Carl was wondering what was taking him so long. He continued explaining his plan.

"The government would only cut the gas in the event of an earthquake. We fill the restaurant with gas, get as many of those ID in there as we can, and we blow it up."

"But the fire," Barnes said, "we wouldn't be able to control the fire. We have a convention center filled with hundreds of tourists down the hall."

"We grab as many fire extinguishers as we can, and we wait outside. We spray any fire that tries to make it down the hall."

"I don't know, kid. It's awful chancy. Things can get messy."

"Barnes, if we don't do something, those tourists are as good as dead anyway, and you know it."

Barnes looked down at his feet, weighing the options. Smithe and Munger were Indians, not Chiefs. Barnes was the oldest, and the closest thing to a leader without Peter. They looked at Barnes for his approval.

"Okay. Let's go."

"But what about Pete? We have to wait for him," Carl interrupted.

Barnes, Smithe, and Munger all exchanged nervous glances.

"I don't think he's coming, kid."

Carl did not believe what he was hearing. "What are you talking about? He'll be here any minute."

"He would've been here by now," Smithe said, the humor in his voice replaced with sympathy. "It didn't take us that long to get here."

Dammit. Carl didn't want to believe it, but he knew they were probably right. But there was no time for panic or grief.

"Okay, let's go."

"Help me up," Barnes said. Smithe and Munger each put an arm around their shoulders and hoisted him up.

Carl ran behind the counter, looking for something.

"What are you doing?" Smithe asked.

Carl grabbed a marker and a piece of paper.

"He's leaving the Lieutenant a note," Barnes explained. Smithe shook his head but said nothing.

After Carl scribbled on the paper, he taped it to the countertop just below the airshaft.

"Okay, let's go," he said.

They made their way to the steakhouse without incident. The ID from the gym had apparently not made it back around yet. Night had fallen, and everything was dark. They walked by the illumination of their shoulder lights.

As they entered through the broken glass doors, they heard the wind roaring through the broken doors to the outside on the far end of the restaurant.

"Crap," Carl said, "that's going to make it difficult for gas to build up in here."

"We're going to have to do the best we can," Barnes said. "The kitchen."

They entered the kitchen, and Carl opened up a large stainless steel refrigerator. "There's a ton of meat in here. And there are three other fridges. Plenty of bait. Help me haul it out there."

Smithe and Munger leaned Barnes up against a stainless steel counter and joined Carl by the refrigerator. They began to load themselves up with meat. They hauled the meat out into the middle of the restaurant and began to make a pile in the middle of the floor.

After dropping a load, Carl stood there surveying the room. "Keep going, guys. I have an idea."

Smithe shrugged at Munger, and they went back into the kitchen to load up with more meat.

Carl began to move tables. He dragged them around the pile and tipped them over, forming a perimeter but leaving a wide opening facing the doors to the hallway.

Smithe and Munger came back out loaded up with beef. They dropped their loads onto the growing pile.

"That's not going to keep them in," said Munger in reference to the semi-circle of tables turned sideways.

"They're not a barrier. They're more like blinders," Carl explained.

"Guys, come in here," they heard Barnes call from the kitchen. They came running in and found him by the stove.

"What's up?" Carl asked.

Barnes turned the knob on the stove. There was no hiss of escaping gas. "No gas, boys."

"Shit!" said Smithe.

"The government must've cut power and gas anyway," Barnes said.

"Well, there goes that plan," said Munger. "What are we going to do now? We have a pile of bait out there but no trap."

Carl started looking around the kitchen.

"What are you looking for now?" demanded Smithe with more than a little impatience in his tone.

"A-ha," said Carl, "here it is."

He reached up, grabbed a red lever on a pipe, and pulled it. "The master switch. They must've pulled it before closing the restaurant."

He pointed to Barnes, who turned the knob on the stove again. He heard the faint hiss of the gas.

"We're in business, kid. Nice work."

"What about the ignition?" Munger asked.

Carl went back out to the dining room and grabbed a few candles off the tables. He put them on a table next to the circle with the pile of meat. "Somebody find me some matches."

Munger ran back into the kitchen. Barnes was already holding a book of matches. He grabbed the matches from Barnes and ran back out, but he almost tripped over himself.

He didn't see Carl or Smithe anywhere, but there were three ID already hobbling in. He covered his shoulder light with his right hand and backed behind a tiled pillar, praying they didn't see him.

When he peeked around the pillar, he saw that they were heading straight for the pile of meat. He looked around, and he saw Carl peeking over the top of one of the tables, his body concealed by the tablecloth.

Carl silently pointed to the next table, and Munger saw Smithe peeking over that table. They were both only a row over from the table with the candles.

Munger knew he had to get the matches over to Carl somehow so he could light the candles. Then, somehow, they had to leave undetected before the gas filled the dining room and reached the lit candles.

Munger held up the matches. Carl nodded and motioned for him to get the matches over there. The three ID descended on the meat and, crouching like cavemen, began to rip at the beef with their teeth.

Munger considered crawling on his belly around the outside of the enclosed portion of the circle where the three ID fed. But it was a long way across, and if they caught him in such a compromising position unarmed, he was toast.

He grabbed a cloth napkin off a nearby table and an empty glass. He put the book of matches in the glass and wrapped it in the napkin. He figured the glass would provide the weight for it to be thrown far, and the cloth napkin would muffle the sound of its landing…in theory.

But he didn't have anything to keep the napkin around the glass. If he threw it as it was, the napkin would fall off and the glass would shatter on the hard tiled floor.

He grabbed the edge of a tablecloth and cut a long ribbon with his knife. He then cut a second one. He put his knife back in its sheath and began to tie the napkin around the glass by crisscrossing the ribbons like a Christmas present.

Just then, two more ID staggered into the steakhouse sniffing the air and grunting. They too saw the meat just lying there like it fell from the heavens, and so they too walked over to the pile.

Munger waited until they descended upon the meat pile, and then he showed Carl the glass. Carl gave a thumbs up.

Munger used to play baseball in high school, so he knew how to throw. He gauged the distance between him and Carl and how hard he would have to throw.

Then he wound up and tossed the napkin-wrapped glass overhanded in a nice arc over the feeding ID. It landed on a table near Carl and rolled off and onto the floor. There was a muffled thud, and one ID looked up like a meerkat, but he quickly returned to his feast.

Munger breathed a sigh of relief and crept low behind the tables back to the kitchen.

"What's going on out there?" Barnes asked, sensing something was amiss.

"We already have a few guests. I tossed the matches over to Birdsall. We gotta get out of here."

"Here." Barnes handed him a rather large chef's meat cleaver.

Munger took it. Barnes grabbed one for him and put his arm around Munger. They nodded to each other and began their three-legged walk to the kitchen door. Thankfully, it had one of those diamond-shaped windows. They peered into the dining room.

Several more ID were entering the restaurant. By the table with the candles, they saw Carl crouching.

"Wait, kid. Let them pass," Barnes said to himself.

Carl, as if he heard Barnes, waited patiently behind the table as the new guests shuffled on past to join the others.

"Good," Barnes muttered with relief. If the kid got himself in a jam, he was in no condition to help.

Carl must've struck a match behind the table, because when he raised his hand the match he was holding was already lit. It glowed eerily in the dark dining room.

He quickly lit the wicks of the candles and blew out the match. But a few of the ID had taken notice of the light.

They straightened up and looked in the direction of the light, sniffing the air like decrepit bloodhounds. Munger saw Carl and Smithe moving in the shadows around the periphery of the room as a couple of the alerted ID stood and walked over to the candles.

Shit, Munger thought. If they messed with the candles, the plan wouldn't work. So he left Barnes and stepped into the dining room, took his shoulder light off his suit, and tossed it towards the doors to the outside. He then grabbed a glass off a table and lobbed it in the same direction.

When the glass shattered on the tile by the detached shoulder light, the two ID and a couple of others took notice and began to move in the direction of the light and sound, ignoring the candles for the moment.

At this point, the smell of gas was growing more palpable, and it was time for them to make their exit. Carl and Smithe were on their own. Munger propped the kitchen door open with a chair to allow the gas into the dining room. Then, he helped Barnes walk in the dark as they too kept to the periphery.

Munger nearly jumped out of his skin as someone grabbed him by the arm in the darkness.

"Munger."

It was Carl.

"We have to exit the other way," he whispered. "There's more ID in the hallway. They're going to be piling in here in a moment."

"But I just threw my shoulder light and a glass in the other direction to get them away from the candles," Munger whispered back.

"There's only a few. We'll have to take 'em out," said Barnes.

"With what?" Carl asked.

"With these." Barnes held up his meat cleaver. Carl uncovered his shoulder light with his right hand enough to see it glinting in the light. Then he covered it up again.

"Okay. That'll have to work."

"But the hurricane. Is it safe?" Smithe asked concerned.

"It's safer than in here. There'll be dozens of ID, and this place is going to blow. I'll take my chances with the hurricane," explained Carl.

"But what about the fire extinguishers and controlling the fire?"

"No time. We have to move and hope for the best."

So they crept back the other way. Carl and Smithe walked in front with their hands titrating out trace amounts of illumination from their shoulder lights. They each held a meat cleaver. Munger and Barnes trailed behind.

Carl remembered his combat training. He flanked an ID groping for them in the dark and struck it in the head with his baton. It dropped to the floor.

Smithe took care of another one, and the third was wandering back toward the meat pile. They regrouped and made their way to the broken doors to the exterior. The winds were howling and debris flew by.

"Okay," Carl said, "if I remember the map correctly, there should be a swimming pool and two buildings across from here. We make it across as quickly as possible, and we get to one of the buildings."

They all nodded. The room was beginning to reek of gas. They heard more shuffling and grunting as more ID entered the steakhouse, and the sounds of ravenous chewing and slurping was enough to turn the strongest stomach.

It was time to go.

Chapter 15

Carl, Smithe, Munger, and Barnes burst out into the storm and they were immediately assailed with debris. Carl and Smithe ran ahead, being tossed to and fro like rag dolls in the wind. As they jumped from spot to spot in the powerful gusts, they looked like astronauts walking on the surface of the moon.

Munger walked with Barnes, the weight of the massive man helping to steady their course, but the winds had their way with them as well. It was dark, there was very little visibility, and before he knew it, Munger was being pulled down by Barnes. He suddenly felt cold and wet, and he was choking on water.

They had been blown into the swimming pool, and apparently into the deep end. Barnes was flailing his arms and grabbing onto Munger so tight that Munger wasn't able to get his head above water.

Munger pulled and pulled, and finally wrenched himself free. He gasped as he breached the surface, and he reached down, grabbed Barnes around his tree trunk of a neck and pulled his head above water.

Barnes choked as he struggled to keep his head above water. Munger paddled over to the shallow end dragging Barnes with him. He pulled them both against the wall of the pool, and they waited there catching their breath for God knows what.

As Carl neared the building on the right, he was blown right into it. Before he knew it, he was thrown onto a ground floor balcony on his back, his boot breaking the glass sliding door as he landed.

Smithe was blown somewhere off course and out of sight. Carl got up, kicked the glass out of the frame, and stumbled into the hotel room landing face first onto a queen size bed.

Palm leaves and dirt were blowing into the room as Carl hoisted himself off the bed and walked into the bathroom. He stepped into the shower stall and sat down hard on the wooden bench. He tried to clear his head as the wind roared and detritus blew into the room.

He wondered if the others had made it to safety when he heard a loud explosion that shook the entire bathroom. It was the steakhouse. It actually blew. Carl only hoped that the explosion took out more than a few of the marauding ID.

The water in the pool thrashed about in the storm when Munger heard the boom. The whole pool shook with the force of the blast. Carl's plan worked.

He thought he heard Barnes say something, but his ears were ringing from the explosion, and the dull roar of the storm blocked everything else out.

A great ball of flame rose into the air followed by a vast cloud of black smoke. Underneath, the restaurant was on fire, but it did not seem to be spreading to the rest of the Business Center. Little movement was in the wreckage, and what little there was ceased within minutes.

Munger saw movement outside the building, however. Stranded ID were being blown about in the wind outside. He pulled Barnes closer to him and waited, shivering in the pool. He didn't want to move and be caught by any ID that would be blown into them.

Carl sat in the shower stall contemplating his next move when he heard footsteps in the hall outside his room. Carl strained his ears, and he thought they were growing closer.

He got up, knife in hand, and stepped into the room in front of the door. He put his eye to the peephole and saw a shadowy figure walking slowly down the hall.

He braced himself, raising the large knife above his head and putting his hand on the doorknob. The footsteps slowed by his room, and the figure stopped in front of the door. It was waiting, listening.

Suddenly the doorknob began to move. Carl tightened his grip on it and yanked the door open as the dark figure fell through the doorway and landed on the floor in front of him.

Carl began to bring his knife down.

"WAIT."

But it was too late. Carl brought down the knife on Smithe, missing his head as Smithe turned over, but burying it deep in his neck.

"Aaaaaaah! Shit!"

Smithe was writhing around on the floor squirting blood everywhere. He was screaming and grunting in pain.

Carl threw down the knife and knelt over his comrade. "I-I thought you were one of them."

Smithe was rocking back and forth on the floor ranting hysterically. "I-I heard the…wind…I…figured you…made it in…through this room."

"Jesus, Smithe. I'm so sorry!"

Carl got up and threw the comforter off the bed. He pulled off the sheets and began cutting strips. He went into the bathroom, grabbed a towel, and placed it over Smithe's wound. He then began to wrap his neck in the strips of sheet.

"Christ, I'm not a medic. I'm doing the best I can."

Smithe was losing a lot of blood. Carl wrapped the wound as tightly as he could. The blood soaked through quickly, and the more pressure Carl applied, the quicker Smithe seemed to bleed out. In frustration, Carl threw his back against the wall behind him and slid down to the ground.

He put his hands to his face and stifled the overwhelming urge to scream. He choked it down in violent, tearless sobbing that shook his body like convulsions.

He didn't know what to do. He wished his big brother was there to guide him. He wished Barnes was there to guide him. Hell, he would've even settled for Jorge, the hotel manager, at the moment.

But he was all alone.

As the night passed, the winds grew calmer and the night quieter. He held Smithe in his arms, but Smithe was cold and still.

The eye of the storm was approaching, a brief respite. There had been no further incident since he struck Smithe. When things quieted down, he figured he'd go outside and check things out.

It was 00:10 when all grew silent. He awoke with a start, unaware that he had succumbed to sleep, sitting in a pool of Smithe's blood. The room smelled of copper.

He slowly rose to his feet, every part of his body aching terribly. His head was pounding as if he was experiencing a vicious hangover.

He picked up his knife, wincing as he bent over, and wiped Smithe's blood off on his face. He smeared the blood on each of his cheeks like war paint.

He didn't know what made him do it. All he could say was that, at the time, it was the only thing that made sense when one's mind teetered on the brink of madness from extreme exhaustion and psychological trauma. He was going to war with the ID, and he wanted Smithe with him. Blood begot blood.

He left Smithe's body on the cool tile floor and opened the door. He stepped out into the hallway and stretched his neck, rolling his weary head around on his shoulders.

He heard the echo of footsteps down the hall, but they were not the footsteps of a human, nor the shuffling gait of an ID. They were small footsteps ending in clicking against the tile. They were clawed footsteps.

A slinky form materialized at the end of the dark hallway. It stopped for the moment, appraising him in the darkness, sizing him up in the context of the long corridor.

Carl remembered that the hotel grounds bordered a wildlife preserve. This was wild life. It let out a low, menacing growl, and it slinked closer down the hallway.

Carl, drained from adrenaline exhaustion and at this point completely unconcerned with his safety, turned to face his new adversary.

The creature drew close, paused, whipping its tail around behind it in darting motions…and then it leapt at Carl. He let it take him, sending them both crashing down to the hard floor.

He quickly rolled over on top of it and slit its throat with his knife, spilling its hot blood on the cool tile. The fight was over in minutes.

Carl stood up triumphantly over his kill. The feeling was primal, and gave him a perverse rush through his mind and body. He no longer thought. He was animal. He was a deadly automaton, clinically detached and unfeeling. His sole purpose was to kill.

He walked back into the room, stepped over Smithe's body as if it wasn't even there, and stepped through the sliding screen doors. He hopped over the balcony and tasted the cool night air on his tongue. The grounds were silent. He walked up to the swimming pool in the moonlight that passed through the hurricane's eye, casting its pale light on the devastation all around him.

He looked down at the pool and saw Munger and Barnes floating on the surface of the water, faces down. They were no longer with him, casualties claimed by the violent frenzy.

Carl stood alone, the only survivor, and gazed dispassionately as several harried flamingoes dashed past him away from some unknown horror. They sidestepped him in their flight, the monochromatic moonlight dulling their wild pink.

That's when he saw them.

A dozen ID were ambling in the silence of the pale moonlight in his direction. Calm and steady, he withdrew his knife from his leg sheath and gripped his baton.

He looked around and saw a replica of a Mayan temple not too far away. It was the sort of thing that hotel guests and tourists posed and took pictures on.

He waited for the ID to get near. They saw him and picked up on his scent, his sanguine war paint wafting in the air. It grabbed their attention like a dinner bell.

When they came within fifty feet, he smiled a depraved come hither and turned, walking toward the replica of the Mayan temple.

They pursued in earnest, as he knew they would. When he reached the temple, he began to climb the steps. He made it to the top and gazed down as the ID reached the bottom and began their clumsy but unremitting ascent.

That's right. Come and work for your food.

There was a barrier of clouds in the near distance, the inner wall of the storm's eye, lined with numerous little lightning storms. The air was electric as the wind began to pick up.

Carl began to step down toward his predators, now his prey, and he began to stab and smash away at their heads, necks, and backs.

He stuck and moved, kicking down bodies of ID, some silenced and some who would make their way back up for more.

He worked his way from step to step and around the temple, herding them into a spiral. He worked his way down the spiral stabbing and crushing heads.

He moved like lightning, and the drones could not keep up. They tripped on the steps and over themselves as the warrior automaton put them to shame with his single purpose.

After a half an hour there were no more drones moving, but a dozen motionless bodies strewn all over the steps of the mock temple.

Carl stood on its zenith, triumphant and looking for more adversaries, but there were none left. He had won, and the storm was regrouping, gathering its strength for one last hurrah before leaving the area.

Carl casually stepped back down the temple, passed the pool, and re-entered his building. He stepped into the room where Smithe's body lay in rest, and he lay wearily down on the bed. He closed his eyes and let the thundering roar of the storm lullaby him into deep slumber.

Chapter 16

Carl was woken by a paramedic who was questioning him in Spanish. He sat up on the bed, his body still aching, but less so. The man was taking his vitals.

Carl let him finish. Then he pushed the man aside and got to his feet. There were Mexican military in the room. He looked out the broken sliding glass doors.

The storm had ended, but the resort was a wasteland of torn thatched roofing, broken tile, and smashed furniture strewn all over the grounds. Strange animals from the zoo next door wandered around disoriented.

"Do any of you speak English?" Carl asked rather authoritatively. He did have authority. He was the last surviving member of his platoon and was now acting lieutenant by process of elimination. The army called it field promotion.

One of the soldiers gestured for Carl to follow him. They walked out of the room, down the hallway, and out of the building.

Carl's escort was armed, but none of them trained their weapons on him. Peter always said they were working in conjunction with the Mexican military.

They arrived at a closed tent in the middle of the grounds. There were soldiers and relief workers everywhere. Carl saw them helping the tourists out of the Convention Center.

The lead soldier gestured for Carl to enter the tent. Carl nodded and passed through the slit. Inside there was a man sitting down at a folding table covered with papers. There were two other men poring over the papers and talking on Mini-com Field Phones.

"Please, have a seat," the man told him in a heavy accent.

Carl sat in a folding chair in front of the folding table.

"I am Colonel Rojas of the Mexican Army," the man continued. "And you are…"

Carl was about to say Private Birdsall, but he corrected himself. "I am Lieutenant Carl Birdsall of the United States Army."

"United States. I did not recognize the uniform."

Carl didn't offer a response.

"What exactly are you doing in Xcaret, Lieutenant Birdsall?"

"Helping with the relief effort."

Colonel Rojas looked at him with obvious disbelief.

"The hotel management reported that you stormed the Convention Center, frightened the tourists, left and told them to keep the doors shut. They then heard gunfire, screaming, and an explosion. There are dead bodies everywhere, some that looked like they had been dead longer than others, some in suits similar to yours. We find you here in one of the rooms sleeping on a bed with a dead man on the floor dressed in the same uniform as you. So as you can see, Lieutenant Birdsall, I require more explanation."

Carl was stoic. There was no explanation he could possibly offer that would have glossed over the ID and the mutinous Lorenzo and Lockwood and made any kind of sense.

"I see. So you don't want to answer me?"

Carl just looked at him.

"Well, Lieutenant, let me offer an explanation based on how all of this appears to me."

Carl didn't even nod. He sat there like a statue hewn from stone.

"I see a lone survivor with the dead body of a fellow U.S. soldier at the foot of his bed. I see the bodies of other fellow soldiers all over the Business Center. I see skeletons, bones picked clean in the gymnasium. I think that you were down here for an operation of some kind, maybe with the knowledge of our government, but I think you flipped. How you say? Went berserk. You killed your unit. And now we found you in one of the hotel rooms with blood smeared all over your face and large knife on the end table."

Carl knew that was how it appeared. If he had been in Rojas' position, he would have put it together in the exact same way. But a switch inside him turned off...or perhaps on. He was weary, his body ached, and he lost his brother. He could say nothing to explain it all effectively to this Colonel Rojas.

He no longer cared about his college loans; he no longer worried about unemployment. These things were all trivialities, mere distractions. He knew how he looked at the moment, and he knew he was in deep trouble, but for some odd reason none of it mattered.

A normal individual would be terrified by this sensation, but he felt emancipated. A shrink would say he was numbed by severe trauma or that he was in some kind of dissociative state.

However, he knew he was not dissociating or psychotic, at least as much as any man could know that (most psychotics don't think they are psychotic). There was a sudden quiet. Not peace, mind you, but a steadiness that one could only achieve from truly horrific experience, the ultimate perspective a man has for a split second before he knows he is going to die.

"The fact that you seem completely unmoved by the fate of your friends leads me to believe I am right about you, Lieutenant."

Carl smiled to himself. This man knew nothing about him. He knew nothing of loss or pain. He knew nothing of sacrifice. He was just some soft officer in a bullshit army.

"There are a couple of men from your army here to take you into custody. They will take you back where you came from and out of my hair. I thank God that none of the tourists was hurt. It was a good thing they locked themselves in the Convention Center. They didn't even want to let *us* in."

Carl smirked to himself. Rojas was unsure if it was even in response to anything he just said or if Carl was having some perverse private moment, lost in his own dementia.

"Personally, I hope they nail you to the wall. Perhaps an execution. But it is not my problem. We have enough to deal with between the drug cartels and corrupt law enforcement. We don't need some American cowboy stomping around killing innocent people."

Carl sat in his folding chair cool as ice, waiting for this yahoo to stop jabberjawing and dismiss him already. He felt he had humored this small man long enough.

Rojas said something in Spanish, and one of the men standing next to him left the tent. In a few moments, he returned with two U.S. Army. Carl smiled like a recalcitrant problem child.

"Lieutenant," Rojas said, "Sergeants Lockwood and Lorenzo are here to take you out of my hair."

They stood there in the tent in normal army uniform. No fancy sci-fi black suits.

"Lieutenant?" jeered Lorenzo, "I assure you he's only a private. Just because he murdered his Lieutenant, it does not promote him, Colonel Rojas."

Rojas put his hands up defensively. "Hey, I just went on what this man told me. He's all yours. Take him out of my sight."

"Stand up, Private Birdsall," ordered Lorenzo.

Lockwood stood there with his hand on his sidearm, like a jumpy backup officer at a traffic stop in a bad neighborhood.

Carl sighed emphatically, mocking the gravity of his situation, and stood up.

"Hands behind your back."

Lorenzo bound Carl's wrists together with a plastic tie. He then grabbed him on the shoulder and steered him out of the tent with Lockwood in tow.

But before they left the tent, Lockwood turned back to Rojas.

"We regret any trouble he may have caused. His actions do not represent the United States Army, Colonel Rojas. He went rogue and acted completely on his own. Our State Department will be in touch with more formal apologies and reparations."

Rojas nodded and went back to his work. Lorenzo steered Carl out of the tent. They walked silently across the grounds to a parked jeep.

"Get in," instructed Lorenzo.

Carl was guided into the back seat. Lockwood got in and sat next to him. Lorenzo got behind the wheel, turned the ignition, and put the jeep in gear.

They drove back down a long highway littered with tree branches and dirt. It was the main highway that connected all of the resorts and beaches to the airport.

But just as Carl thought these snakes were actually going to take him to the airport for extradition, Lorenzo turned off the road. He drove through a superficial layer of flora. Behind it lay a dirt road. Lorenzo drove the jeep as if he had been down that road before, and Carl did not doubt that he had.

As they bounced around in the jeep, Carl had no thoughts whatsoever of escape. Sure, he could have jumped out of the jeep and attempted to make a run for it. Maybe he would have made it, but he just stayed put.

Lorenzo pulled up to a few corrugated tin shacks in a clearing. He parked the jeep and stepped out.

"Get out."

Lockwood got out and stepped aside, this time with his handgun trained on Carl. Carl casually slid over and stepped out of the jeep.

Lorenzo pointed to the shack all the way to the right. "In there. Move."

Carl stepped ahead of them, and Lorenzo and Lockwood followed behind. Lorenzo stepped in front of Carl and opened the front door. "Inside."

Carl stepped in. There was a chubby man in filthy shorts and a tight blue tee shirt riddled with holes—Navajas no doubt—standing by a table and a metal chair. In the corner was a coffin standing vertically.

"Please, you must be exhausted Private Birdsall. Have a seat," Lorenzo mocked.

Carl did as he was told. He sat down in a slow, measured movement in the chair.

"So," Lorenzo continued, "Pete's little pussy brother. You were the last person I had expected to be alive."

Carl sat there looking Lorenzo dead in the eyes. There was no fear, no anger, and no vengeful glare. He just looked at him matter-of-factly.

"Sorry about your big brother, but he wouldn't play ball. And to be quite honest, I don't expect you to either."

He paused for dramatic effect, but it wasn't having the desired effect on his prisoner, so he continued.

"So I'm not even going to bother making you an offer. I won't listen to you beg for your life. It'll just be easier to kill you."

Carl was an oak.

"By the way, I'm curious, Carl. Which is scarier, trying to talk to a girl or being hunted by blood thirsty ID?"

He chortled at his own joke. Lockwood, however, did not share in the amusement. In fact, Carl's whole demeanor appeared to unsettle him. He kept his handgun trained on him.

"What's the matter, cat got your tongue? Well, I have something that will break the ice."

Lorenzo nodded to the Navajas, who walked over to the coffin and removed the lid, tossing it aside. Inside was a young woman in a white dress that looked like she had been dead for some time.

"You see, Carl, since you are such a coward, I took the liberty of finding you a girlfriend."

Carl recognized what it was. It was one of the ID. But these perverts had taken her out of her black uniform and put her in a simple white wedding dress. Her skin was ashen and tight, her eyes clouded with cataracts and dormant.

The Navajas backed away towards the opening of the tin shack, as did Lockwood with his gun still on Carl. Lorenzo produced an AI kill switch.

"I figured that if your brother couldn't do it, I'd bust your cherry for you. I think it's time for you two to get acquainted. Any final requests?"

Carl sat there grinning at his torturers.

"He's smiling," Lockwood commented in awe, "the bastard's lost it."

Lorenzo sneered at Carl. "You cost me ninety ID, you lousy son-of-a bitch, and you set us back quite a bit. But Lewis will have to give us more. We'll be back down here before you know it. Too bad you won't be here to see it."

He hit the switch, and the dead woman sprung to life. She began to step forward towards Carl as Lorenzo stepped back. The Navajas and Lockwood stepped out of the shack altogether. The Navajas walked away, but Lockwood remained.

"I want to see your first time, Carl," Lorenzo spat venomously.

But Carl didn't flinch. He only turned his head to look at the woman as she loomed over him, growling and spitting.

Then she stopped.

She just stopped, standing over him. She wheezed and swayed in place.

Lorenzo looked confused. He fiddled with the switch, and the woman did not respond. "Shit, what now? Damned switch. Maybe it's the chip in her head."

Carl just gazed into her eyes as she stood there. If Lorenzo wasn't mistaken there appeared to be some kind of understanding that passed between them, like he was willing her to be still.

"What are you doing to her?" Lorenzo snapped impatiently. "Lockwood, get in here!"

Lockwood peeked his head in. "There's something wrong with the ID."

Lockwood stepped completely into the shack. He saw the woman standing over Carl waiting. "Is it the switch?"

"No, it's not the switch," Lorenzo snapped. "She won't move."

"Why's he staring at her like that?" Lockwood was frightened. Carl's glare bothered him before, but it was as if his fears about Carl's demeanor were being fully realized.

"Th-that's impossible," Lockwood stammered.

Lorenzo walked up to the woman and shoved her hard. She stumbled backward and stood in place. Carl looked from her to Lorenzo. He was grinning maliciously.

"What the f…"

The woman suddenly lunged forward at Lorenzo. Lorenzo put up his right hand in defense, reaching for his handgun with his left, and she bit the fingers of his right hand clear off.

He screamed and backed into Lockwood, who was trying to get a clear shot at the woman's head. Carl stood up and walked right past the screaming Lorenzo and out of the shack.

As Lockwood pushed Lorenzo aside and turned to shoot Carl in the back, the woman sunk her black teeth into his neck and pushed him down to the ground. He clawed at her face frantically in a futile exercise that would be his last on this earth.

The Navajas man and a few others came running out of another shed and saw Carl standing there with his hands bound behind his back.

One pointed a shotgun at him, but the woman dropped Lockwood and began to advance on them, growling and eyes wide.

They turned their attention to her as Carl walked away, never looking back as he heard shotgun blasts and yelling in Spanish. As he strolled over to the jeep, he heard shouts and then shrieks. And then silence.

He walked around the jeep and down the dirt road until the three shacks were behind him and out of sight.

Part III
Carl's In Charge

Chapter 17

Fort Bliss
Texas
Four Days Later

Carl had been in the hospital for three days for medical and psychiatric observation. In that time, Captain London had been in once to visit him. She had offered her condolences regarding his brother, and she ordered him to report to her office upon his discharge. She set the time and date.

She was a breath of fresh air for Carl. He basked in her intelligence, her beauty, and her sincerity. He thought the sessions were a joke, but he knew she was only doing her job and he decided that he wasn't going to give her a hard time.

The psychiatrist was another story. The man came in for only thirty seconds at a time and asked him some very obvious and rudimentary questions. He asked about his sleep and his appetite. He asked if he was anxious or depressed. And then he left.

There was one visitor that he expected but who never came—Major Lewis. But he was instructed to report to Major Lewis' office upon discharge.

He anticipated what would come out of the meeting. He didn't believe Lorenzo when he said that Major Lewis was oblivious to the plans to siphon off ID to the Navajas.

It just didn't make sense. It didn't follow that ninety ID were lost in what was a "successful" operation and he'd just give them more, no questions asked.

Carl figured that it would be Major Lewis' reaction that would belie his guilt or innocence. If he pulled Carl out of the ID Program, he figured it would imply Lewis' guilt.

Why else would he pull out the lone survivor of the program and start over from scratch? If Lewis were indeed a part of the conspiracy, he would not have expected Carl to survive. And, the fact that Carl was alive meant that he knew everything. Hence, Lewis would have to rebuild the program from scratch.

Or, Lewis was going to make him an offer to take Lorenzo's place, but this was less likely. The fact that Carl was still alive meant that he killed Lorenzo and Lockwood and therefore wasn't going along with the conspiracy.

Either way, the ball was in Carl's court, and he was going to dictate terms.

When the door to Major Lewis' office opened, Carl stepped in, removed his headgear, and saluted the Major.

"Have a seat, son."

Carl sat.

"Let me begin by saying that I'm sorry for the loss of your brother. He was a good man. A tough soldier. He will be missed."

Carl nodded.

"I've read your report about Lorenzo and Lockwood. It's unfortunate. Two rotten apples that caused the deaths of American soldiers to make some money on the side. Frankly, I'm surprised at the both of them."

Carl sat up straight in his chair, offering no response verbally or with body language. Major Lewis continued.

"I'm tempted to shut down the program altogether, but since you've been away, there've been several more terrorist attacks on soft targets in the American heartland. It's unclear at the moment whether or not it was homegrown, but the usual suspects are taking credit. One thing's for certain, the attacks were coordinated. The press is running wild, stirring up paranoia and panic."

Carl smirked at the Major. "So you're pulling me out of the ID Program."

"I have to, son. The press is all over what happened in Xcaret. They're reporting dead bodies of an entire platoon of what was apparently US Army in some very interesting uniforms. They're reporting that there were some corpses that were inexplicably dead less recently than makes sense. We need damage control, and after the mutiny, I want to start from scratch."

Carl sniffled pointedly and sat forward in his chair. "You want me out because Lockwood named you."

Major Lewis' expression turned to outrage. "Are you accusing me of conspiracy, Private?"

"I said that *Lockwood* named you."

"Be very careful, son. I'll have you court marshaled for insubordination."

"It's okay, though. It all makes sense," Carl continued, "but you're not pulling me out of the program."

Major Lewis didn't believe the balls on this private. "Listen, you little shit. Just because you had a harrowing few days in Mexico..."

"No, you listen, Major. You want me in this program, because I can control the ID."

"You can—what do you mean you can *control* them?"

"I can control them. They listen to me. I don't need an Amygdala Inhibitor. Not only do they not attack me, but they take my direction."

"What in the name of all that is holy are you talking about, boy. The psychiatrist needs to re-examine you..."

"You don't believe me? I can show you."

"Listen, son. You're obviously mentally unstable. There's no way I'm going to put you back in the program like this. You're looking at a discharge the way you're talking...or the brig."

"Go ahead. Call the ID containment facility."

"What? What are you talking about now?"

"I said call the ID containment facility."

"I'm through wasting my time..."

Just then, the Major's phone rang. He ignored it and pressed the button for his secretary. "Mary..."

"Yes, Major."

"Have two MP's sent to my office immediately."

"What about the Third Hangar?"

Lewis' face turned white. That was what they called the ID containment facility. "What about the Third Hangar, Mary?"

"They've been trying to contact you. Apparently they're having some difficulty with some of the cargo in storage."

Major Lewis gawked at Carl incredulously. Carl just sat there looking self-satisfied.

"Sir?"

"Yes, Mary."

"You still want me to get two MP's?"

He sized Carl up with wide eyes. "No. No, Mary. Cancel that."

He terminated the call. His phone rang again. He picked up. "Hello?...Yes...calm down...they're what?...did you hit the master AI kill switch...you did...seal the area and evacuate immediately."

He terminated the call. "I don't know how you're doing this, but make it stop, Birdsall."

"Oh, Major, I can make it start or stop at any time."

"There are innocent people…"

"Oh, save it. They're in no danger. You, on the other hand…if I were you, I'd listen to me very closely. Your life just might depend upon it."

Major Lewis swallowed hard. He looked as if he was about to be ill. "I'm listening."

"Because of you, my brother was killed, his whole platoon wiped out for the second time. But, I'm willing to overlook it for now."

"Wh-what do you want?"

"I want the program to remain open."

"Why? What are you playing at?"

"Because lucky for you, I need you. I still have a bone to pick with these terrorists…and the drug cartels. I need you to let me lead the program. It's the only way."

"How?"

"How what?"

"How do you…control them?"

"With all due respect, Major, that's none of your concern right now. I want you to focus. This is very important."

Major Lewis was completely taken off guard. He was taken off guard by the apparent veracity of this young man's story. More importantly, he was taken off guard by his cold, calculating confidence and negotiation with a superior officer.

"This program is very important, and it needs to continue. We are on the cusp of turning the tables on these bastards. I want to take the fight to them. I want to hunt them down in their own caves and smite them from the face of the earth. It is now my sole purpose."

"And what about me?" Lewis couldn't believe he was at the mercy of some little grunt private.

"Believe me, Major, I'd like nothing better than to kill you, but it won't bring my brother or any of the other men back. I need you because I have bigger fish to fry. But I wouldn't expect you to understand sacrifice."

It was true. This measly administrator no longer knew the pangs of sacrifice. He'd gone soft from sitting behind a desk, and in his decadence, his morality had decayed. He had been swayed by greed into conspiring with scoundrels, the very enemy he was sworn to hunt in the name of freedom.

However, Carl understood sacrifice. His brother Peter understood sacrifice. Barnes and Munger and Smithe all understood sacrifice. There was a greater good at stake, and an opportunity to pursue the elusive enemies of liberty to the bitter end.

"Firstly, I am not a Private. In the field, as the sole survivor of the Xcaret mission, I have been promoted to First Lieutenant."

"Yes...yes, I suppose that can be arranged."

"It has already happened. Second, I am to be shortly promoted to Captain."

"But..."

"Captain, for valor. Thirdly, we rebuild the program with a new team. And then we go to Afghanistan and get these bastards where they live."

"It took time to scout those men..."

"I have a list of men, from my experience in Basic Training. They're good men, and we've already functioned as a team, so I expect the learning curve to be brief."

"I-I—"

"And if at any time I get the sense that you are having second thoughts about our little arrangement, you will be paid a visit from some of our ID. Do you know what it feels like to be eaten alive, Major?"

Lewis just gaped at Carl. There was no response he could give other than a nod.

"Good, so we have an accord."

"Wh-what about the ID in the containment facility?"

"Oh, them? They've already stopped."

Major Lewis' phone rang.

"You take that call. It'll be the men at the containment facility telling you what I just did—the ID are immobilized again. I expect to see those transfers within the week so we can begin training exercises. The future of American lives and freedom are depending on you, Major. This is your chance to do something right."

Carl stood up and saluted the Major, who flummoxed, returned a limp salute. Carl smiled and left the Major's office.

***

In the week that followed, Carl assembled his platoon, which was largely composed of his mates from Basic Training— Mendoza, Koontz, Kettle, Cartieras, Fromm, and even Cronos.

It was like old times, only Carl was the CO and they were wrangling zombies. Carl preserved the Labyrinth hazing, putting each unsuspecting man in there with an ID. Lieutenant Farrow stood nervously by with his finger over the AI kill switch, but thanks to Carl's newfound talent, it was completely unnecessary.

Once they began the training exercises of release, infiltration, target neutralization, and extraction, everything went like clockwork. The men already had a rapport and worked well together, and Carl's uncanny control over the ID made everything run that much more smoothly.

There were no humpers, none of the ID got out of hand and attacked any of the men, and Carl often found himself inside the funnel of the reverse Vee formation amongst the ID, their fearless leader and fellow automaton.

Carl's new gift frightened the men, and it cultivated a mystique around him that induced immediate respect. The man was a machine, driven in the exercises, and one only wondered how any terrorists would stand a chance in an actual combat scenario.

Carl was intense, totally without fear, and unrelenting. His platoon became a formidable force in a short period of time, and he counted the days until deployment to Afghanistan.

In the meantime, Major Lewis kept his end of the one-sided bargain, promoting Carl to the rank of Captain. He nervously granted whatever Carl asked for and was reluctantly impressed by what Carl had done with his platoon in such a brief period of time.

During it all, Carl attended sessions with Captain London. She, too, was impressed with his accomplishments, but she was also concerned with his singular focus on the program.

"You know, you're different than your brother."

"Easy, Fiona. Let's not disrespect the dead."

"Oh, by no means. Peter was a great man, a hero. Just an observation."

He smiled at her sincerity. "Go on."

"Peter also suffered a great deal of loss. He, too, was an only survivor."

"Yeah, so?"

"Well, he was suffering with conflicting emotions. He was riddled with guilt. We call it 'survivor's guilt.'"

"Yes, I know what survivor's guilt is."

"But you, Carl, on the other hand, seem to have closed off all your emotions. With Peter, we were concerned about his sense of vengeance clouding his judgment. But you don't even want revenge."

"And this is a problem how?"

"It's a problem because it is unnatural not to feel sadness or loss."

"I did, at first, but…a switch inside me flipped. It's not a defense mechanism, Fiona. Something's changed."

"What's changed, Carl? Explain it to me."

"I'm not repressing emotion. It's just not practical now. I have no one, which I think makes me the perfect weapon. I have nothing to lose. My entire purpose is to devote myself to hunting terrorists."

"But that's not healthy."

"What's healthy, Fiona? Am I supposed to cry myself to sleep every night? Do you want me to wash out due to mental instability?"

"I fear you've been traumatized beyond what your defenses can handle."

"Don't you see? Fiona, I've been set free. We are at war with an adversary who doesn't fear death, who has no regard for their own lives. We've never been able to combat that, or even fathom it for that matter. But I do now."

"You almost sound suicidal."

"I am suicidal like any soldier who goes into combat knowing full well that there's a good chance he's not coming back. I don't want to die, but I don't fear it either. Believe me, I want to stick around to hunt every last terrorist until I take my last breath."

Fiona wanted to change the subject for the moment. "What about this...ability of yours?"

"What about it?"

"They tell me it's like you control the ID, and they follow your every command."

"It's not *like*, Fiona, I really do."

"But how? How does it work?"

Carl sighed and looked down at his hands on his knees for a moment, as if searching for the right answer. "To tell you the truth, I don't know. I just can."

"But it's impossible."

"Really? Because I'm doing it. If you don't believe me you should come down to our exercises and observe some time. Or if you'd like, I could summon some ID up to your office for a demonstration."

Captain London squirmed in her seat. "No, that won't be necessary. I just want to know how."

"How? That's like asking someone how they reach out for a cup of coffee or pick up a pen to write their name. They just do it, they don't know how."

"Some think it's because of the trauma you've experienced, all of the loss."

"Other soldiers have experienced loss."

"True, but then you talk about something snapping inside of you..."

"I never used the word *snapped*. That word implies that I have gone crazy. But on the contrary, I feel saner than I ever have in my life."

"I don't know if I'd call what you're experiencing sane, Carl."

"What is sane, Doc? *Normal* people walk around oblivious to the horrors of life. They buy houses with picket fences, go to their little jobs, and attend dinner parties. But when the harsh realities of this world intrude on their delicate little fantasies, their 'assumptive world,' as you shrinks would call it, is shaken. Then insecurity, paranoia, and fear creep in."

"What are you trying to say, Carl? That you're better than all of those people?"

"Not better. Just free. I know the horrors of evil. I've experienced pain and loss. But emotions like fear and sadness only make you succumb to terror."

"So you've turned off your fear?"

"How does a tightrope walker in the circus walk the tightrope? He turns off the fear. How about in the early 1900's, those pictures you see of men walking on steel girders stories up in the air with no safety harnesses. In those situations, fear is not practical. Come on, Fiona, what about Victory Tower?"

"In Basic Training?"

"Exactly. Surely, you remember Victory Tower. I don't think anyone forgets it. You swallow your fear and run the course. That's the purpose, right?"

"I guess."

"Listen. Just because you don't understand my state of mind does not make it dysfunctional."

Fiona hesitated. She was waiting for the right moment to bring it up, but time was running out. "Carl, I'd like you to submit to some brain imaging. MRI's of your brain."

"Sure, I'll do whatever you want. I don't know what you expect to find though."

She was surprised and relieved. "Thank you. I just want to make sure that this new ability of yours isn't something detrimental to your health."

"Do what you think is right, Doc. I won't fight you."

"And before you go, I wanted to briefly discuss your father."

Carl pretended to look at his watch. "Boy, I'm really getting a bang for my buck this session. You're not going to charge me double, are you?"

Captain London glared at him.

"Okay, okay. What about my father?"

"You said before that you had nothing left. But you still have your father. I want you to go home for a few days, and reconnect. See how he's doing."

"I don't think now's the best time. We're almost functional, and…"

"And nothing, Carl. Just a few days. I think it'll be good for you."

"So I don't lose my humanity?"

"I didn't say that, but now that you mention it, yes. I think that you need to care for your father."

"Doing what I do every day is caring for my father and every other American. True care is sacrifice, doing what needs to be done even to your own detriment."

"Go home, Carl."

"Yes, ma'am."

"I already arranged for a pass. Major Lewis approved it."

"Thank you, Doctor."

"And when you come back I want you to report to radiology for testing."

"Can't I have Kettle hold up a MR.UD to my head?"

"CARL."

"Okay, okay."

"Now get out of my office. Talking to you is exhausting."

Carl stood up, saluted, and smirked. "Thank you, Fiona."

"Scram."

***

Carl walked up his front walk to his house and rang the doorbell. There was a period of silence, and just as he was about to scan and let himself in, he heard his dad shuffling to the door. The door opened.

"Hi, Dad."

Carl was astounded when he saw the state of his father. It was 11:00 and the man was still in his robe, his hair jutting out to one side, at least a few days of whiskers on his face, and he reeked of body odor.

"Jesus, Dad. Are you okay?"

"Come on in," his father said almost absent mindedly.

He followed his father into the living room, which contained waist high piles of garbage, laundry, and all other kinds of discarded things.

"Dad, what happened?"

"You, know Carl, I expected to hear the news about your brother from you, not some bureaucrat I don't know."

"Dad, there was no time."

"Dammit, Carl, there's always time."

"We spoke over the com."

"A quick call isn't enough. It was hard enough losing your mother. But now, Peter too…"

"Dad, I was there, remember? I know what happened."

Carl's father got right in his face, his breath pungent. "Oh yeah? So what did happen, exactly? You gonna give me some bullshit about Peter being a hero in some vague combat situation. Shit, I don't even know where you guys were!"

Carl thought for a minute. His father had received the "official version" of what happened, the runaround designed to make grieving parents feel proud without revealing any sensitive information.

"I'll tell you, Dad. I'll tell you everything."

His father looked dumbfounded. He hadn't quite expected that answer. "You wouldn't. You can't."

"Technically you're right, Dad, but you deserve the truth. But only under one condition."

"Okay."

"You must take it to your grave."

"What?"

"It's very classified, Dad. Not even all of the army knows about it."

His father walked into the kitchen and cleared some garbage off of a chair. Carl came in and leaned on the kitchen counter like he and Peter always used to do.

"Dad, Pete and I were working on something very classified. Something very important. Something that might make us start to win against these terrorists."

"Yeah, Carl, did you hear about the other attacks? The President is bombing Afghanistan, but those terrorists hide like rats in the caves. We can't get to them."

"Funny you should bring that up, Dad."

And Carl began to tell him about the ID Program, the Labyrinth, and the training exercises. He told his father about Peter's involvement in operations against the Navajas cartel in Mexico, what happened in Tijuana, and the botched mission in Xcaret that left his father with only one son.

At first, his father thought he was joking. But as Carl told the story and filled it in with such inexplicable detail, he began to realize that this was no tale. Carl was definitely breaking protocol by telling his father, but Major Lewis was in no position to do anything about it.

There was also the risk of the information leaking out to the public, but Carl trusted his father. Besides, once he got to Afghanistan and scorched the earth, the government would want to publicize their use of the Insidious Drones.

When Carl was done bringing his father up to date, his father just sat there staring at him.

"Well, that's what has been happening."

"And…you're going to be leading these Insidious Drones?"

"Yup."

"And you can control them…with your mind."

"Exactly."

His father let out a loud sigh. "Carl, don't you think there's been enough loss?"

"I-I don't know what you mean, Dad."

"You're all I have left. These bastards took my wife and one of my sons. And now they're going to finish the job with you."

"Dad, I have to do it. No one else can, not like I can."

"But why not someone else this time, Carl? You can come home, live here as long as you like. Maybe go back to school."

School. Wow. Carl hadn't thought about school in quite some time. At this moment, classes and homework seemed silly. Ridiculous even.

"Dad, there's nothing for me here. School is pointless. There are no jobs. And what am I supposed to do? Go from hunting terrorists to sitting in a cubicle making copies all day?"

"You'd be safe."

"Like Mom? No one's safe, Dad. Don't you see? Unless we do something about the evil that's out there, there is no safe. There won't be any companies or employees or colleges or students."

His father put his palm gently on Carl's face. "You used to be my little boy. You were so young, and smart, and full of life. Now I don't recognize you. You are so hard, and full of scars."

"I'm a man now, Dad. I'm no longer a boy. You raised me to do right, not play it safe. And I'm doing right. And believe me, once I get out there with the ID, nothing will be the same again."

"I just wish it didn't have to be you."

"Dad, there will come the day when you will be proud it's me. I know this is all hitting you at once, and it's a lot for you to digest, and you don't fully understand all of it. But trust me. Someday soon you will understand."

His father threw his hands down at his sides and stood there resigned.

"And by the way," Carl continued, changing the subject, "at what point did you start living like this? Pete didn't tell me anything about this."

Barry looked sheepish. "He didn't want you to worry."

"Come on, Dad. You've got to start taking better care of yourself. Let me help you clean up. Then we're going to go out for lunch. My treat, of course."

Carl began to help his father clean up the kitchen and then the living room. It was such a herculean task that Carl sent out for lunch, and they went out to dinner later that evening.

Carl recognized that Fiona was right. It did feel good to see his father. His dad needed him. He'd never understand what Carl had been through or why Peter died, but Carl needed to be a son to his father.

He'd have all the time in the world to be a fearless warrior on the battlefield. But being with his father reminded him of what he was doing it all for, and his resolve grew even stronger.

***

Somewhere in Mexico

A man sat alone in the dark, hands tightly bound behind his back, drenched with sweat, with a burlap sack over his head. He found it difficult to breathe, his hot, uneven breath hitting the inside of the burlap and bouncing back on his face, smothering him.

If the Navajas had wanted him dead, he would have been dead already. They were keeping him alive, but to what purpose he was not certain. He had been moved around, dragged in and out of vehicles blindly. There had been no contact since he had been taken, save for an occasional sip of water in the dark. But whatever it was, he was resolved not to cooperate, even if it meant his demise.

He heard a door open and footsteps in the dirt. He braced himself for whatever was coming. He was forcibly bent forward at the waist so that the person was able to grab him by his bindings and hoist him up. He rose to his feet with a grunt of pain and was shoved forward, stumbling as he went.

They left whatever structure he was being kept in, because sunlight began to penetrate the gaps in the burlap and he began to hear the ambient sounds of the outdoors. After a few minutes of being led blindly, his captor yanked him to a halt by his bindings, and he stood there waiting for whatever was in store for him. He whispered a silent prayer for the strength to resist whatever came next.

After standing for some indeterminate amount of time waiting, he heard multiple sets of footsteps approach. The burlap sack was yanked off of his head. As sunlight flooded his vision, he struggled to make out his surroundings.

He was correct in concluding that he was outside. He was in a sizable clearing, about the size of a football field, with lush vegetation surrounding it. There were men in tattered black outfits, approximately sixty of them, standing motionless at attention.

They looked like soldiers, but as his eyes adjusted he saw that they were not human, and they were not standing at attention…they were completely still. The commander of this outfit, a Navajas, approached him accompanied by a smaller man. The commander began to bark at him in Spanish. A heartbeat delayed, the smaller man began to translate.

"You will help us to use these monsters. You will teach us how to make them follow commands. You will teach us how to control them. You will teach us how to make them kill. If you do not, you will be tortured."

Although the smaller man was translating, the prisoner never took his eyes off the Navajas commander. He hesitated, gathering saliva in his mouth, and spat on the ground, spraying the commander's boots. The commander sneered, baring yellow teeth, and struck him hard on the side of his head, catching his ear. The ringing was so loud that he could not hear what the translator said next.

The translator apparently realized this and began to speak in hushed tones to the commander. The commander nodded. The man who dragged the prisoner out shoved him forward towards the decrepit men in black standing in rows.

The prisoner was guided right up to one in the front row and was shoved face-to-face with it. It had no breath, but a stench emanated from its mouth that nearly made him lose his lunch.

He was then pulled away, and again the commander barked at him. The smaller man translated. "You will teach us, or we will feed you to this one piece by piece, and you will watch as it feeds on your appendages."

Shit, these guys weren't playing around. The prisoner shrugged. "I don't even know what these things are. How the hell am I supposed to teach you how to use them?"

The small man translated back to the commander, who shook his head in defiance. Then he got in his face and shouted, covering the man's face with spittle.

"He says that you will teach his men, or he will start by feeding the monster your…manhood."

Certainly not the way he wanted to go. He was thinking of something like a decapitation, or being shot in the back of the head. Maybe there was another way out of this, a way that if he was going to die he could take as many of these bastards with him.

He smiled wryly. "When do I start?"

The commander, upon hearing the translation, smiled triumphantly. He signaled to another man, who handed a small apparatus to the prisoner. The prisoner looked down and saw a remote control with a button. He held it up towards the monsters standing in rows and pressed the button. They began to move forward, reaching out for the commander and his little translator.

The translator shouted, "Stop!" The commander backed away behind his translator, training his gun on the prisoner and shouting in Spanish.

The prisoner smiled defiantly, "Go ahead and shoot me. You won't escape."

"We have someone important to you," shouted the translator.

This got the prisoner's attention. What did they have up their sleeves now? He had a feeling he knew, but he hoped he was wrong. "Prove it."

The translator took out his Mini-com, activated the video feature, and tossed it to the prisoner. The prisoner looked down at the screen, and his face went white.

The monsters were closing in on the commander, who now had his handgun trained on them. The prisoner pressed the button, and the monsters came to a stop. He was furious as he looked down at the Mini-com screen. They weren't bluffing.

"Do you see that monster standing over him in the wedding dress?" the translator gloated. "We will feed him to it, and you will watch."

"And what makes me think you won't harm him if I do what you ask?" the prisoner asked through gritted teeth.

"He will die quickly, senor…" the man looked at his rank on his uniform, "…Lieutenant. But if you don't, his death will be slow and painful."

Peter Birdsall looked down at the screen, as if one more look would reveal that the scene depicted was not real. He looked around to see if he could figure out where they were keeping Carl. They had him by the short hairs…for now.

"Okay, I'll do it."

The video was looped, which suggested that the footage was not current. Carl was probably dead. But he would bide his time and discover the truth of all of this. And then he would catch these bastards off guard and turn the drones on them. For some unknown reason God had given him nine lives, not that he felt he deserved it. But he'd keep on keeping on…for Carl.

Chapter 18

Carl returned from his visit with his father refreshed and energized. He submitted to the neurological testing that Captain London ordered.

He lay down and was pulled into the MRI. It was tight, reminding him of a coffin, but he wasn't dead yet. The sensation caused him mild discomfort, but it quickly passed.

The voice of the technician talked into his ear. "We are going to begin. It should take approximately twenty minutes. Are you okay?"

"Yes."

"Good. Now remember, it is important that you do not move."

"Okay."

Within seconds, the machine began to bang all around him. It began with a series of five bangs and then six clicks, five bangs and six clicks, and on and on. He closed his eyes, hoping the time would pass quickly.

The sequence of bangs and clicks eventually turned into a rat-tat-tat, like the sound of a machine gun. With his eyes closed, scenes of Tijuana and Xcaret flooded into his mind.

He saw Peter firing his gun in training, and then he saw him one last time before entering the ventilation shaft. He heard the yelling and gunfire of the terrorists by the Convention Center.

When he was pulled out of the MRI, he was rigid and pale as a ghost.

"We're done. Are you alright, sir?"

Carl sat up and nodded. "Yeah, I'm fine."

He picked up with the training exercises. Another week passed, and they had mastered live insurgents and surprise attacks, moving targets, and cave extractions. In fact, the extractions became simpler as the ID simply followed Carl out of the simulated "caves" like he was the Pied Piper and kindly collected themselves back into their crate.

Carl found himself back in Major Lewis' office making quite the unusual request.

"You want to do what?" Major Lewis gasped.

"I want the ID to come from the bodies of victims from the terrorist attacks."

"You must be…do you know how difficult…we can't just ask their families for their bodies," Major Lewis said horrified.

"Any organ donors?"

"*Organ donors*. Captain, what you are talking about is a little more than organ donation."

"Well, where do we get these bodies from, anyway?"

"That's classified."

Carl sat forward menacingly. "Did you forget our arrangement?"

"Listen, I can't tell you everything."

"Try me."

"Let's just say that some of them are our citizens. Some are bodies presumed missing from the rubble of past attacks. Some are the bodies of indigents without any family."

"So bodies can be exposed to the virus posthumously. And the rest?"

"Remember when the Camp X-Ray of the Guantanamo Bay holding facility was shut down?"

"Yes."

"Well, let's just say that it never really shut down."

Carl sat back and smiled widely, barely hiding his amusement. "So you mean to tell me that we're training the corpses of terrorists to hunt their own down?"

Major Lewis nodded.

"I love it!" Carl laughed. "This'll be another great PR piece when it goes public."

"Public? I don't know if it can ever go public."

"Trust me, after we hit the caves of Afghanistan without expending American lives and bring back the heads of dozens of those tunnel rats cowering in the mountains, the public will be behind us every step of the way. Maybe not the bleeding hearts, but most everyone else."

"Captain Birdsall, I don't know if there is a right way to spin all of this, even with good results."

Carl was losing patience. "Then why the hell did you get involved with this, anyway? To turn the tables. This isn't like dropping the A-bomb on soft targets. You don't get any more precise than what we're doing. We're not raiding villages, raping women, and looting. We're going into the caves, away from any innocents. Sure, it's ugly. But we're talking about terrorists. Political correctness is wavering, and the world is finally trying to find a way to deal with them."

"I know. This is what we've been working towards. But when you talk about bringing back heads and then publicizing it all…"

"No mercy. They don't show us any mercy. Shit, *they're* hitting soft targets. Not us."

"I know. I know. You're preaching to the choir. But the public…the media won't be won over so easily. Let's run our first mission in Afghanistan, see how it goes."

"My men are almost ready. We don't have any of the old problems with the humpers."

"But there's your…ability."

"Yeah, what about it?"

"We haven't done enough testing. We don't even know if it's stable."

"What do you mean *stable*? Of course it's stable. Why wouldn't it be stable?"

"How are you so certain that it is stable? Do you even know how you are doing it?"

Carl shrugged it off.

"You shouldn't be so glib about it, Captain. What if we sent you into combat based on all of your training with your ability, and then it stops or wears off? American soldiers can get hurt."

Carl couldn't believe what he was hearing. This "ability" was exactly the break they were waiting for, and now this bureaucrat wanted to wait some more. "This is our chance! What if it does wear off? My men are prepared just in case. We still have the AI kill switches. We still have all of the safety measures in place."

"We just need to tread carefully."

"We need to mobilize soon. How many more attacks on soft targets on U.S. soil do we have to endure before we strike back?"

Major Lewis knew the kid was right. This was why he got involved with the ID Program in the first place. They had come so far, there was no turning back now, and he knew it.

"We will mobilize soon. Work out all of the bugs. Get your platoon in tiptop shape. We won't have a second chance. Xcaret almost shut us down permanently."

"Xcaret won't happen again," Carl snapped. "We have good men this time. *I* chose them, not you."

Despite the major breach in protocol in addressing a superior officer, Major Lewis let it slide. The kid was their best chance at implementing the program, and he was right.

"Dismissed, Captain Birdsall."

Carl stood up, saluted, and left Lewis' office all charged up. Major Lewis had to admit that the kid got him all fired up as well. Not only had he gotten the platoon functioning at an optimal level, but Carl and his ability was beginning to become the stuff of legend.

All of the other men looked up to him. They both admired and feared his leadership with the men and the ID. There was a new energy disseminating amongst the ranks, and for once, soldiers were beginning to believe that they might actually win this war.

The man was fierce, determined, and had a good command over his platoon. He inspired confidence and boosted morale. For such a young man he was a natural born leader.

Major Lewis was jarred from his private reverie by a call from Captain London. "Yes, Captain. What can I do for you?"

"I'm holding the results of Captain Birdsall's MRI."

"How does it look?"

"I think we should meet in person, sir."

"Why? What's wrong?"

Captain London was hesitant on the other line. "Would you like me to come to your office, sir?"

"No, Captain, I'll come to you. I'll be there in a few minutes."

"Very good, sir."

He terminated the call. What could the MRI have shown that she was unwilling to discuss over the phone? He got up from his chair, straightened his uniform, and left his office, telling Mary that he would be at Captain London's office on his way out.

***

"He has a tumor?" Major Lewis asked in disbelief.

"Yes," replied Captain London, "in his temporal lobe. It's quite large and extensively vascular."

"So it would be difficult to excise via surgery?"

"Yes, Major, quite. But it's pressing on his brain, particularly in areas heavily involved in speech and hearing."

Major Lewis looked perplexed. "But his speech and hearing seem unaffected. I just had him in my office a few minutes ago."

Captain London was reluctant to offer her explanation, which only exasperated Major Lewis.

"Oh, out with it, Captain. We're talking about anti-terrorist zombies and a man who seems to control them with his mind. Nothing will shock me at this point."

"Okay. Well, just because the tumor hasn't detracted from his speech and hearing doesn't mean that it hasn't affected it."

"You mean you think there's a possibility that the tumor is *enhancing* his speech and hearing?"

"Think about it, Major. It makes sense. Maybe he can hear the ID, in an extra-sensory way, and perhaps he can communicate back with them using a similar pathway."

"Jesus. You mean this large tumor allows him to talk to them? Is it dangerous? The tumor, I mean?"

"Yes. The neurologist states that it's at an advanced stage of growth, and there'd be a significant risk in removing it."

"And if it were to be removed, would he lose his ability to communicate with the ID?"

"Most likely, sir."

Major Lewis appeared deep in thought, and Captain London thought she knew the direction his thoughts were taking. But little did she know that this was news to his ears.

"We have to tell him, sir."

"Yes. Yes, I suppose we do."

"He'll have to decide whether or not to operate once he's been given all of the facts."

"I'd like to be present during this meeting with Captain Birdsall."

Captain London knew this was a bad idea the moment she heard it. She knew that he was going to try to discourage Carl from consenting to operate on the tumor.

But, unbeknownst to her, Major Lewis' motives were two-fold. True, the ID Program would certainly benefit from Carl's ability to control the ID. But the prospect of Carl's premature death meant that there would be no one else who knew of Major Lewis' scandalous involvement with the Navajas. Carl would take it to his grave, and Major Lewis would be free from Carl's constant threats of turning the ID on him.

"Sir, I don't know if…"

"Are you refusing a commanding officer, Captain London?"

"No. No, sir. Of course not."

"I also want this information to be kept confidential. If Captain Birdsall declines surgery, we don't want to dissolve the mystique that his ability has cultivated around him. The program and morale would surely suffer."

"I think I understand, sir," Captain London said with a trace of disapproval.

"Captain, he's a hero amongst the men, and he is going to change the face of the war on terror. If he chooses, we will preserve the legend."

"Yes, sir."

"So when are we having this meeting?"

"The neurologist is coming at 18:00. I was planning to hold the meeting in my office."

Major Lewis stood so abruptly that Captain London nearly jumped out of her skin. "Excellent. I will see you at 18:00." He turned and left her office.

Captain London sat behind her desk most displeased. That rattlesnake was going to attempt to convince Carl to decline surgery. She had to do her best to advocate for him. In the end it was indeed Carl's decision, but she feared that the Major's influence would be too strong.

She had to find a way to counteract Major Lewis so that Carl would make a decision in his own best interest. She had an idea...

Chapter 19

Captain Carl Birdsall stepped into Captain London's office.

"Have a seat, Carl. This is Dr. Rinke, the neurologist who interpreted the results of your MRI."

Carl shook his hand. As Carl sat, he noticed that the office was once again decorated like his childhood home. Captain London wanted him to feel comfortable, which likely meant bad news.

Major Lewis was a no show. Captain London hoped he had forgotten about the meeting, had an attack of conscience, or just lost interest. She sat behind her desk. Dr. Rinke sat next to Carl.

"What's this all about, Doc? Am I gonna live?"

Dr. Rinke looked nervously at Captain London. Carl knew from the lack of humor in the room that there was bad news.

"Well" Dr. Rinke began, "we found a rather large, highly vascularized tumor on your left temporal lobe."

"A tumor...highly vascularized. That means it has a lot of blood vessels, right?"

"Yes. That also means that an attempt to remove it surgically carries great risk."

"I see."

"Carl," Captain London interjected, "we think it's affecting speech and hearing areas in your brain."

"But my...oh, I see."

"Yes," she continued, "we think that this tumor explains why you are able to communicate with the ID."

Carl thought about this. "Well, it's not like I can hear them in my head. And I don't speak to them either."

"We think it might be some extra-sensory process," Dr. Rinke added.

"What, like ESP?"

Just then, Major Lewis came barging into Captain London's office. "Sorry I'm late. Captain London, Captain Birdsall."

They stood and saluted.

"And this is…"

"Dr. Rinke," Dr. Rinke extended his hand, and Lewis shook it.

Everyone sat down again. Captain London shifted uncomfortably in her chair. "Dr. Rinke and I were just explaining our theory about Carl's tumor and his ability to communicate with the ID."

"Yes, a hell of a thing," Major Lewis commented rather indelicately. "I mean, what are the odds?"

The digital décor flickered slightly. Carl addressed Dr. Rinke as if he hadn't heard Major Lewis' comment. "So it isn't from any kind of psychological trauma?"

"No, I'm afraid not. Such an explanation is unlikely and, frankly, unheard of."

"But there've been documented cases of tumors causing phenomena like this?"

"Well, nothing quite like this, Captain, but minor psychic phenomena."

"So then how do you know it's the tumor?"

"Yes, good point," Major Lewis added.

The digital décor rippled ever so slightly. Carl awaited Dr. Rinke's answer.

"Well, Captain, it's our most likely suspect."

"Can I die from it?"

"It's in the advanced stages. Yes, ultimately it will be terminal."

"Can it be operated on?"

"Yes, but at this stage the surgery would be quite risky."

"Yes, very risky," Major Lewis snapped. Carl's mother's curtains glitched. "Something you should think about, son."

"But there's a solid chance you'd survive, Carl," Captain London jumped in.

"How much of a chance?" Carl asked.

"I can't say better than average," Dr. Rinke said gravely, "but there is a chance."

"And if I do nothing, I'll definitely die?"

"Yes," confirmed Dr. Rinke.

Carl considered something for a moment. "If you can successfully remove the tumor, will I lose the ability to control the ID?"

Dr. Rinke looked at Captain London, who answered. "Most likely."

"But at what risk?" Major Lewis asked, ignoring the rolling of Captain London's eyes. "Think of all you've accomplished in the program. Think of the opportunity that will be lost." The impressionist painting on the wall from his parents' living room jumped slightly.

"It's up to you," Captain London jumped in," there is risk, but if you opt out of surgery you will definitely die. At least with surgery you have a chance."

"How long do I have, Dr. Rinke?"

Dr. Rinke hesitated. "These things are hard to estimate. I would say a year or less."

Carl looked down at his hands folded in his lap. "I see."

Major Lewis was getting nervous. "Son, think of what we are about to do in the program...," the image of Carl's old backyard outside the window sputtered, "...think about the history you are going to make."

"Can the operation wait, Doctor?"

"If you were to opt for surgery, Captain, I would recommend that it occur as soon as possible. Time is of the essence."

"Don't feel rushed," Major Lewis pleaded, leaning forward in his chair. Carl's mother's oriental vase wavered.

"GODAMMIT! THAT'S ENOUGH," Major Lewis boomed. "Captain London, kindly turn off your holographic milieu program.

Damn. Major Lewis wasn't completely oblivious. She pressed a button on her desk, and the holographic décor from Carl's childhood vanished into thin air.

Carl looked startled, as if he did not hear Major Lewis' outburst. "What just happened?"

Major Lewis grabbed Carl's arm. "Son, it appears Captain London programmed her holographic milieu program to glitch whenever I speak, subliminally interfering with you registering anything I say. Am I correct, Captain London?"

Captain London looked flustered. She implored Carl, "He wants to convince you to opt out of surgery so the ID Program can progress with your ability. I just wanted you to hear the facts and make up your own decision."

Carl believed that Fiona had always been sincere in wanting the best for her patients, and he believed her now. And then it hit him why Lewis wanted him to opt out of surgery. It wasn't just the success of the ID Program. If Carl were dead, he would be out of Lewis' hair.

"You will face charges for insubordination, Captain London."

Dr. Rinke looked positively shell shocked at the exchange unfolding before him. He wasn't quite sure what was happening.

"No she won't," Carl stated with an authority incommensurate with his rank with respect to the Major.

Major Lewis looked at him startled. His outrage was clear, but for reasons unclear to both Fiona and Dr. Rinke, he dared not express it.

"Captain London was merely looking out for my best interest as my doctor and adhering to her ethical code of practice as she saw fit," Carl explained.

Captain London looked nervously at Major Lewis, aghast at Carl's blatant breach of etiquette regarding the chain of command. But she saw Lewis give in, and she didn't understand why. She was, however, relieved. "Good, Carl. I'm glad you feel that way."

"But I'm going to opt out of surgery," Carl added, dropping a bomb on her.

"B-but, I don't understand."

"Fiona, the ID Program, this ability to communicate with the ID…this is my purpose."

"But, Carl," she sounded desperate, "what purpose will you have if you are dead?"

"Which is why I must use my gift now. This is an opportunity I fear we'll never have again. I lost my mother and my brother to terrorists. By taking them from me, they have entangled themselves with me. I aim to see this through."

"But what if you can survive the surgery?"

"I cannot risk losing the ability to control the ID."

"But the program would still work. It worked before."

"But the ID turned on us in Xcaret. It was clumsy and dangerous."

"Captain," Major Lewis said pointedly, "might I remind you that you are discussing classified information in front of a civilian."

Dr. Rinke looked extremely uncomfortable, like he wanted to run out of the room.

"Oh, shut up, Lewis," Carl snapped.

Fiona was confused and mortified.

"Fiona, remember what we discussed…about sacrifice?"

"You're not some kind of martyr, Carl."

"I don't want to be a martyr, Fiona. I want to bring these terrorists to justice. I want them to be afraid for once. We can win this."

She no longer knew what to say. All of her attempts at getting him to advocate for himself failed. His mind was made up.

"Good choice, son," Major Lewis said with phony sincerity, "you are a great American." Then he stood up. "Well, I think we've all said what we came here to say, and Captain Birdsall has made up his mind. Good day, Captain. Dr. Rinke." He left her office.

She gawked at Carl. "What was *that* all about? How can you talk to a superior officer like that?" She almost sounded accusing.

He stood up, "Fiona, for your own protection, I cannot tell you. Don't worry about it." He nodded to Dr. Rinke. "Thank you, Doctor." And he walked out of the office.

He bumped into Major Lewis in the hallway.

"You won't be around to threaten me forever, Birdsall. Your days are numbered," he hissed in hushed tones.

"Lewis," Carl said loudly, "you're beginning to convince me that I need to deal with you sooner rather than later."

This not so veiled threat silenced Lewis. He dared not push it any further. He would have his day; all he had to do was wait.

Carl brushed past him, smiling insolently. All he had to do was wait a little longer. Once the success of the ID Program became public, he could deal with Major Lewis. But not before then.

***

Two Weeks Later
08:00

Captain Carl Birdsall and Lieutenant Nolan Kettle stepped into the debriefing room and took their seats. Major Lewis was seated at the front.

"You will be deploying to the White Moutain Range in Afghanistan in twenty-four hours to infiltrate the Tora Bora cave system."

Carl exchanged a knowing look with his Lieutenant. This was it. It was finally happening.

"As you know, the U.S. military operation in 2001 was only a partial success. Many terrorists were neutralized, but even more escaped through the elaborate cave system, crossed the mountains, and took refuge over the Pakistani border.

"But we have intelligence indicating that there is a significant Order for International Liberation presence operating out of those caves. You will guide the ID into the cave system and hunt them down.

"Your platoon will be dropped off at an entry point to the cave system by Black Hawk gunships, and one hundred ID by Chinook helicopters. Captain Birdsall, you will lead the ID into the cave and travel with them. Your objective is two-fold: scientific observation and assisting the ID. Lieutenant Kettle, you and the rest of the platoon will form a perimeter around the entry point and protect it."

Carl consulted his Cybernetic Digital Organizer clipboard. "I will load up several of the ID with heavy packs filled with food and water, as a thorough scouring of the cave system will likely take days, even weeks. I will also leave an ID with Lieutenant Kettle so that I can send signals back through the ID that I'm still alive."

"This time," Major Lewis added, "no electric ignition weaponry. They're obviously too vulnerable. More research needs to be done. Standard weaponry. AK's, shotguns, and Desert Eagle sidearms."

"What about the locals?" Carl asked.

"The government is sympathetic to our cause and they expressed that they will give us their full cooperation."

"So in other words, be on our guard."

"Exactly. Any questions?"

Carl and Nolan shook their heads.

"Dismissed. And good luck."

Carl and Nolan stood up, saluted, and left to begin preparations.

On the way back to the barracks they ran into Captain London. Nolan saluted her.

"Hello, Captain Birdsall. Lieutenant Kettle."

Nolan knew when he was the third wheel, so he excused himself and left.

"Come to see me off, Fiona?"

"Carl, I heard about your mission to Afghanistan…"

She looked embarrassed. "I'm sorry about calling you a martyr. It's…just that I can't fathom your decision. I understand it, but I can't fathom it."

"Thank you, Fiona. I think you do understand."

"You really are a hero, like your brother. I think he'd be very proud of you."

"It's funny, all my life he was my big brother. I always looked up to him. He was always the stronger, more confident one. And now I'm finishing what he started."

"You're not the weak little brother any more, Carl. You've become so much more."

Carl smirked. "Why Fiona London, have you fallen for me? I knew it. Ever since Frisky's…"

She gave him a stern look. "Now Captain Birdsall, you know that I cannot…"

"Oh shut up," Carl said. He grabbed her and kissed her deeply. Despite all of her ethical protest, she went limp in his arms, surrendering herself completely to something she had probably thought about for some time.

When he pulled himself away from her, he said wryly, "You can have me court marshaled when I get back. But right now, I've got some terrorists to kill."

He strode off towards the barracks to prepare for battle.

Chapter 20

Tora Bora Cave System
White Mountains, Afghanistan

Captain Carl Birdsall assembled his men outside the designated entry point. He stood outside the three shipping crates filled with a combined force of one hundred Insidious Drones clad in their black suits, hungry for living flesh.

"Lieutenant Kettle, open the crates."

"Yes, sir."

Kettle signaled for the crates to be opened. He deactivated the Amygdala Inhibitor kill switch. The ID stepped out of the crates and into the funnel of the reverse Vee formation.

Carl walked amongst them unmolested in the funnel. He checked the packs on several ID, counting his supplies: condensed food, bottles of water, and thermal field blankets for bedding. He felt like he was going camping, and these reanimated dead were his demented Boy Scout troop.

"We're a go," he shouted to Kettle.

Carl marched forward, the mass of ID following around him like an enormous entourage. One ID remained behind. Kettle had guns trained on it, just in case it decided to get nasty.

Carl led the mob into the cave, and after a few minutes, they all disappeared from view. Kettle ordered the men to form a perimeter and scan the area for insurgents. He even sent out a few scouts for reconnaissance.

In the cave, Carl led his angry mob. The whole scene reminded him of an old black-and-white movie. All they needed were torches and a castle to storm. They penetrated the cool, dark caves, the wheezing and growling and heavy footsteps of the ID echoing off of the walls.

They walked for a few hours before they encountered their first band of terrorists. There was shouting as they scattered, opening fire on the ID. Carl returned fire from within his entourage, taking out several of the terrorists while the hungry ID neutralized the rest. The screams and cries of men being eaten alive echoed throughout the cave, and then there was silence.

Carl had flashbacks of Xcaret, Mexico and his unit being eaten alive. He remembered the mirrored walls of the workout room in the hotel gymnasium reflecting the marauding dead, making it appear as if they were surrounded on all sides. He feared their numbers then. Now it gave him strength.

Carl ordered the ID to cease their attack when the terrorists were sufficiently dead and beyond reanimation. He searched their persons. On one, he found a map of the cave system.

"Well this will come in handy, won't it," he said to his brigade of dead, but they offered no answer. Seven kills. Not a bad start.

He began to follow the map throughout the cave system, avoiding dead ends or tunnels where there was no indicated occupation. The map had saved them from wasting time. As they went he marked the walls with a solution that would illuminate under a black light that he carried, a trail of crumbs to find his way back out.

At 12:00, Carl stopped his band of marauders to consume a quick lunch. He rested for approximately twenty minutes, his bodyguards standing by supportively, clicking their jaws in anticipation, but otherwise remaining quite still.

At 12:30, they resumed their trek further into the cave system. As they made blind turns by the light of their field lanterns and the flashlight on Carl's assault rifle, he trained his weapon, ready to shoot first and ask questions later.

Their campaign was take-no-prisoners. The fact that they were in the caves, where only Order for International Liberation terrorists would be hiding out, made their task infinitely easier. No innocents in their right minds would take refuge this far into the cave system. That meant no collateral damage, only hard targets.

Carl consulted his Mini-com unit, but he had lost reception some time ago. He was on his own, left to the drones' ability to track live prey. He also had the map.

They walked on for another several hours without incident. Occasionally he heard a flurry of footsteps running in the other direction, but no contact with the enemy was made. They passed through a few areas with overturned tables and chairs and some crude lighting, but the posts had been deserted.

He figured it was time to use his mental connection with the dead to send back a signal to Kettle to let him know he was still alive.

***

Outside the cave, Kettle and the two men training their rifles on the lone drone nearly jumped out of their skin when it suddenly made a movement with its right arm.

Kettle signaled for the two men to stand down. He didn't want them blowing away their only contact to their Captain because they were jumpy.

"Look," Kettle said, "it's waving."

Then the ID rather clumsily held out its right hand, made a fist, and awkwardly stuck its thumb up in the air.

"He's giving us a thumbs up," Kettle said, "the Captain's all right."

***

Although he wasn't able to tell from inside the dark cave, night had fallen. It was close to midnight, and Carl was weary. He decided to catch some shut eye.

He ordered the ID to halt. He picked a man-sized nook in a corner of the cave and sat himself down with his back to the wall. He draped a few thermal field blankets over him, as the caves became quite cold at night, and he rested his assault rifle on his lap.

Then, by his command, a few dozen of the ID crowded around the spot where he sat, blocking him out completely from view. He ordered the others to fan out a bit and attack anything human that moved into the area. Content with the protection of his guard and his kills for the day, he allowed sleep to take him.

***

The next day Kettle was awakened in the large tent by an anxious private from the late night/early morning detail.

"Lieutenant Kettle. Lieutenant Kettle."

He sat up in his sleeping bag, rubbing the sleep out of his eyes. "What is it, Private?"

"The drone, sir. It waved again and gave us the thumbs up."

"Good. That means Captain Birdsall survived his first night. Thank you, Private."

Kettle stood up and stretched. He put on his headgear and stepped out of the tent. "Private Fromm, report."

Fromm walked over. "Good morning, sir. The scouts have reported back and left again. They reported no unfriendlies in the area. All's quiet, sir. The perimeter remains intact."

"Good. Carry on."

***

Days passed in the cave, but due to the perennial darkness Carl's Circadian Rhythms were thrown out-of-whack, and he was beginning to find it difficult to sleep. He slept at odd hours, which was really immaterial given the fact that their mission was ongoing for days. His signals back to Kettle were going out at odd intervals. But there was a serendipitous result. Carl's movements with the ID became more nocturnal and, as a consequence, they were catching terrorists off guard.

Carl was beginning to lose track of the days without the use of his Mini-com. He estimated that it was around one week in the cave system. They had exhausted the map and were now winging it, but Carl had twenty-eight more kills since the initial seven, which brought his total to thirty-five.

The effects of approximately seven days of submersion in the caves left him a little disoriented, but he rationed out his food carefully and stayed hydrated. The ID were no worse for the wear, and they didn't know the difference. They only ate in combat, they never dehydrated, and they never slept. Their muscles never tired, as the buildup of lactic acid was no longer a factor.

Carl, on the other hand, did suffer from lactic acid buildup, so for short stretches he had two ID carry him on their shoulders. He mused that he was the emperor of a cave dwelling dead culture, but the rides allowed him to recover from long stretches of hiking in the dark.

***

Outside the cave, Lieutenant Kettle was talking to Sergeant Koontz in front of the guarded drone. There was a pop and Koontz suddenly dropped, dead before he hit the ground.

"SNIPER," Kettle yelled as everyone took cover, scanning the area for the location of the sniper. There were a few more shots fired at men taking cover.

Kettle was behind a large rock formation. He looked through his binoculars. There was no one on the flatlands for miles. He panned across, past the drone still standing there...

"Christ," he spat under his breath. He forgot about the drone. It was just standing there, as Carl ordered. He had to get it out—

It's head exploded like a melon from the sniper's bullet.

"Goddammit!"

That was their only connection to Carl. Now they wouldn't know if he was alive or dead, which left them blind, deaf, and dumb. They had no fix on his location, no status on his progress, and no idea when he would be coming out, if he was even coming out at all.

Cronos had his sniper rifle trained on the mountains. "I see him."

The sniper was facing the sun, and his scope had for a moment reflected the sun, shining briefly on an undulation in the rock of the mountainside.

That would be his last mistake.

Cronos took a deep breath and began his mental calculations of height, distance, force, and arch. He steadied himself as the sniper fired a few more shots nearly missing Kettle's head.

"Dammit, Cronos, take him out before he takes my head off!"

Cronos waited for one more flash of sunlight from the scope. Seconds passed like hours, and then it came. He lined up where he thought the target was, and he squeezed the trigger.

They waited. The sniper had stopped firing and appeared to be slumped over the ridge of rock he was hiding behind.

"Cartieras!"

"Yes, sir."

"Take a squad up there to confirm the kill. Cronos, you cover them."

Cartieras later returned, confirmed the kill, and reported that the sniper was shot through the scope in his right eye. Cronos' shot was incredible.

But the fact was that now they were cut off from Carl. Kettle couldn't believe that they had trained to defend against flanking but had never anticipated this scenario. He should've had the drone in the tent or under some kind of cover. Now they were lost, or rather Carl was lost, cutoff from his own platoon.

Kettle knew he'd have to radio in to HQ to be advised on what to do. They were sitting ducks out there waiting for their Captain who might never return.

***

Days passed and Carl was beginning to encounter more and more terrorists within the recesses of the mountains. He had seventeen more kills, bringing his total to fifty-two.

He came around a sharp bend, where there were bright lights and voices echoing off of the cave walls. Carl tightened his fist and urged the ID forward. They began to pick up pace, and as their footsteps thundered in the cavern there were the sounds of panic from the lighted area.

Gun shots rang out and people hollered. Carl turned the corner in his sea of undead drones, and as terrorists became visible, he began to take them out. Shots took down several ID around him, but Carl was unharmed and unafraid. The drones swarmed the area, toppling over lighting, computer equipment, and a video camera.

On the other side of the cavern daylight crept in. There was an opening to the outside. Several terrorists ran towards the exit, but

Carl cut them down. After several minutes of gunfire and cries of terror, the room was once again silent. Carl rewarded his drones by letting them feed. This was a mother lode, some twenty odd terrorists, bringing his count to around seventy-two.

He saw the camera equipment lying sideways on the floor. It was broadcast equipment. Apparently, they were working on broadcasting something. They always did, to rally their men around the world or to claim credit for an attack.

Carl, worn out from wandering the caves for two weeks, picked up the camera on its tripod and righted it. The red light was still on. It was recording.

Carl backed up and stood in front of the camera, assault rifle pointed down in bravado, and ordered some of the ID to stand behind him in the shadows.

And then he began to speak.

"This is a message to all of those who are enemies of freedom around the world. For decades, you have planned attacks on the free world in hiding, cowering in these caves. You've massacred many men, women, and children in the name of your perverse ideology. It has been said that you do not fear death, as many of you have extinguished your own lives for your cause.

"All that has changed. I have found you in the recesses of these White Mountains, cowering like swine. You need not fear death, but you will fear me.

"I have come for your lives, and I have claimed many. There is nowhere you can hide that I will not find you. My men do not tire, they do not thirst, they do not sleep...but they hunger for your blood, and they will not be satiated.

"Heed this warning: disband, immediately. Your reign of terror is at an end. For every attack made on free soil, I will claim fifty of your heads. I will not stop until the attacks do, or until there are none of you left. I vow this from your own backyard. You will answer to the dead. Not only to your victims, but to those in life who counted themselves amongst your ranks. You owe the free world a profound debt, and I am here to collect."

Then he trained his rifle on the camera and shot it to pieces.

Chapter 21

Fort Bliss
Texas

Major Lewis was watching a news conference addressing the mysterious broadcast coming from just outside the Pakistani border. The media was running wild with the story. The figure in the video didn't identify himself, and his uniform did not bear any of the traditional markings of the United States Army. It was the black suit of the ID program.

There were rumors that American forces were in Afghanistan in the area of the White Mountains, but the notion that they could have achieved such penetration was dismissed as a logistical impossibility.

However, shockwaves rippled through the international media. There was some condemnation of this unidentified character by the Order for International Liberation and some of the more liberal groups in the United States, citing the campaign as a breach of diplomacy.

But the world was fascinated by the broadcast. Some groups debunked it as a hoax, propaganda against terrorist factions. Some ascribed it to the work of a paramilitary vigilante group. Surely the terrorists of the world knew that they were missing many of their operatives hiding in the Tora Bora cave system. They also knew the broadcast came from one of their clandestine stations.

Right wing groups came out praising the actions as definitive action against a ruthless enemy. The President himself, while not claiming responsibility, condoned the action as a positive result in reigning in an elusive enemy.

Major Lewis sat there in his office in awe. The kid did it. He really did it. His phone was ringing off the hook. There would be questions, and he would have to provide answers. He was not quite sure how all of this was going to play out. The world was shocked, but no one of real import came out against the message of the broadcast. It would be a new era for the war on terror.

Major Lewis turned off his television and stepped out of his office. His secretary, Mary, put her call on hold, the board lighting up like a Christmas tree, and she held her hand up.

"Major Lewis…"

"You have to wait, Mary. I'm going to use the john." He marched off to the men's room before she could continue.

He pushed open the bathroom door and hurried in. Fortunately the bathroom was empty. Not that it really mattered, but he liked it that way.

He entered a stall, closed and latched the door, and sat down on the bowl. At his age he appreciated a good bowel movement when it came, and he figured it would give him some time to think.

The door to the bathroom opened, and someone came in. The footsteps were slow and measured, which at first just seemed odd. But then, with a grisly realization, a wave of panic came over the Major. The kid did what he said he was going to do. He carried out a successful mission and went public. Perhaps he thought he no longer needed the Major, which made Lewis suddenly dispensable.

The shuffling footsteps ended in front of his stall. Did Birdsall dare send a drone for him, in the officers' restroom? He was locked in the stall, but unarmed. He would have to think quickly, be resourceful. He supposed he could…

The faucet was opened and the person in front of his stall began to splash water. False alarm. The man used the hand dryer and left the restroom, and Major Lewis was once again alone.

He finished up and washed his hands. He was now hyper vigilant, looking over his shoulder constantly, seeing ID everywhere he looked.

He didn't want to return to his office. The ID would most certainly be looking for him there. He figured he'd go to Captain London's office.

He could tell her everything. She was bound by confidentiality…except if any of his superiors were to ask. Dammit. But she wouldn't rat him out…because she was implicated too. She had been working with him on the ID program every step of the way. She even helped to select the men, including Lorenzo and Lockwood.

He remembered her reservations about Lorenzo. She felt he came from an unstable background. He, however, saw potential. A man that easily corrupted would likely go along with the deal with the Navajas if he was pitched properly. Lockwood was in on it from the get-go.

Major Lewis stomped down to her office. He would tell her everything. It would feel good to tell someone else. If someone else knew, then Birdsall would have two witnesses to dispose of, which he would not likely do. Lewis noticed Birdsall had a soft spot for Captain London. He would bet his life that the kid would not let any harm come to her, even if she knew about the sordid arrangement with the Navajas.

He approached the door to her office and scanned in.

"Enter, Major Lewis."

He stormed into her office and sat down in one of her chairs.

"What can I do for you…"

"Captain…Fiona, I need to talk to you."

Fiona? Major Lewis never called her Fiona. He was always such a stickler for rank and protocol. The chain of command was his manifesto.

"Is everything alright, Major?"

"Yes, I mean, no. There's a bit of a problem with the program that has me worried."

The man was shaking. Something definitely had the man rattled. She never saw Major Lewis lose his composure before. He was always so smug and superior.

"Okay. Is it one of the men?"

"Yes, I fear he has become unhinged and we are all in danger."

"Okay, but I was just about to use the restroom, and I'm afraid it cannot wait. Will you excuse me, sir?"

"But I really have to talk to you."

"It will only take a minute, sir. I'll be right back, and we can discuss this. I assume you are referring to Captain Birdsall."

"Yes. Yes, that's the one."

"He *has* been behaving very strangely. I'm not so sure he's dangerous though. But we can discuss it when I return."

"Oh, fine. Hurry up."

Captain London excused herself and walked down the hall to the officer's restroom for ladies.

Major Lewis sat in her office waiting quite impatiently. He squirmed in his chair like he had red ants in his pants. The sooner he told her everything, the sooner he'd be safe.

He noticed the digital décor of the office generated by the Therapeutic Ambience Program. The retinal scanner at her door had picked up an impulse and projected his favorite bar in New Orleans in the French Quarter. The familiarity soothed him a little as it brought back memories. A big band track played in the background, something for him to listen to while he waited.

He noticed a glitch in the corner of the room where an ornamental tree stood. The glitch, a minute ripple in the digital veneer, was localized to that one area only. The rest of the illusion was intact.

Before he could register the meaning of the glitch, a figure emerged from behind the digital projection of the tree and grabbed Major Lewis. Startled, he screamed in her office, but the music had increased in volume, the horns drowning him out.

"You can't kill me," he yelled at the drone, "they'll know!"

But the ID made no attempt to devour the man. In fact, it held something in its hand, and it placed it in Lewis' hand, forcing it closed over the object.

Lewis looked down and saw he was holding a handgun...*his* handgun. Then he understood how it was going to go down.

Clever kid.

The ID began to force Lewis' arm to bend and twisted his hand so that the handgun was directed right at Lewis' face. Lewis struggled against the drone, but its strength was unrelenting and he was easily overpowered.

The ID grabbed Lewis' head and forced the handgun barrel into his mouth, his front teeth scraping the metal. Major Lewis looked up into the milky, dispassionate eyes of his assassin and wondered if Carl saw him through those eyes.

The drone pulled the trigger, splattering blood across Captain London's desk.

The ID dropped the twitching body of Major Lewis back into the seat and reached into its suit, pulling out a piece of paper. It tossed the paper in the now motionless Major's lap and returned to the corner behind the illusion of the potted, decorative tree. The music lowered in volume.

Major Lewis sat with his head hanging backwards in Captain London's chair, handgun still in his right hand and the note in his lap.

I have written this note because I am a traitor and cannot take the guilt any longer. My name is Major Hardy Sinclair Lewis, and I have been overseeing the Insidious Drone Program. I have been training soldiers in the use of infantry drones to hunt down and neutralize terrorists.

Unfortunately I took a good program that had demonstrated effectiveness and attempted to use it in the interest of personal greed. I struck a pact with the Navajas, a Mexican drug cartel, a sworn enemy of the United States, in which the drones would also be used as mules to traffic drugs into the country.

In the process I have led too many good soldiers unknowingly to certain death in the interest of my pact with the enemy. I regret my actions and can no longer stand the guilt. I apologize to the families of the men I have murdered, and I apologize to my own family.

It is my hope that with this final selfish act I can depart this world with some shred of honor.

Hardy Sinclair Lewis

Captain London returned to her office and saw the body of Major Lewis in her chair. "Terminate New Orleans bar ambience program." Her office went back to normal. She went into her closet and produced a private's uniform. She dressed the immobile ID in the outfit, covering up its black suit.

She then walked it out of her office, steering it down the hallway. She took it back to Carl's new office, passing only a few others in the hallway. They took no notice. She walked it into the closet where it stood obediently. She closed the door and entered the security code that Carl provided into the digi-lock and returned to her office.

When she returned to her office, she called security and did her best to sound panicky. When they arrived, she explained to them how Major Lewis came to her office unannounced with something important to discuss about the program. She told them that she just left the office to use the ladies room, and when she returned she found him as he was.

She was asked if she recorded the session, and she replied that she hadn't as it wasn't a session at all. Given the circumstances and the note, the incident was deemed a suicide.

Carl had told Fiona everything. He had told her about Lewis' role in Tijuana and Xcaret. He also told her that once he completed his mission in Afghanistan that Major Lewis would come to seek her out and imply her in the conspiracy.

Their plan worked flawlessly. Carl told her that no matter what, things would work out. Either someone else would take the helm of the ID program, or it would be shut down.

Either way, he was loose and carrying on the work of the program. He would pursue the Order for International Liberation and all enemies of peace and freedom to the ends of the earth with his drones.

Fiona had heard that he was last spotted just over the border in Pakistan. Rumors of his exploits circulated quickly through the international press and intelligence communities. The Order for International Liberation appeared in broadcasts daily, denouncing the actions of this mysterious man and his death squad and making wild threats. But in actuality, the attacks stopped, if only for a moment…

…because for once they were afraid.

There was a ringing, and Fiona answered her phone at her desk. "Hello, Colonel Betancourt."

"Captain, I just thought you should know that we received a communiqué from Xcaret, Mexico. Lieutenant Peter Birdsall is alive. There will be an extraction within the hour."

"You'll need me to do a full evaluation."

"Yes, Captain."

"I'll forward you the report when I'm finished."

"Thank you, Captain."
Fiona terminated the phone call and couldn't help smiling.

The End

NIGHTMARE OF THE DEAD
VINCENZO BILOF

In a world of war and mayhem, a twisted nightmare of undead cannibals begins.

The outlaw Neasa Bannan uncovers a horrifying conspiracy engineered by the psychopathic mastermind behind the Confederacy's deadly flesh-hungry weapons. A homicidal gunslinger and a brotherhood of killers emerge out of Neasa's tragic, blood-soaked past while the living dead ravage the land.

With the fate of the country in the balance, Neasa must decide: save the Union from the undead menace, or surrender to Saul's vision of ultra-violence.

www.severedpress.com

ICE STATION ZOMBIE
JE GURLEY

For most of the long, cold winter, Antarctica is a frozen wasteland. Now, the ice is melting and the zombies are thawing. Arctic explorers Val Marino and Elliot Anson race against time and death to reach Australia, but the Demise has preceded them and zombies stalk the streets of Adelaide and Coober Pedy.

The Coalition

When the dead rose to destroy the living, Ron Cutter learned to survive. While so many others died, he thrived. His life is a constant battle against the living dead. As he casts his own bullets and packs his shotgun shells, his humanity slowly melts away.

Then he encounters a lost boy and a woman searching for a place of refuge. Can they help him recover the emotions he set aside to live? And if he does recover them, will those feelings be an asset in his struggles, or a danger to him?

THE STATE OF EXTINCTION: the first installment in the **COALITON OF THE LIVING** trilogy of Mankind's battle against the plague of the Living Dead. As recounted by author **Robert Mathis Kurtz.**

www.severedpress.com

MACHINES OF THE DEAD

The dead are rising. The island of Manhattan is quarantined. Helicopters guard the airways while gunships patrol the waters. Bridges and tunnels are closed off. Anyone trying to leave is shot on sight.

For Jack Warren, survival is out of his hands when a group of armed military men kidnap him and his infected wife from their apartment and bring them to a bunker five stories below the city.

There, Jack learns a terrible truth and the reason why the dead have risen. With the help of a few others, he must find a way to escape the bunker and make it out of the city alive.

JUDGMENT DAY

Dr. Jebediah Stone never believed in zombies until he had to shoot one. Now they're mutating into a new species, capable of reproducing, and the only defence is 'Blue Juice', a vaccine distilled from the blood of rare individuals immune to the zombie plague. Dr. Stone's missing wife is one of these unwilling 'munies', snatched by the military under the Judgment Day Protocol.It's a new, dangerous world filled with zombies, street gangs, and merciless Hunters desperate for a shot of blue juice. Has the world turned on mankind? Is Mortuus Venator the new ruler of earth?

www.severedpress.com

TIMOTHY
MARK TUFO

Timothy was not a good man in life and being undead did little to improve his disposition. Find out what a man trapped in his own mind will do to survive when he wakes up to find himself a zombie controlled by a self-aware virus.

www.severedpress.com

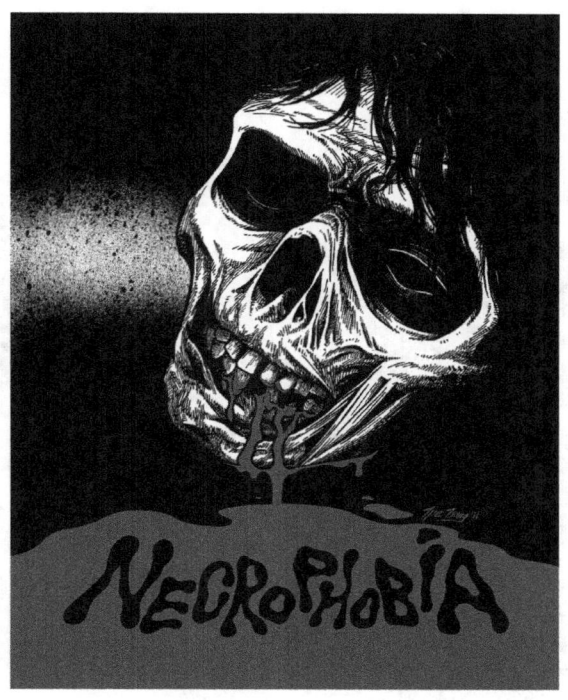

NECROPHOBIA

An ordinary summer's day.
The grass is green, the flowers are blooming. All is right with the
world. Then the dead start rising. From cemetery and mortuary,
funeral home and morgue, they flood into the streets until every
town and city is infested with walking corpses, blank-eyed
eating machines that exist to take down the living.
The world is a graveyard.
And when you have a family to protect, it's more than survival.
It's war.

Zombie Fallout
Mark Tufo
CURRENTLY IN DEVELOPMENT WITH
Illuminandi Media
ShaedStudios.com

www.ingramcontent.com/pod-product-compliance
Lightning Source LLC
Chambersburg PA
CBHW060404180626
46817CB00007B/2507